FORT BRIDGER SERIES

CONSIDER THE LILIES

BOOK TWO

AL AND JOANNA LACY

MULTNOMAH PUBLISHERS
Sisters, Oregon

This book is a work of fiction. With the exception of recognized historical figures, the characters in this novel are fictional. Any resemblance to actual persons, living or dead, is purely coincidental.

CONSIDER THE LILIES

published by Multnomah Fiction
a Division of Multnomah Publishers, Inc.

Cover design by Left Coast Design
Cover illustration by Frank Ordaz

International Standard Book Number: 1-57673-049-2
Printed in the United States of America.

For information:
Questar Publishers, Inc., Post Office Box 1720, Sisters, Oregon 97759

LIBRARY OF CONGRESS CATALOGING-IN -PUBLICATION DATA
Lacy, Al.
Consider the lilies/Al and JoAnna Lacy.
p. cm.—(Hannah of Fort Bridger; bk. 2)
ISBN 1-57673-049-2 (alk. paper)
I. Lacy, JoAnna. II. Title. III. Series: Lacy, Al. Hannah of Fort Bridger; bk. 2.
PS3562.A256C6 1997 97–17922
813'.54–dc21 CIP

97 98 99 00 01 02 03 04 05 06 — 10 9 8 7 6 5 4 3 2 1

For my precious daughters, Connie and Kelli,

who for nine months I carried beneath my heart...

and always and ever carry in my heart.

As in Hannah Cooper's life, they too in their Christian walk

with the Lord have learned to

"consider the lilies."

I love you both with all my heart.

Mommie

PROLOGUE

No other region of the United States has so shaped the image of our national identity as the Old West. Together, as husband and wife, we have traversed the vast regions of Colorado, Wyoming, Montana, Texas, New Mexico, Nebraska, Kansas, the Dakotas, Utah, Idaho, Nevada, Arizona, California, Oregon, and Washington.

We have read and reread many history books on the nineteenth-century old West, and between us have read literally hundreds of novels about it. From Daniel Boone to Davey Crockett; from Kit Carson to Wyatt Earp; from Wild Bill Hickok to Buffalo Bill Cody, our national folklore is replete with rugged men finding their dreams fulfilled in the wide open spaces or craggy mountains of an untamed land.

Though this image is well founded, both of us find it one-dimensional and incomplete. Little is said by historians or novelists about the role played by gallant, resourceful women in settling the West.

In this new series, Hannah of Fort Bridger, we will give men their due, but our intent is to show our readers the truth of women's contributions in forming this nation's vast land west of the wide Missouri.

As we present this second book in the series, let us follow valiant Hannah Cooper, whose faith in the Lord has been severely tested by the sudden death of her husband, Solomon, in central Wyoming.

The California-bound wagon train in which Hannah and her four children are traveling as far as Fort Bridger, Wyoming, is still some two hundred miles from the fort. It has been nearly four months since they left their home in Independence, Missouri, to begin this venture westward. On the day they pulled out of Independence, their dreams were yet to be fulfilled—as Solomon had put it—*"out there under the distant sky."*

As the wagon train pulls away from Solomon Cooper's grave, will Hannah's faith sustain her? Only the Lord knows what dangers and trials lie ahead on the trail. And when they arrive at Fort Bridger, how will she cope with the seemingly insurmountable obstacles in her path? Will she be able to handle the task of running Cooper's General Store without her husband? Especially since she's carrying their fifth child in her womb?

Our heart's desire in presenting this book and the ones that follow in the series is to encourage our Christian readers to more fully trust the Lord as they walk life's pathway. And for those readers who have never opened their hearts to the Lord Jesus Christ for salvation and forgiveness of their sins, our prayer is that they might do so.

Chapter One

At high noon, the California-bound wagon train was still camped on Wyoming's Sweetwater River, just west of where the water roared through a narrow boulder-strewn section known as Devil's Gate.

Stuart Armstrong reached out to help Hannah Cooper climb onto the wagon seat, but she turned to look over her shoulder one last time at the freshly mounded grave.

As usual, the wagon train had stopped at dusk the previous night to make camp. After such an oppressively hot day, the Coopers had decided the whole family would sleep outside beneath the wagon. The children fell asleep quickly, but Solomon and Hannah lay awake in each other's arms for quite some time, talking softly.

In the dark hours of the night, Solomon awakened to a sensation of movement against his bare arm and heard a slight rattling sound. It took only seconds to realize that a rattlesnake had slithered next to him, yet he couldn't see where the head was.

Even the slightest movement would cause the snake to strike. If any of his family stirred in their sleep...

Solomon swung his arm toward the snake in the darkness and felt the sting of the rattler's bite. The snake bit him twice more before he got to his feet and managed to kill it.

Hannah had a few precious minutes with Sol before he was gone, but it was enough time for him to urge her to fulfill their dream and go on to Fort Bridger.

"Ezra's about ready to go, ma'am." Stuart took her hand and helped her onto the wagon seat, then climbed up and grasped the reins.

Hannah looked at this kind man, her eyes red and swollen from a night of weeping. "Thank you for offering to drive, Stuart. I should be feeling up to it in a couple of days."

"It's my privilege, ma'am."

He and his wife, Tracie, had traveled to Independence, Missouri, from Toledo, Ohio, to join Ezra Comstock's wagon train. On the trail, Solomon Cooper witnessed to Stuart and led him to Christ. Tracie, who was now driving the Armstrong wagon by herself, had come to the Lord through conversations with Hannah.

As the Cooper wagon took its position in line, fourteen-year-old Christopher Cooper mounted his bay gelding, Buster, and drew up beside the wagon. His dad's horse, Nipper, trailed behind, tied to the tailgate.

Little five-year-old Patty Ruth Cooper sat between her mother and Stuart, holding tightly to her stuffed bear, Tony, named for Tony Cuzak, who drove one of the Cooper's four supply wagons.

In the back of the wagon were Hannah's other two children, twelve-year-old Mary Beth, and eight-year-old B. J. (short for Brett Jonathan), and the family's black and white rat terrier, Biggie.

As he waited for all the wagons to line up, wagon master Ezra Comstock swung into his saddle at the front of the line and talked to his nephew, Micah, who drove the lead wagon.

Hannah thought back to Ezra's words that morning. Just after the burial, he came to her and said, "I'd really like to see you go on to Fort Bridger, but not too far along the trail we'll come upon a supply train headin' back east. If you wish to join it, I'll make arrangements for you." Then he left her alone beside the grave.

She knelt and prayed, asking God to show her what to do. She was aware that her children were standing some distance away, watching her. They wanted to go on, but knew the decision belonged to her alone.

The words of Isaiah 26:3 came to mind, and soon her heart flooded with peace as she kept her mind stayed on Jesus. Yes, they would go on to Fort Bridger and make a new life there.

Now, as she waited for the wagon master's familiar call to head out, she felt that same God-given peace even in the midst of overwhelming grief.

Ezra looked back along the line of wagons to make sure they were all in position, then raised up in his stirrups and gestured west, shouting, "Wagons, ho-o-o!"

The Cooper family wagon was ninth in line, with their four supply wagons directly behind and more wagons trailing them. As the wheels began to turn, Hannah twisted on the seat and leaned out. Tears came as she took one last look at her beloved Solomon's grave. Her grief was so new and deep that she felt as though the breath had been taken from her. Through quivering lips, she whispered, "O dear Lord, I need the grace and strength right now that only You can give."

Solomon's grave seemed so lonely there, under the trees. She knew he was in heaven, but still, with each step of the oxen and each turn of the wagon wheels, Hannah felt herself moving farther and farther from the one who had been the essence of life to her for so many years. Her aching heart bid him good-bye with the knowledge that one day they would share a glorious reunion in God's bright heaven.

When the grave passed from view, she sat up straight on the wagon seat and looked toward the western horizon. Twenty days to Fort Bridger, she thought, and many tomorrows. Abruptly, her own words, spoken earlier on the trail, came back to her: *The Lord always knows what's ahead of us and can prepare us for the trials and heartaches that come our way, even before they happen. He's already in eternity, which means He's already in the future. So, He's already in our tomorrows.*

"Thank You, Lord," she said under her breath. "Thank You for that wonderful truth."

The wagon rocked and swayed as Hannah lifted her gaze to the magnificent canopy of sky. As she studied the blue horizon, Solomon's words before they left Independence filled her with hope. "Out there, Hannah, under the distant sky, is our new home and our new life."

She felt a small hand press firmly on her shoulder and turned to see Mary Beth's compassionate eyes. Tears were streaming down her cheeks. She smiled through her own tears and reached up to squeeze her young daughter's hand.

Mary Beth drew in a shuddering breath and half-whispered, "I love you, Mama."

"I love you, too, sweetie."

B. J., who was holding on to Biggie, turned to look back at his father's grave and started to sob. Mary Beth wiped at her own tears and swung around to put an arm around her little brother.

Hannah glanced at Chris riding beside her on Buster, wondering how he was holding up. His eyes looked straight ahead, but his lower lip gave him away. She'd seen him hip around in the saddle as the wagons began to roll and take a last look at his father's grave. But Chris had wept the least of any of her children. Hannah knew he was trying to show his mother that she could depend on him, for he was now the "man of the family." Her shattered heart glowed with warmth toward her courageous teenage son.

There were no shadows as the sun's burning rays scalded

the rugged land and the temperature climbed higher and higher. Hannah dabbed at her forehead and turned her gaze to the majestic mountain peaks. She hoped it would be cooler when they reached the base of the mountains and started over South Pass. The Rocky Mountains—where the wind blew free and the eagles ruled the skies. At least that was what Hannah had once read about this mountain range.

Twenty more days, she thought. If all went as Ezra planned, they would arrive in Fort Bridger on September 17. School, no doubt, would start in early September. She hoped her children wouldn't find it too difficult to catch up with their studies.

Patty Ruth looked up at Hannah with a sheen of moisture covering her face. "Mama, I'm thirsty."

Hannah half-turned to reach for the canteen, but Mary Beth, who rode directly behind her, had already lifted it from a small table and now offered it to her. She thanked her oldest daughter and helped the little redhead take her fill.

Patty Ruth smacked her lips and burped slightly. "'Scuse me."

"Well, I should hope so," Hannah said, smiling, and capped the canteen.

Stuart chuckled. "Mrs. Cooper, I want to commend you for the way you and Mr. Cooper have brought up your children. They're so mannerly and polite. I hope that when Tracie and I have children, they'll be just like yours."

Hannah smiled. "That's a wonderful compliment, Stuart," she said, pride in her children welling up in her heart. She thought of the new little life she was carrying. A lump rose in her throat when she realized it was just last night that she'd informed Solomon they were going to have a fifth child. He could hardly contain his excitement.

She touched her midsection and told herself she would wait to tell the children about the baby until just before it started to show. She looked down at Patty Ruth, who watched her, and cupped a hand under her chubby little chin.

Patty Ruth blinked earnestly and said, "Please don't cry, Mama. Papa's lookin' down from heaven, an' he wouldn' want you to cry."

"I'm trying not to, honey. Oh, I love you so much!"

"I love you so much, too, Mama."

"And so do we," spoke up B. J. from behind. "Even Biggie loves you."

"And so does Tony the Bear, Mama," said Patty Ruth, lifting up the stuffed animal.

Mary Beth didn't say anything, but she put her hand on her mother's shoulder and squeezed gently.

"You're the best mother in all the world, Mama," Chris said. "The Lord sure blessed us when He made us your children."

Hannah began to cry all over again.

Even Stuart Armstrong could feel some moisture welling up in his eyes, and he turned his head so they couldn't see.

As the wagons continued on the journey and the dust boiled up in clouds, Hannah's mind went back to her parents. Ben and Esther Singleton had refused to go along with Hannah and Solomon to Fort Bridger. They would not budge from their home in Independence. They fought the "foolish" idea of Hannah and Solomon taking their grandchildren and moving to the Wild West.

Hannah swallowed hard as she recalled her father's harsh words: *If you loved us, you wouldn't be so eager to go off and leave us! I'm telling both of you, you'll be sorry you did this foolish thing. It'll backfire on you! You're making the biggest mistake of your lives!*

Two hours ago, when Hannah knelt beside Solomon's grave, she told herself that her father was right. She and Solomon had misunderstood what they thought was God's leading and had made a horrible mistake. For a moment she had actually thought that Solomon's untimely death was the backfire her father had predicted.

But then the Lord spoke to her by His still small voice in her heart, saying, *Hannah, if you had stayed in Independence, what about Tracie, Stuart, and Tony?*

Suddenly it had come over Hannah that none of those three would be Christians now if the Coopers hadn't been in the wagon train. They're going to heaven because we followed God's leadership and struck out for Fort Bridger!

Yes, she and Solomon had done the right thing! It was all in God's perfect plan, even Solomon's homegoing.

Even so, she felt keenly the loneliness. She had leaned so much on Solomon; loved him so much, and now he was gone. Her throat tightened. Thank the Lord she still had her four children…and the new baby was a special gift from God. She would have this part of her darling Sol to carry with her to their new home.

Hannah noticed Chris pull up on Buster's reins and let the wagon move on, then he fell in beside the first Cooper supply wagon and started talking to Tony Cuzak. Tony's plan had been to go to California, but when the wagon train had stopped at the Kline ranch, he had fallen in love with young widow Amanda Kline. After driving the Cooper supply wagon to Fort Bridger, Tony planned to go back to court Amanda.

Tony. Hannah smiled to herself. Though Tony was young in the Lord, he had shown much spiritual growth since his conversion. At the graveside this morning, he had approached Hannah and asked if he could read Scripture and say a few words over Solomon's blanket-wrapped body before it was lowered into the grave. Hannah was pleased to give her permission.

Tony's touching words ran through her mind: *Solomon Cooper was a brave man. Not only did he show valor on the battlefield in the War, but he demonstrated unparalleled courage and heroism by taking the venom of the rattler in order to protect his family. He knew he would probably lose his life in the process. He loved his dear wife, Hannah; his dear daughters, Mary Beth and Patty Ruth; and his dear sons, Christopher and Brett Jonathan, more than he loved his own life. God bless the memory of this gallant man in each of our hearts.*

As Hannah once again felt tears on her cheeks, Patty Ruth looked up and said, "I'm sorry, Mama. Your heart hurts, doesn't it?"

Hannah couldn't speak.

Patty Ruth then laid Tony the Bear in Stuart's lap. "Would you hold Tony for me, please, Mr. Armstrong?"

"Certainly," Stuart said with a nod.

Patty Ruth stood up on the seat, wrapped her arms around her mother's neck, and said, "I miss Papa, too."

Hannah's weeping became loud sobs. Mary Beth and B. J. leaned toward their mother and wrapped their arms around her and Patty Ruth, and Chris joined them on Buster. Hannah and her children huddled together, finding quiet strength in their closeness.

In a few minutes, Ezra Comstock rode by and exchanged glances with Stuart Armstrong, then drew up next to Buster, and said, "Hannah, is there anything I can do?"

The sun's rays glistened the tears streaming down her cheeks. "No...thank you, Ezra. There's nothing you can do. We're just having a hard time with Solomon's death."

"I understand. When I lost my wife, it took me a long time to get adjusted to it, even though, like your Solomon, she went to heaven."

"It would have been easier if he had suffered a long illness," Hannah said, "but to be taken in the prime of his life, when he was strong and healthy—"

"Yes'm," said Ezra. "My heart goes out to you and these children."

"Please understand, Ezra, I'm not bitter against the Lord. I know He never makes mistakes. But...but we just miss Sol so much."

"Yes, ma'am. If there's anything I can do at any time, you let me know."

"Thank you, Ezra. I will."

As the wagon master rode away, Hannah looked at all her children and said, "We'll be all right. The Lord will help us through this."

Mary Beth and B. J. wiped their tears and returned to the back of the wagon. Even Biggie's head hung low. He knew something was dreadfully wrong with his family.

Patty Ruth sat down on the wagon seat and reached for Tony the Bear as she thanked Stuart for holding him.

"My pleasure, sweetie," Stuart said, warming her with a smile. Then to Hannah, "Mrs. Cooper, like Ezra, anything I can do..."

"Thank you," Hannah said. "You're already doing exactly what I need right now."

"Well, if there's anything else, you just say so."

"I will. I appreciate your kindness more than I could ever tell you."

"So do I, sir," Chris said.

Hannah studied her oldest son. She hoped he would let out his grief soon.

Chapter Two

As the afternoon wore on, the blazing sun baked the dry ground and scorched the bodies of man and animal. Dust floated in the hot air, mixing with sweat that ran down the travelers' faces in dirty rivulets. Their lungs felt like brass cylinders filled with fire.

Everyone looked forward to evening when the sun would set behind the looming Rockies, and they could stop and enjoy the cool water of the river. For now, they could only watch the shimmering sunlight reflected off the swift current, while a pair of hawks swooped from the sky and snatched a fish from just beneath the surface.

Late in the afternoon, Chris rode beside each of the four supply wagons for a few minutes and thanked each driver for helping his mother get the store supplies to Fort Bridger. Then he headed for the lead wagon to spend a little time with Micah Comstock. Chris and Micah had become close friends on the trail. The fact that Micah was a Christian sealed the bond between them.

Just as Chris drew up alongside his family wagon, the train was passing two freshly dug graves near the river.

Hannah's heart went cold as she gazed at the dismal mounds. She knew by their short length that children were buried there. Stuart Anderson eyed the graves and heard

Hannah say to no one in particular, "Their brokenhearted parents are not far ahead of us."

He nodded. "And probably blaming themselves for leaving their home somewhere back east and venturing into this wild, rugged country."

Hannah noticed Chris draw up on Buster.

"You all right, Mama?" he asked, glancing at the graves, then back at his mother.

"I'm fine, honey."

The boy smiled thinly, then rode on ahead.

Hannah moved her lips silently. Thank You, Lord, that all four of my children are with me. Then she gently touched her abdomen...that all five are with me.

At sunset the dusty, sweaty travelers welcomed the cool breeze that swept down from the north and picked up the smell of water as it moved across the surface of the river. As the sun dropped behind the Rockies, Ezra called for the sixteen wagons to make a circle beside the Sweetwater.

Twilight accentuated the lonesomeness of the gray winding river. The cook fires added some cheer, and the people ate hungrily as night shadows descended from the looming mountains.

Maudie and Elmer Holden had invited Hannah and her children to eat supper with them and their grandson, Curtis, who drove their wagon. Deborah Smith, who traveled with her sister and brother-in-law, Lloyd and Suzanne Marlin, and their baby, James, had also been invited. She and Curtis were sweet on each other since getting acquainted on the trail.

The Holdens had become like grandparents to the Cooper children ever since the train had left Independence. When the children entered the circle of firelight, Elmer, in his slow Arkansas drawl, spoke tenderly to them, giving each one a grandfatherly hug. Then he hugged Hannah as he would have his own daughter, and spoke words of comfort to her.

Maudie was a small birdlike woman with a ready smile. She wore her long silver hair upswept in a topknot. She, too, embraced each of the Coopers, murmuring how she loved them. Her words soothed their weary, broken hearts.

None of the Coopers had much of an appetite, but at Maudie's gentle persuasion, they all ate.

After supper, Ezra Comstock stood in the center of the wagon circle. Firelight flickered across his face as he explained how they would section off the river so the men and boys could bathe around the east bend, and the women and girls around the west.

Before dismissing them to the river, he said, "At this point, we are 829 miles from Independence. By noon tomorrow we'll pass a tall rock formation known as Split Rock. This prominent landmark serves as a geographical guide for emigrants like yourselves, and for fur traders and Indians. One more thing—we'll be in the mountains day after tomorrow, which will give us cooler air."

Several people cheered.

After baths were done, and people were preparing to retire for the night, many of them drifted by the Cooper wagon to speak words of comfort and encouragement to Hannah and her children.

Later, Hannah sat inside the wagon, brushing Patty Ruth's hair, while Mary Beth wrote in her diary by lantern light. B. J. played outside with Biggie.

Hannah was still getting Patty Ruth ready for bed when Chris eased up to the tailgate. "I've got the horses and oxen fed and watered, Mama," he said. "Is it all right if I go see Micah for a little while? He asked me earlier today if I'd come see him."

"Sure, honey. Just be back within half an hour so you can get to bed at a decent time."

Patty Ruth turned her sky-blue gaze on her oldest brother. "You're gonna miss Micah when we get to Fort Bridger, ain'tcha, Chris?"

"Yeah," he said in a melancholy tone. "He's a real pal."

Micah Comstock was alone in the lead wagon, reading his Bible by lantern light, when he heard a familiar voice. He looked through the opening in the canvas and smiled as Chris climbed over the tailgate.

"Oh, I didn't mean to interfere with your devotions, Micah," Chris said, noticing the open Bible beside the lantern.

"It's all right. I was almost finished. How are your mother and your brother and sisters doing?"

"It's pretty tough, but I think they're doing all right."

Micah looked Chris straight in the eye and said, "And how about Chris? How's *he* doing?"

The fourteen-year-old cleared his throat, then said, "I'm doing as well as could be expected."

Micah nodded. "We're good friends, aren't we, Chris?"

"Sure. Why?"

"Well, I'm a bit concerned that you're trying to carry too much on your own, and I'd like to talk to you about it. Since I'm your friend, you'll listen, right?"

"Ah...sure."

"Good. I've never told you about my parents, but my dad, Uncle Ezra's brother, was killed in the Civil War when I was just a year younger than you are."

Chris's eyes widened. "I didn't know. So, you've experienced what I'm going through."

"I have. And Chris, my mother was such a help to me. She showed me something in the Bible that I want to show you."

Suddenly Chris threw his arms around her and breathed into her ear, "Mama, I'm so thankful I still have *you!*"

Hannah could feel her son trembling as they clung to each other. When they eased apart, Chris took hold of her hands and said with a quiver in his voice, "Mama, I'll take care of you. I'll work hard in the store so you won't have to. I'll—"

"Honey, you don't have to carry this family all by yourself. I'm able to work."

"I know, Mama, but if I have to stay out of school for a year to help get the store on its feet, I'll do it. I can catch up."

Hannah shook her head. "No, Chris. I appreciate your willingness to give up school time to help, but it won't be necessary. I can handle the store during the day. You and Mary Beth can pitch in after school and on Saturdays. Next summer, I'll work you two so hard you'll be asking for wages."

Chris smiled slightly. "The only pay I want is to see you happy, Mama. That's all that matters."

"I'll be happy because I still have you children. We're going to have a wonderful life in Fort Bridger. I just know it."

"Sure we will," Chris said. "It'll help having a good church, won't it?"

"Oh, yes! And everyone we meet won't be strangers, since we've already met Pastor and Mrs. Kelly when they came through Independence."

"That's right. And we know Colonel and Mrs. Bateman, and Major and Mrs. Crawley, too. I can't wait to get inside that fort."

"I'm sure you'll visit there lots of times," she whispered. "Well, General Cooper, it's time for us to get some sleep. I've fixed you a spot by B. J."

She kissed him goodnight and watched him settle in, then lay awake for a time, nursing her grief. But the weariness of the day's journey soon took her into sound slumber.

"Okay."

"I know what God's Word can do for you, Chris, because it helped me so much in dealing with Dad's death. Then it helped me again when Mom died of fever just over a year ago."

"Oh, Micah! I had no idea you'd lost both your parents."

"Of course you didn't. But I'm glad I can tell you that both of them were saved. I'll see them again in heaven, just like you'll see your father."

Micah reached for his Bible and flipped to the eleventh chapter of Matthew. Before reading, he said, "Chris, I know that when your papa died, you suddenly felt responsible to take his place, since you're the oldest boy. Am I right?"

Chris studied him for a moment, then said, "Yes."

"And for your family's sake, you feel you can't let go and grieve over your papa's death, right?"

Chris was quiet for a long moment. Finally he nodded yes.

"Pretty big load, I'd say. In fact, it's too big a load for you to carry all by yourself. Mom showed me this passage when Dad was killed. Listen to what Jesus said in Matthew 11:28: 'Come unto me, all ye that labor and are heavy laden, and I will give you rest.' Chris, have you asked Jesus to help you carry the load?"

"Well, I prayed and asked Him to help me be a strength to Mama and the kids."

"That's good, Chris, but did you ask Him to help you carry the load?"

"No. I guess not."

"Listen to what else Jesus says. 'Take my yoke upon you, and learn of me; for I am meek and lowly in heart: and ye shall find rest unto your souls. For my yoke is easy, and my burden is light.' You know that the oxen that pull these wagons are yoked together so they can pull the load as a team."

"Yes."

"Well, Jesus says to put your neck in *His* yoke, and you will find rest for your soul. And you know why?"

"Not exactly."

"Because when you put your weary neck in His yoke, He will pull the load and make your burden easy and light. He can do that because He's so much stronger than you. Make sense?"

"Yeah, it does. But how do I put my neck in His yoke?"

Micah showed him the page he was reading from and put his finger on the word *learn* in verse 29. "See that? Jesus said *learn* of me. He will teach you how to let Him bear your load. He sure did it for me when both my parents died. And He's done it since with lesser burdens."

Chris's eyes got moist as he said, "Micah, would you pray with me right now? I need to ask Jesus to help me to learn how to do this."

They bowed their heads and Micah put his arm around Chris's shoulder, asking the Lord to help Chris know how to find rest for his soul by letting Jesus carry the load.

When he finished praying, Chris prayed, thanking the Lord for his good friend, and thanking the Lord that He was willing to carry his burden over the loss of his father. He asked Jesus to teach him how to take His yoke upon him.

Hannah finished making beds for her children. It would be a tight fit, but she wanted all of them inside the wagon, close to her.

After she read Scripture to her three youngest, they prayed together. As they talked to the Lord, mother and children cried over their horrible loss. Hannah caressed their tear-stained faces and told them the Lord gave tears as a means of healing their broken hearts.

She opened her Bible again. "Look here in Psalm 56:8,"

she said. "The Bible tells us that God cares so much abou weeping that He even puts our tears in a bottle for rer brance." Then she kissed them goodnight, saying she was to see what was keeping Chris.

Hannah quietly made her way across the circle towar lead wagon, receiving words of comfort from the peopl passed. When she drew near the Comstock wagon, the inside revealed the profiles of Micah and her son on the ca wall. A few more steps and she could hear Micah praying, ing that Chris could learn to let Jesus carry the load he bearing.

She breathed a prayer of thanks for Micah and qu returned to her wagon.

The three younger children were fast asleep.

Hannah took out a pair of B. J.'s pants and sewed up knees, marveling at how quickly he could wear out clotl She remembered how Solomon would always laugh when commented on it. He said B. J. was just a chip off the old bl

Solomon. She remembered the day they first met. throat began to tighten, and her eyes filmed with te Suddenly she heard footsteps. She cleared her throat softly brushed the tears away in time to look up and see her ha some, dark-haired son climb in the rear of the wagon.

"Sh-h-h!" She placed a finger to her lips. "They're asleep

Nodding that he understood, Chris kept his voice l "Sorry to be late, but Micah was talking to me about Pap dying and all. He prayed with me, too."

Hannah touched his shoulder. "I know, son. I came ov to see what was keeping you, and I heard Micah praying. He's wonderful friend to you, honey."

"He sure is. He never told me before, but his father wa killed in the Civil War when Micah was thirteen. And hi mother died of fever just over a year ago."

"Oh, my. Bless his heart!"

Sleep eluded Chris Cooper. He lay awake deep into the night, listening to the soft, even breathing of his mother and siblings. Through the rear opening of the canvas he could see a myriad twinkling stars in the black velvety sky. Crickets gave off their pleasant music with the gurgling river as background. And now and then he heard a woeful wail somewhere in the vast rugged land, baying in a lonesome, wild way.

His thoughts went to his father. A sick feeling curled in the pit of his stomach. He would never see his father again in this life. He missed him terribly. Not only had he lost his father, he had lost his best friend.

Chris slipped out of the wagon, carrying his boots, and moved to the closest fire and sat down. Although he could see no one within the circle of wagons, he knew there were three men on watch while the rest of the wagon train slept.

A sudden gust of wind fanned the paling embers, blowing sparks and white ashes and thin trails of smoke into the circle of blackness. The wind settled to a whisper again, and after a moment the quiet was split by another mournful howl. It was full-voiced, crying out for its misplaced mate.

Chris's heart felt as if it would burst. He got up swiftly and left the circle of wagons to find a secluded spot by the river. As he stood on the bank, blinking against scalding tears, a dam broke within. Great heavy sobs came from the deep regions of his soul. He threw himself facedown on the grassy river's edge and finally surrendered to his grief.

Chris had been crying for some time when he felt a soft presence. He raised his head and then sat up as he recognized his mother. Hannah knelt down and took him in her arms.

"I'm sorry, Mama," Chris said, still crying. "I didn't mean to break down."

"Honey, that's nothing to be ashamed of. I'm glad you're letting it out."

"Oh, Mama, I miss him so much!" he wailed, clinging to her.

Hannah held him tight. "Go ahead, sweetheart. Cry it out."

Chris wept hard for several minutes. When he was able to speak again, he sucked in a sharp breath. "Mama, this is the worst thing that's ever happened to me. I love my papa so much!" A few moments later, he said, "Thank you for understanding."

"Of course I understand, Chris. All of us have had to do this. You just fought it because you thought if you let go you wouldn't be a strength to me or your brother and sisters."

Chris nodded and sniffed, then said, "I'm the man of the family now, and I don't want to fail you or the kids."

Hannah kissed his cheek. "You're a good boy, Chris. You've assumed this 'man of the family' role for yourself, and I appreciate it. But you don't have to carry the whole load yourself. It's too heavy for a fourteen-year-old boy. I have no doubt that you'll be all the help to this family you can be, but we must all work together as we go on with our lives."

Chris hugged her again. "You're the best mama in all the world!"

Hannah held him close. "I'm glad you feel that way. Tell you what..."

He eased back to look at her face in the faint light.

"Let's talk to Jesus about it right now."

Hannah asked the Lord to help Chris to be a source of strength to his brother and sisters, but she also asked the Lord to help Chris understand he could not carry the load his father had carried, and he wasn't expected to carry it—not by God, and not by his mother.

As soon as she said "Amen," Chris said, "Lord, You know how hard it is on all of us to have lost Papa. We don't understand why You took him, but we know You don't make mistakes. Thank You, Lord, that Mary Beth, Patty Ruth, B. J., and I still have our precious mother.

"Lord, please help us to be the comfort and support to Mama that we ought to be—especially me. Thank You for Micah, and for what he taught me tonight about putting my neck in Your yoke so I will find my burden easy and light. Please give Mama and us kids a happy life together at Fort Bridger. And Lord, please give me the wisdom and strength I need to carry as much of the load that was Papa's as possible."

Hannah blinked against the moisture in her eyes and swallowed hard. She patted Chris's arm. "We'd best get back to the wagon. You need to get some sleep before dawn."

As they headed back to the circle, a shadowed figure moved toward them.

"The boy all right?" came the familiar voice of George Winters.

"Yes," Hannah said. "Thank you for letting me know he'd left the wagon."

"Glad to, ma'am."

She urged Chris toward their wagon. They crept inside and managed not to wake any of the children.

Chris slipped out of his boots and into his narrow bed. Soon he was fast asleep, and Hannah lay in silence, listening to his soft, even breathing. And to B. J's and Patty Ruth's.

She strained her ears toward Mary Beth, then raised up on one elbow and peered through the darkness. "Mary Beth, why aren't you asleep?" she whispered.

A shaky whisper came back. "I...I heard Mr. Winters and what he said about Chris. Is he all right?"

"Yes. He finally let out his grief over Papa. He'll be fine. You get to sleep now."

"Mama?"

"Yes?"

"Could...could I come over there? I know it's crowded, but I need you to hold me."

"Come on, sweetheart."

Mary Beth squeezed into the tight quarters of her mother's bed. Hannah embraced her tightly, and said, "I love you."

"I love you, too," came a tremulous whisper.

Soon Mary Beth Cooper slept in her mother's arms.

Chapter Three

The wagon train was on the move just after sunrise the next day, but the heat descended early.

The travelers were close enough to the mountains to pick out snow-clad crevices on the north side. A few long-fingered clouds hung low over the jagged peaks that took an uneven bite out of the deep blue sky.

When the sun finally dropped behind the mountains, everyone sighed in relief as a cool breeze kissed their hot, sweaty faces.

Ezra Comstock led the wagon train up the slopes that would gradually take them into the mountains and over South Pass.

Stuart Armstrong rode alone as he drove the Cooper family wagon. The children were with various friends, and Tracie Armstrong had invited Hannah to ride with her. Hannah had ridden with Suzanne Marlin that morning. It helped to have women to talk to. Her grief over Solomon's death dulled somewhat as her friends kept her mind occupied.

Brush covered the lower slopes of the Rockies. But midway up, quaking aspen skirted the mountains and looked like orange diamonds in the light of the setting sun. Higher still, the towering blue spruce cast their deep shadows—mysterious forests that stretched up to timberline at just over eleven thousand feet.

After the wagons had circled for the night, Hannah stood and stretched, then climbed down from the Armstrong wagon. "Thank you, Tracie," she said with a smile. "I enjoyed riding with you."

"It was my pleasure."

"Oh, no, the pleasure was all mine. It's such a joy to see how you've grown in the Lord since you came to know Him."

Tracie smiled. "Thank you, Hannah. You're very special to me."

"That goes both ways. It's going to be difficult to watch you and Stuart drive away from Fort Bridger. We may never meet again this side of heaven."

"I know, but won't we have a grand time when we meet up there?"

"That's for sure," Hannah said, and she waved as she turned to go.

A faint glow crested the mountain peaks and gave enough light for Hannah to take in the beauty of her surroundings. She could just make out the narrow passages on all sides that led into deep, dark spaces in the rugged mountains. Lofty conifers swayed with the breeze, accompanied by evening bird song.

As the evening wore on, Hannah kept busy with cooking and washing dishes, baths, and all the other mundane chores that went with wagon train travel, managing to push the loss of Solomon to the back of her mind.

That night, however, when the children were asleep, she lay awake, letting her mind slip back to her happy life with the wonderful man she'd married. Except for the war years, Solomon had always been at her side at this time of the day. Sweet memories made the grief heavier, almost unbearable.

Hannah knew she shouldn't do it, but she dwelt on how the evenings with Solomon were always so special. After they had tucked their energetic tribe into bed, she and Solomon would sit at the kitchen table over an extra cup of coffee and talk about the events of the day and make plans for the next.

They always read the Bible together and prayed, asking for God's blessing and wisdom in their lives. Bedtime would come, and they would fall asleep holding hands or locked in each other's arms.

Now my arms are so very empty.

The next day the wagon train wound its way into the mountains amidst cooler air and little dust. Though the going was slow, no one minded.

That night Hannah got her little brood to sleep and lay in the silent dark once more. She'd heard the boys and Patty Ruth laughing some during the day. Patty Ruth, who felt her mission in life was to give her brothers a hard time, was starting to tease the boys again, little by little.

Now Hannah's main concern was for Mary Beth. She seemed quite melancholy most of the time. She'd smiled a couple of times that day when Patty Ruth teased Chris, but she didn't laugh. Not even a giggle.

Hannah thought of Solomon as she lay in her small place with the children sleeping soundly around her. All at once the loneliness of her empty arms turned into cold, heart-piercing fear. How could she face the future without him?

Her stomach rolled and a bitter taste filled her mouth. How would she handle the store and be a mother to the new baby? She began gasping for breath, and a cold sweat beaded her brow. She had to get out of the wagon!

Hannah put on her robe and slippers and carefully climbed over the tailgate. As she headed for the river, Jock Weathers—one of the watchmen—walked toward her. "You all right, Hannah?"

She paused and sleeved perspiration from her forehead.

"I...I just need a little fresh air, Jock, thank you."

"If you need somebody to talk to, I'll go get Lucille."

Hannah raised a palm and said quickly, "Thank you, Jock, but that won't be necessary. I'll just go over by the river for a little while."

"All right, ma'am, but if you need me, I won't be far away. Just give a holler."

When she reached the river bank, she began to pace back and forth. *I should have told Ezra I wanted to turn back—*

The unfinished thought hung in her mind. She stopped and drew in a ragged breath. Facing the future in a strange place without her husband was suddenly too much. She'd been wrong to tell Ezra she and the children would go on. It was one thing for women who had their husbands, but for a pregnant widow? First thing in the morning she would seek Ezra's help to get on the next returning supply wagon. She and the children would go back to Independence and her parents.

Hannah was almost running back to the circle of wagons when suddenly her mind filled with potent words: *Thou wilt keep him in perfect peace, whose mind is stayed on thee: because he trusteth in thee.*

Hannah stiffened and came to an abrupt halt. She swallowed hard as a still small voice spoke to her heart. *Hannah, child, you've put your focus on the wrong thing. You've forgotten to trust in Me.*

She trembled all over and started to weep anew. "O Lord," she said half-aloud, "please forgive me. Forgive my lack of faith, my negligence in staying my mind on You. Help me! Please give me the grace and mercy I need. Comfort me. It's all so new—facing life without Solomon! Give me wisdom. Increase my faith."

Her hands slipped down to her midsection. Sniffling, she said shakily, "Lord, I need extra strength from You to carry this precious child and bring it into the world without a father to help raise it." Suddenly a verse in the psalms came to Hannah's mind:

> The LORD will perfect that which concerneth me: thy mercy, O LORD, endureth for ever: forsake not the works of thine own hands.

The words, "the LORD will perfect that which concerneth me" reverberated in Hannah's mind. All at once a deep peace settled over her like a warm blanket, suffocating her fears. The mighty hand of the Lord was upon her, and she knew it. God, in His graciousness, was giving her the peace and fortitude she needed to carry on. His healing presence in the midst of her pain was unmistakable, and she knew He would sustain her as she and her children continued on to Fort Bridger.

In the morning, Hannah felt stronger than she had since Solomon's death. She could tell that Chris, B. J., and Patty Ruth were in better spirits, too. Mary Beth, however, continued to worry her.

Solomon Cooper had loved his children equally, but he had shown each of them that they were special to him in a unique way. Mary Beth and her father had been buddies, and though it was recognized by the others, never had there been an ounce of jealousy.

Mary Beth had often worked with her papa in the store. Father and daughter shared a great love for books of various kinds, and Solomon was pleased with Mary Beth's desire to learn and with her goal to be a schoolteacher. He was very supportive of her plans to go to college and earn her teaching certificate.

They had often taken long walks on summer evenings

and enjoyed the many wonders of God's handiwork in nature. Their walks also included conversations about the Bible.

From the time Mary Beth was four years old, people had commented on how much she resembled her father. Though she adored her mother and thought she was the most beautiful woman she'd ever seen, she also thought her father was the most handsome man. To hear that she looked like him always made her feel good about herself.

Since his death, she had stolen glances of herself in the small mirror in the wagon. It comforted her sore heart to see his resemblance in herself. In fact, she was looking in the mirror as the wagon jounced along when she heard her mother shout, "Chris! Where are you going?"

B. J. and Biggie were at the front of the wagon, looking past Hannah and Patty Ruth as Stuart Armstrong pulled rein and drew the wagon to a halt. Mary Beth hurried to join them and saw her older brother galloping Buster down a steep slope through small conifers and brush.

Ezra Comstock wheeled his horse around as Micah drew the lead wagon to a stop.

Chris heard his mother's call, but didn't look back. He pulled his Winchester .44 repeater rifle from its saddle scabbard and kept his sight on the big male cougar menacing a fawn trapped in bramble halfway between the trail and the river. The fawn shrieked in terror as the cougar lashed at her with his powerful paws.

As Buster stirred up a cloud of dust on the way down the slope, the cougar lifted his head and hissed and roared. Chris worked the rifle lever and shot above the cat, making it turn tail and run. Within seconds, the cat was on lower ground, running along the river bank, and soon disappeared.

Chris leaped from the saddle, keeping his rifle in hand, and slowly approached the terrified fawn. There were claw marks on her rump and left side. She struggled to get loose from the bramble bush, but the prickly limbs held her fast. Her large brown eyes were bulging, and she was panting hard.

Chris moved closer, saying, "It's all right, little deer. I won't hurt you."

At the sound of pounding hooves he looked up to see Ezra riding down the slope in a cloud of dust. People stood at the ridge of the slope, looking down, and some of the men on horseback rode at a slower pace behind the wagon master.

Ezra reached bottom and slid from the saddle. "I think you scared that cat off for good! Poor little gal, she's really scared. Looks like he scratched her pretty bad."

"Sure did," Chris said. "We need to get her out of the bush."

The men on horseback pulled up. Behind them, through the dust cloud, Chris could make out two or three others on foot.

Jock Weathers helped Ezra and Chris spread apart the bramble bush, and soon the little fawn was out. She struggled as the men held her to examine the claw marks.

Micah Comstock reached the small group ahead of the other men on foot. "Look, fellas!" he said, pointing further down the slope. A doe stood a few yards below, looking at them through the trees.

"Shouldn't we put some salve or something on these scratches, Ezra?" Jock asked.

"No need. Her mother's saliva will heal her faster than any salve man can produce. The Lord fixed it that way." Ezra turned to Chris. "Let her get to her mother now."

Chris nodded, and patted the fawn's head. "Good-bye, little gal. You get well real soon, won't you?"

The men released the fawn, and she bounded to her mother, making a shrill sound in her throat. Instantly, the doe examined her baby and began licking the wounds.

When the men returned to the wagons, Hannah rushed to

her son, who was leading Buster, and wrapped her arms around him. Ezra explained to everyone what Chris had done, and he was greeted with cheers and applause.

As the wagons started to roll again, Chris rode Buster beside the Cooper wagon. Patty Ruth, who sat between her mother and Stuart, said, "I'm proud you're my brother, Chris."

Chris grinned at her. "Why, thank you, Patty Ruth. Is that because I saved the little fawn's life?"

"Well, sort of."

"Sort of?"

"Mm-hmm. Even though you missed when you shot at the cougar, you did scare him away."

"Patty Ruth, I missed him on purpose. I was just trying to frighten him so he would run."

The five-year-old snorted and said, "If all you were doing was trying to scare him, why didn't you just let him see your face? That'd scare *anything* away!"

Stuart hurriedly stifled a laugh. B. J., who was in the back of the wagon, laughed out loud, and Mary Beth smiled.

Chris was about to retort when Hannah gave him a look that said, *Leave it alone.*

He did...reluctantly.

"Patty Ruth, you shouldn't say things like that about Chris," Hannah said. "He's a very handsome boy."

"Well, I heard Randy Perkins tell Chris one time that he had a face only a mother could love."

Chris made a mock-angry face at Patty Ruth and said, "Mama, can't you do something with her?"

B. J. giggled. "Yeah, Mama. Like maybe feed her to that cougar back there."

"B. J., that'll be enough of that!" Hannah said.

Patty Ruth looked back at B. J. and stuck out her tongue. B. J. returned the same, and Biggie barked and wagged his tail.

Hannah glanced at Mary Beth, but her oldest daughter sat

in silence. When will we get our Mary Beth back? she wondered.

That evening, as they prepared to make camp, Ezra Comstock rode along the line of wagons and told the people they'd made excellent time the past couple of days. They would camp a mile ahead at a spot called Burnt Ranch.

When the wagons circled for the night, a few people noticed a burial plot with about three dozen grave markers. Ezra pointed out that all the graves were those of travelers on the Oregon Trail who had died at or near this spot.

Some of the wagon train members asked if Burnt Ranch was a particularly dangerous place. Ezra told them he'd never seen anything dangerous about it, but for some unknown reason, the area happened to be a jumping-off spot for eternity.

The children ran to gather kindling and firewood from beneath the trees while the men carried water from the river and the women started supper. Soon the aroma of cooking food filled the air.

When supper was over, Ezra stood before the travelers and said, "Folks, we're now nine hundred and five miles from Independence. If everything goes well tomorrow, we'll reach the base of South Pass early in the afternoon."

Morning came with clouds covering the sky. The air was quite cool, and the wind that swept down off the high peaks made it feel even cooler.

About an hour after pulling out from Burnt Ranch, Stuart began talking about God and his newfound faith. Hannah had her Bible open on her lap and was answering Stuart's questions with Scripture. She was pleased at how much he and Tracie were growing in their Christian life.

Patty Ruth sat between them, holding Tony the Bear and listening.

Hannah had just finished reading a verse when B. J. stuck his head above Patty Ruth's and said, "Mama, could I talk to you about somethin' very important?"

"Sure, honey. What is it?"

B. J. frowned. "I mean by ourselves…in the back of the wagon?"

"You mean right now?"

"Yes, ma'am."

"All right." She rose from the seat and turned toward the back of the wagon. "Patty Ruth, you stay up here and keep Mr. Armstrong company."

"She'll do that, all right," Stuart said with a chuckle.

Patty Ruth smiled at him and asked him where he was born.

Hannah was climbing into the back as Stuart said, "Well, Patty Ruth, have you ever heard of Ohio?"

The child thought on it a moment. "Is that by Arkansas, where Grandma and Grandpa Holden are from?"

"Not exactly. Ohio is a long way north and east of Arkansas."

Hannah followed B. J. to the rear of the wagon and sat down on a wooden box. "Okay, honey," she said, keeping her voice low, "what's this important business you want to talk to me about?"

B. J. took a deep breath and sighed. "Mama, I don't want you to be mad at me. I did somethin' I shouldn't, but I was worried about Mary Beth and I—"

"So what have you done, son?"

"I…well, I just happened to see Mary Beth's diary layin' over there next to where she sleeps, and—"

"B. J.! You didn't!"

"Well, like I said, Mama, I've been worried about her. She's still so sad all the time."

"So you read her diary."

"Not a whole lot. Just what she wrote since Papa...died."

"And?"

"Well, she wrote day before yesterday that...would you like to look at it?"

"No. You just tell me."

"You're mad at me, aren't you, Mama?"

"Not mad, honey, just a bit upset. Someone's diary is a very private and personal thing. It was wrong of you to open it without Mary Beth's permission."

The eight-year-old boy ran his fingers through his dark-brown hair. "I know. It's just that I've noticed tears in her eyes when she writes in the diary at night. And with her bein' so sad all the time, I thought maybe I could find a way to help her if I knew what she was writin'."

Hannah stroked his freckled cheek. "I'm glad you want to help your sister, B. J., but you mustn't ever look in her diary again."

The boy dropped his gaze. "Yes, ma'am."

"But now that you've seen some of what Mary Beth has written, and you wanted to talk to me about it, what did she write that you want to tell me?"

"Well, it almost seems like she's mad at God for taking Papa from us. And she wrote three times that she misses Papa so bad that she wishes she could die and go to heaven so she could be with him."

Hannah's heart grew heavier. "Anything else, B. J.?"

"No. That's it. I just thought you should know."

"All right. Now, we must keep this to ourselves, do you understand? We tell *no one* that you looked in Mary Beth's diary, and we tell *no one* what you read there. Understand?"

"Yes, ma'am."

"You just pray for her and ask the Lord to help her through this hard time, okay?"

"I will."

"And you pray for me, that I can help Mary Beth without ever telling her I know what she wrote in her diary."

"Yes, Mama."

"I'm glad you love her that much, son. And thank you for sharing it with me. But you do understand that you're never to look in her diary again?"

"Yes, Mama. I won't ever do it again." He paused. "Mary Beth won't die, will she, Mama? I mean, so she can go to heaven to be with Papa like she said in her diary?"

"No, honey. You know that she and Papa were special pals."

"Yes, ma'am."

"It's taking her a little longer to come to the place where she can pick up and go on with her life. Why don't we just pray for her right now?"

"Okay, Mama."

Chapter Four

The next day, Ezra Comstock rode some three hundred yards ahead of his lead wagon, watching the broken clouds ride the wind currents. About two o'clock in the afternoon, he topped a rise and saw the base of South Pass, like a wide gate, amidst the rugged mountain peaks. He drew rein and pivoted his horse to wait for the wagon train to reach him. As the lead wagon drew near, he signaled his nephew to haul up.

"Start the circle, Micah," he called. "I'll explain to everybody what happens next."

When the travelers had left their horses and vehicles to meet with Ezra, he said, "Folks, that open space directly to the west is the base of South Pass. We're gonna take a pause here for about a half hour and let the animals rest. We've been followin' the Sweetwater River for quite a long time, but now we leave the river behind.

"We'll cross the Continental Divide at a summit of seventy-five hundred feet above sea level. Does anyone know why South Pass was chosen as the Oregon Trail route?"

"I know, Mr. Comstock," said Becky Croft as she raised her hand.

"All right, tell us, Becky."

"It's lower than the other passes. A *lot* lower."

"Right. All the other passes are three to four thousand feet higher. Not only that, but South Pass makes wagon travel over the Continental Divide relatively easy and simple because of how wide it is. Both sides of the pass—ascent and descent—are gradual compared to the other passes.

"We'll come to South Pass City about an hour before sundown and make camp just east of town. They've got a general store there, and we can stock up on food and supplies, get us a good night's rest, and start out fresh in the mornin' for the climb to the summit."

As predicted by the silver-haired wagon master, the train drew near South Pass City as the sun lowered onto the jagged peaks of the Wyoming Rockies.

To Hannah Cooper, the higher they climbed the more beautiful the land became. Long centuries before, the mighty hand of God had smoothed out the plains and scooped out the valleys behind them, and rounded off the hills through which they'd climbed earlier in the day. She appreciated the beauty of all God's handiwork, but these mountains were indescribable. The beauty and grandeur of it all took her breath. She only wished Solomon could have experienced the wonder of it with her.

As the setting sun cast long shadows, Ezra guided the wagons into a circle at the east edge of South Pass City. The people alighted from their wagons with a bit more excitement than usual and walked the broad street that ran through the center of town. Two blocks of weather-worn clapboard buildings made up the town's business district.

McDougal's General Store was situated on a corner of the main intersection, across from the South Pass Bank, the Sweetwater Hotel, and the marshal's office and jail, whose sign informed them that William L. Stone was town marshal.

A few people were gathered outside the general store, watching two elderly cowboys do rope tricks and crack jokes. The wagon train people swelled the size of the usual small audience, and the old cowboys reveled in so many people to watch their act.

All of the Coopers except Mary Beth laughed at the jokes and applauded the tricks along with the rest of the people. Hannah noticed that her eldest daughter hadn't once smiled during the performance.

When the act was over and the crowd had dispersed, the wagon train travelers stocked up on their supplies and returned to the circle of wagons.

Later, as Hannah and her children ate with the Holdens and Deborah Smith, Tony Cuzak joined them to chat for a minute. "Those old cowhands were pretty good, weren't they?" he said to everyone.

"They sure were!" B. J. replied. "I wish they were travelin' with us. They're funny!"

"Yeah!" Patty Ruth said with a giggle. "Tony the Bear was laughin' at 'em!"

"Did you like them, Mary Beth?" Tony asked.

She forced a thin smile. "Yes, Mr. Tony. They're very good with those ropes."

"And the jokes. Weren't they funny?"

Her smile faded. "I'm just not ready for jokes, Mr. Tony," she said softly. "I still think about Papa a lot."

"Sure, honey. I understand. But your papa would want you to get on with life and enjoy it."

"Thank you for caring, Mr. Tony. And I've been meaning to thank you for the nice words you said about Papa at the grave."

"You're welcome, Mary Beth. Your papa was a fine man, and I owe him my life for caring about me and leading me to Jesus. Won't we have some reunion when we meet him in heaven?"

Mary Beth nodded at Tony's words and forced another smile on her lips. But in her young heart she felt she would be disloyal to her father if she didn't continue in her deep grief. She was even feeling a little anger at the rest of the family for laughing and enjoying the old cowboys when Papa's body lay back there in the grave.

Tony moved on, and when supper was over and the dishes were washed, Hannah thanked the Holdens for the meal and led her children toward their wagon.

As they walked across the circle, she said, "Mary Beth, let's you and me take a little walk. Chris, please take B. J. and Patty Ruth to the wagon. Mary Beth and I will be there shortly."

As mother and daughter walked slowly in the gathering gloom, a slim quarter moon gave off just enough light for Hannah to see her daughter's features. She laid a gentle hand on Mary Beth's shoulder and said, "Honey, did I detect that you might be a bit disturbed that your brothers, Patty Ruth, and I were having a good time watching the old cowboys perform?"

Mary Beth stopped abruptly and looked at her mother in the dim light. "I have to be honest, Mama. Yes, it disturbed me. How...how can you be that way with Papa hardly cold in his grave?"

Hannah prayed in her heart, asking the Lord for wisdom. She cleared her throat and said, "Honey, it's like Tony said a little while ago. You have a life to live, even though Papa is gone. And Tony was right; Papa would want you to go on with your life and enjoy it."

Mary Beth didn't respond.

"Honey, you were there when Papa left us. What did he say he wanted us to do?"

Mary Beth bit down on her lower lip. "Go on to Fort Bridger. Build the new life that we had planned."

"Then, wouldn't you say that Papa wants us to be happy and enjoy our new life?"

"But I miss him so much, Mama. It's like a part of me died with Papa."

"Honey, I feel that way too. And so do Chris, B. J., and

Patty Ruth. But we must not live in the doldrums. Papa wants us to be happy."

"But how much happier would we be now if God had let that dirty ol' rattlesnake die the day before he bit Papa? He's God. He could have done that."

Hannah took Mary Beth in her arms and held her close. In a half whisper, she said, "Honey, are you angry at God for taking Papa?"

Silence.

"I had a little of that kind of thinking, too, Mary Beth. Just for a few hours. But I got over it. We don't have a right to be angry at Jesus for anything. He went to the cross and paid for our redemption. And He sure didn't have to. If He had just turned His back on us and said, 'Let them go on to hell,' He would have been justified in so doing. Am I right?"

"Yes," Mary Beth squeaked, her lips trembling. "I love the Lord for what He's done for us...for *me*, Mama. But—"

"But what?"

"Why? Why did He take Papa? I need my papa!"

Hannah searched hard for the right words. "Honey, the Lord is perfect in His wisdom, as He is perfect in every attribute. He doesn't owe us an explanation for what He does. He simply wants us to trust Him, even though we don't understand His ways."

Mary Beth was quiet again for a long moment. "That's how it was with Job, wasn't it? When God took away Job's children, and just about everything he owned, he wanted to talk to God face to face, didn't he?"

"Yes, he did. Why don't we look at that passage of Scripture together and see what happened."

"Okay, Mama."

Back at the wagon, Hannah explained to the other children that Mary Beth was questioning why the Lord took Papa. Maybe some of them were wondering the same thing.

"Come on, children," she said. "Let's consult the Bible and read about Job."

As Hannah gathered her children about her in the wagon and turned up the lantern, B. J. hoped this meant his big sister wouldn't be mad at God any more.

Hannah turned to Job 13, and said, "Listen to what Job said to his friends who had come to comfort him in his loss. Verse 3 says: 'Surely I would speak to the Almighty, and I desire to reason with God.' Job had the same desire you do, Mary Beth. He wanted to sit down with the Lord face to face and reason with Him—ask Him why he was suffering."

Hannah flipped ahead to chapter 31 and read a portion of verse 35: "'Oh that one would hear me! behold, my desire is, that the Almighty would answer me…' Job wanted an answer from the Lord, Mary Beth, just like you've been wanting. It's only normal and natural."

Patty Ruth spoke up while Hannah turned more pages. "Mama, how come Jesus doesn't come and talk to us? He came and talked to people over in Jer—Jersulum—"

"Jerusalem."

"Yeah. Jersulum."

B. J. snickered.

"Don't make fun of me, B. J. I'm jus' a little girl."

"Here," said Hannah. "Listen to what Job said in chapter 23, verse 2: 'Even today is my complaint bitter: my stroke is heavier than my groaning.' Job was tempted to get bitter toward God over all the things that had happened to him."

B. J. thought of what he'd read in the diary. Mary Beth didn't *say* she was mad at God, but it sure seemed that way.

"Now, listen to verse 3," said Hannah. "'Oh that I knew where I might find him! that I might come even to his seat!' Hasn't this been pretty much what you've wanted, Mary Beth?"

"Yes, Mama."

"Here's what Job says he would do if he could talk to the

Lord in person: 'I would order my cause before him, and fill my mouth with arguments.' Job even searched for Him. Listen to verses 8–10: 'Behold, I go forward, but he is not there; and backward, but I cannot perceive him: On the left hand, where he doth work, but I cannot behold him: he hideth himself on the right hand, that I cannot see him…' Is this how you've felt, honey?"

Mary Beth nodded, her lips trembling.

Hannah nodded with compassion. "I didn't read verse 10 yet. After Job bemoans the fact that he cannot find the Lord to talk to Him in person, he says, 'But he knoweth the way that I take…'

"Mary Beth, the Lord knows the way that *you* take. He knows your life, your heart, your mind, and the direction you're headed. So he knew you would be on this wagon train, and that in His wisdom He would allow Papa to be bitten by the snake and die. He knew that, didn't He?"

"Of course He did, Mama."

"So now, Jesus is trying you to see if you will trust Him even though He won't come in person and talk to you and let you put forth your arguments. He's testing you to see if you will love Him even though He took your papa long before you thought He should. Do you understand what I'm saying?"

"Yes, Mama."

"You don't want to fail the test He's putting on you, do you, honey?"

"No, Mama. I still love Jesus just as much. And I want to please Him."

"Well, honey, Hebrews 11:6 says that without faith it is impossible to please Him. So you must trust Him now, in this trial. Trust that He never makes mistakes, even when He took Papa to heaven. You must not allow yourself to become bitter toward the Lord. Understand?"

"Yes."

"Now, let's finish this verse," said Hannah. "I'll start at the beginning and read it all. 'But he knoweth the way that I take: when he hath tried me, I shall come forth as gold.'

"Mary Beth, if your love for the Lord is what it should be, this is how it will turn out. When you get through your grief over Papa, you will come forth as gold."

"That's what I want, Mama. It's just that I miss Papa so much."

"The Lord understands that, honey," Hannah said softly. "He's the one who gave you and Papa the sweet relationship you had. The main thing is that you not be angry at God for taking him."

"I...I know. It's just been so hard."

Hannah flipped through a few pages. "Let me show you what God says about Job when the trial was over. Look...here in chapter 42, verse 12: 'So the LORD blessed the latter end of Job more than his beginning...' So you see, Job's words were correct when he said, 'When he hath tried me, I shall come forth as gold.'"

"This Scripture is a good lesson for all of us, Mama," Chris said. "I too have struggled to not feel bad toward the Lord for taking Papa."

Hannah closed her Bible and sighed. "We've all been tried, my precious children. But even though we don't understand why, we must trust Him completely. He's a wonderful God. We owe Him everything."

"And we can be happy because we know we'll see Papa again someday in heaven," said B. J.

Chris nodded. "That's right. And then we'll never be apart again—any of us. 'Cause Jesus saved us and promised to take us to heaven when we die."

Patty Ruth turned pale. She looked up at her mother and said weakly, "Will *I* go to heaven to see Jesus and Papa when I die? I haven't been saved yet."

Patty Ruth had been asking many questions about salvation up to the time Solomon had died. Hannah knew the truth of the gospel was slowly working its way into her little heart. But Solomon's death had dominated the thinking of all the family of late.

She touched Patty Ruth's head and smoothed her hair. "If you were to die right now, honey, you would go to heaven to be with Jesus and Papa because you're very young. You don't understand all about sin and being saved. Jesus has made it so you're safe until you're old enough to be saved."

"How old do I have to be, Mama?"

"Well, it really isn't *how old,* honey. I should have said Jesus will keep you safe until you clearly understand about sin and why Jesus died for you on the cross."

"Okay," she said, satisfied that all was well.

"Now, it's time for bed," said Hannah. "But first, let's talk to the Lord."

Hannah prayed for each of her children. When she came to Mary Beth, she asked the Lord to give her the faith to come through this trial as gold, and to help her find happiness once again.

Later, when the lantern was out and the family lay quietly in the darkness, Mary Beth called for her mother.

"Yes, sweetheart?" came Hannah's tender reply.

"You're the best mother in all the world. I love you."

"And I love you, Mary Beth. You're the best twelve-year-old daughter in all the world."

"I hope when I grow up that I'll be almost as good a mother as you are."

"You'll be better!"

"Oh, no, Mama. But I sure am going to try to be almost as good as you."

Hannah brushed away tears, thanking the Lord in her heart for the love of her children. She thought of the little one growing under her heart. Though she loved the four children who lay around her with everything that was in her, still the Lord had enlarged her love capacity to include the little life she carried in her womb.

The wagon train topped South Pass summit at noon the next day and started down the western side. Two bald eagles swooped low over them, screeching loudly as if to complain that the long line of wagons and animals were trespassing on their territory. They made a wide circle, came back screeching a second time, then flew out of sight.

Micah Comstock knew the ritual. He guided the lead wagon to a spot some three hundred feet below the summit and hauled up. Ezra Comstock rode along the line of wagons, telling the drivers to spread out. There was something he wanted to show them.

Ezra led the travelers on foot to a massive rock formation where clear, sparkling water spilled from a hidden source and headed down the side of the mountain in a gurgling stream.

He ran his gaze over the group and said, "You're looking at what is called Pacific Springs, so named because it's the first water source after the Continental Divide in the Pacific watershed. It's customary for travelers of the Oregon Trail to take a ceremonial drink of the first water that flows into the Pacific Ocean."

On such a warm day, all were glad to drink the cold mountain water before moving on.

At the end of the next day, they were once again on level ground, with the Wind River Mountains to the north. They camped at an abandoned settlement called Dry Sandy, right next to Little Sandy Creek. A faded sign that read *Pony Express* identified a weather-beaten log building whose open doors swung on rusty hinges

After supper, Ezra gathered the people around the main campfire and pointed to the old log building. "As you can see, this was a stopover place for the Pony Express riders back in 1860 and 1861. I'm glad I can tell you that we're now just ninety-nine miles from Fort Bridger, where Hannah Cooper and her children will make their new home."

"We'll miss you, Hannah!" called out Maudie Holden. "The children, too!"

Others joined in.

Ezra nodded, and continued speaking. "Now everybody give me your attention. We haven't had to watch for Indians for nearly two weeks now, but I want you to understand that has changed. We're now entering big Indian country. There are Crow, Sioux, Snake, Shoshone, and Blackfoot all around us. We have no reason to fear the Crow; they're very friendly to white people. Many of their braves work as scouts for the United States Army, and Hannah and her children will meet some of them at Fort Bridger.

"There's a large Crow village a few miles north of the fort. Their chief is a brilliant young warrior called Two Moons. He and I have become close friends during these years I've been leading wagon trains to Oregon and California."

Dave Croft spoke up. "So the other tribes you mentioned are hostile toward whites, Ezra?"

"It depends. Some of the Shoshone are friendly, but some are not. However, even the Shoshone who are unfriendly have not been known to attack wagon trains or army posts. They just tolerate white people, wishing they'd stay out of their territory.

"But the Sioux, Snake, and Blackfoot are very hostile toward us. They often attack without provocation. So everyone keep your eyes peeled. If hostiles decide to attack us, we'll only know it a few seconds before it happens. Indians have a strange union with the earth. They can almost become a part of it, and you don't see them till they're comin' at you. If anyone sees them comin', give a shout in a hurry and form a circle fast...and get ready to fight."

The people were on edge after Ezra's talk, but as the wagons rolled across the shallow Little Sandy Creek the next morning, their faces were set doggedly westward, weapons within reach.

They camped that evening on level ground next to a small unnamed creek. After supper, the Cooper children visited their friends at various wagons within the circle, knowing that soon they would arrive at Fort Bridger and have to say good-bye.

Alone inside her wagon, Hannah's thoughts turned to Solomon. She shoved a couple of wooden boxes out of the way and opened the trunk that held his personal things.

On top was his well-worn Bible. A lump formed in her throat as she picked it up and held it, her eyes fixed on the faded words: *Holy Bible*. She thought of how Solomon had read and studied it for so many years. He had used it to lead many to Jesus. As she ran her fingertips over the cracked leather, her eyes flooded with tears that spilled onto the cover. She brushed them off with a shaky hand and laid the book aside.

Her fingers took up Solomon's pocketknife, wallet, and pocket watch. She squeezed the objects lovingly and laid them next to the Bible.

Next were the shirts she had made for him. She caught his scent, though the shirts had been washed since last he wore them. She lifted the top shirt and buried her face in it, tears staining the fabric.

After a few moments she laid the shirts aside and reached for a leather folder containing the papers from the sale of the store in Independence. She opened it with trembling fingers and released a sob, weeping all the more when she saw his handwriting and signature. After several minutes, she regained her composure and tied the strings on the leather folder.

Next came two pair of trousers and a brand new pair of boots. His winter coat lay just beneath the trousers. She drew a shaky breath and caressed it, loving the memory of the man who had worn it. Beneath the coat was his revolver and gun belt.

At the very bottom of the trunk lay a special leather folder tied with a faded yellow ribbon. Her heart pounded as she opened it and pulled out the official paper bearing the seal of the President of the United States and signed by Abraham Lincoln. The Presidential Commendation bore the name Captain Solomon Cooper, acclaiming him for courage and valor above and beyond the call of duty, exhibited on the battlefield at Shiloh, Tennessee.

Hannah felt the same rush of pride she'd felt the day he came home from the War and showed her the paper.

Suddenly, she heard the voices of Patty Ruth and George Winters approaching the wagon. She placed all the items in the trunk and wiped telltale tears from her face as she moved the wooden boxes back into place.

"Hi, Mama!" came the sweet little voice of her youngest, as George Winters lifted her into the wagon through the rear canvas.

"Hello, sweetheart," Hannah said, smiling. "Did you have a nice time with Polly?"

"Uh-huh. Mr. Tony was there, too. He held me and Polly on his lap."

Hannah turned her attention to George Winters. "Thank you, George, for walking her back."

"My pleasure," he said, grinning. "Gladys and I would steal her if you looked the other way."

Hannah was able to laugh, but just barely. "Well, I won't

look the other way then. I couldn't make it without my little Patty Ruth!"

Winters chuckled, told mother and daughter goodnight, and was gone.

The five-year-old squinted up, cocking her head. "Mama, your eyes are red. You've been cryin', haven't you?"

"Oh, a little."

"About Papa?"

Hannah cleared her throat gently. "Yes, honey. About Papa."

"It's gonna be awhile yet till we don't cry about Papa, isn't it?"

Hannah nodded. "Mm-hmm. This kind of thing takes time to get used to."

Patty Ruth brushed a lock of auburn hair from her forehead and flipped a long ponytail over her shoulder. "You know what?"

"What?" Hannah lifted her youngest daughter to her lap.

Patty Ruth turned so she could look into her mother's eyes. "I wanna be a good mama like you when I grow up."

"That's a nice thing for you to say, sweetheart. I'm glad you think I'm a good mama."

"An' you know what else?"

"What?"

"When I grow up, I won' have a husban' as good as you did, 'cause there'll never be a man as good as Papa was."

Tears trickled down Hannah's cheeks. "I can't argue with you on that count, honey. There will never be a man as good as Papa was."

"I'm back, Mama!" came B. J.'s announcement as he climbed over the tailgate. Immediately he saw Hannah's tears. "Did Patty Ruth do somethin' bad?"

"No, we were just having a little talk about Papa."

B. J. moved closer and hugged his mother and little sister.

"It's gonna be all right," he said. "We'll never stop missin' Papa, but we've got happy days ahead at Fort Bridger."

Hannah laughed. "Yes, we do! This whole family is more than anxious to get to Fort Bridger, settle in our new home, and live a happy life!"

Chapter Five

The town of Fort Bridger, Wyoming, was situated in a shallow windswept valley on Black's Fork of the Green River. Rolling hills surrounded it, with the rugged Uintah Mountains in view a few miles to the southwest.

After Jim Bridger and Louis Vasquez established a trading post there in 1843, the town of Fort Bridger grew up around it. The U.S. Army built the actual fort in 1858. The military installation, with its ten-foot-high stockade wall, stood at the west edge of the thriving town.

In spite of the mid-September heat, the town was a beehive of activity when a pair of well-dressed horsemen rode in.

They stopped in front of the Fort Bridger Bank and Trust and watched a man on a scaffold putting finishing touches of paint on the eaves.

"Pardon me, sir," the older rider said in a deep bass voice. "Do you happen to be employed by Clayton Farley?"

"I sure am," the man said, sleeving sweat from his face.

"Where might we find Mr. Farley?"

"Well, sir, he's usually movin' around town to oversee all the buildin' projects he's got goin', but at the moment he's inside the fort at the sutler's store."

"Doesn't this town have a general store?"

"Not yet, sir. It's under construction—down there near the end of the next block on the east side of the street. You'll see it goin' up 'tween the clothin' store and the barber shop."

"And where is the Wells Fargo office?"

"It's under construction, too," the painter said, pointing in the opposite direction. "Down there in the middle of the block. Ain't open for business yet."

"I know," said the man. "I'm Winn Haltom, and this gentleman with me is Stanley Mills. We're Wells Fargo executives. We work out of Cheyenne City, and have been riding the newly proposed route to check on the new offices. We just came from Rawlins and wanted to see how the new office building is coming along here."

"Well, sir, you can ride on down and see for yourself, but you'll probably want Mr. Farley with you when you look at it. He can answer any questions you might have."

"All right. We'll go look for him."

Moments later, Haltom and Mills passed through the front gate of the fort under the careful eyes of two soldiers atop the tower where the flag of the United States waved in the hot breeze. They dismounted in front of the small structure that housed the sutler's store.

Two middle-aged women came out the door, carrying bulky burlap sacks. Haltom and Mills touched their hat brims and went inside.

Clayton Farley, a well-muscled, robust man of fifty, was in conversation with a slender, full-bearded gentleman about ten years his senior, when the two businessmen entered the store.

"Well, look who's here!" he said with a smile. He shook hands with both men, then said, "I'd like you gentlemen to meet Judge William Carter. He owns this store."

Farley saw the puzzled look in their eyes and explained that Judge Carter had come to the town at the same time the army fort was established and had opened the sutler's store in June 1858. He had served as a justice of the peace in Utah Territory, and was appointed district clerk by the federal government. In

September of that same year, Carter received his papers and seals of office as probate judge of Uintah County, Wyoming.

Haltom shook his head. "Pardon my big nose, but how come you're running this store, Judge?"

"My missus and I liked this place so much when we visited that we just decided to move in. The fort needed a store, so we opened one. Truth is, I'm eager to see the new general store open up in town so I can give all my time to the legal matters in this county."

Carter stroked his beard. "This town's growing, gentlemen. Right now, all groceries, staples, foodstuffs, and other items found in a general store are sold right here. Problem is, I can't carry enough inventory to keep the expanding population properly supplied."

Mills nodded. "So someone else is set to open the general store once the building's finished?"

"Yes," Carter said. "A Civil War veteran who's had a general store in Independence, Missouri, for several years. He's on his way now—with his wife and children. Name's Solomon Cooper."

"I see."

"Actually, we owe Cooper's arrival to Colonel Ross Bateman—he's the commandant here at the fort. When the colonel and his regiment were en route from Fort Benton, Illinois, they stopped in Independence. Cooper had served as a captain in the Civil War under Colonel Bateman. I guess it didn't take him long to convince Cooper to sell out and come to Fort Bridger. Mr. Cooper placed enough money in the colonel's hands to purchase the land and have the store built. The Coopers should be arriving here just about any time."

"I imagine the people of the town and the fort will be glad to have a larger store," Mills said.

Carter chuckled. "You can say that again! Folks are planning a royal welcome for the Coopers. It'll be better for everybody to have a store that can carry more inventory. And I'm eager to get out of the sutler business."

Clayton Farley clapped a hand on Haltom's shoulder. "Well, did you see how the Wells Fargo building is coming along?"

"No. We wanted you to give us the tour."

"All right, let's go."

As he and the Fargo executives walked the busy street, Farley pointed out several other buildings under construction, including a saddlery, boarding house, and church building. Right now Pastor Andrew Kelly and his congregation met in the town hall on Sundays and Wednesday nights.

Recently Farley's construction company had completed the one-room schoolhouse at the south end of town, and the small cabin next to it that served as the schoolmarm's home.

He and his crew had also completed the Uintah Hotel and its adjoining café, known as Glenda's Place. Both businesses were owned by Gary and Glenda Williams.

Farley pointed out the town's other businesses—the pharmacy, saloon, blacksmith shop, livery stable, doctor's office and clinic, a combination gun shop and hardware store, land office, ladies' dress shop, the barber shop, and the family clothing store.

He also had men working in the residential area, building houses. He'd brought a crew of thirty-seven men with him and had hired some of the men in town. Even at that, he was running behind on promised dates of completion.

The men arrived at the Fargo building to the sounds of sawing and hammering. Both Haltom and Mills were pleased at the progress on the building, and commended Farley for excellent work.

"Thank you, gentlemen," he said. "We should come fairly close to the promised date. Do you have an agent hired for this office yet?"

"Not quite," Haltom said. "Looks like we may have a husband and wife team coming. They're operating a stage stop up in the Sierra Nevada Mountains in California. We're negotiating, and I think they'll end up taking the job here."

"Your stage line should do well through here," said Farley. "More and more people are moving in all the time."

Mills nodded. "Only thing that has us worried is the Indian problem."

"I can understand that. Maybe with the army patrolling these parts, the hostiles will lay low."

With that, the two Wells Fargo agents bid Farley good-bye and rode east out of Fort Bridger.

Farley decided to check on progress at the general store. As he approached the new structure, he saw Colonel Ross Bateman and his second-in-command, Major Darrell Crawley, walking toward him.

A young worker painted a large sign in front of the store that read:

COOPER'S GENERAL STORE
Solomon Cooper, Prop.

"Hello, Clayton," said the distinguished-looking Bateman. "Major Crawley and I thought we'd stroll over and see how the store's coming along."

Farley cleared his throat. "We've been running a little behind. I'm glad the wagon train hasn't arrived yet. I've had a hard time with some of the local men not being able to work as fast as my regular help. I could even use more men, but there just aren't any more available."

Bateman ran his gaze over the white two-story clapboard building. It had a wide porch where folks could sit and while away time in warm weather. The store windows were gleaming and ready to be filled with samples of what customers would find inside. "Looks like you're pretty close to having it done.

Even the sign is about finished."

"We're close," Farley said, "as far as the store is concerned. It's the living quarters on the second floor where we're behind. If the Coopers don't arrive for another week, we'll have the store ready to operate. It'll take a couple of weeks beyond that to finish the living quarters. I've made arrangements with Gary Williams for the Coopers to stay at the hotel at my expense until they can occupy the second floor."

"That's mighty nice of you," said Crawley.

"I owe them that much for not having the place finished. Have you gentlemen seen the back side of the store?"

The three men walked between the general store building and the barber shop. Bateman blinked in amazement at the barn and small corral that stood some forty feet from the rear of the store. "How did you find time to do this, Clayton?"

Farley grinned. "I figured they'd need it right off. Have to put their animals somewhere."

Crawley peered into a window of the barn. "Well, I declare, Colonel. Clayton's already got hay in the barn!"

Farley chuckled. "Who do you think the Coopers are dealing with, Major? Some hayseed outfit?"

"Well, I guess not!"

Colonel Bateman gazed at Farley with approval. "Next time I have to have a fort built, Clayton, I'm going to tell the army to hire you!"

Suddenly they heard a loud voice from inside the store building. "You're crazy, Harris! I'm not either!"

"I know a drunk when I see one!" a second voice shouted. "And you're drunk!"

Clayton Farley shook his head and turned back toward the store. "Excuse me, gentlemen," he said over his shoulder. "I'll be right back. When things cool down in there, I'll give you a tour of the inside."

Farley rushed through the open door to find two men

shouting at each other. "What's going on, Gil?" he demanded.

Gil Harris was Farley's foreman on all the building projects. Farley had instructed him to concentrate on the Cooper's store to hurry its completion. Now he was standing nose-to-nose with Alex Patterson, a local laborer.

The foreman's face was beet red as he turned and said, "He's drunk, boss. You oughtta fire him! I've lost count of how many chances you've given him to straighten up."

Alex Patterson had sunken cheeks, deep-set eyes, and a bony, hawklike nose, which looked even more unattractive as he spat out, "He's got no reason to fire me, Gil! I'm not drunk!"

"You *are* drunk, Alex! The fact that you're so slow gettin' any work done proves it. I'm better off without you!"

Patterson swore. "You've got it in for me, Gil! And this is your way of tryin' to get rid of me! Let's settle it by steppin' outside."

Harris took a step toward Patterson. "Nothin' would please me more than to beat you senseless, you drunken sot!"

"Hold it right there!" Farley commanded. "You two swinging fists won't settle anything! Alex, Gil's right. I've given you plenty of chances to square up, and you haven't done it. I can smell the liquor on you from here."

Patterson wiped a bony hand over his mouth. "Well, maybe I had a drink or two a little earlier, but I ain't drunk."

"You look drunk to me. But even if you're not, you came to work with liquor in you. I told you before, I don't want any of my men drinking on the job. I hate to do this, Alex, especially because I'm already shorthanded, but you're fired. Get outta here!"

Sudden woe showed in Alex's eyes, and a twitch started in the hollow of his cheek. "Fired? Oh, please, Mr. Farley, don't fire me! My...my family. I—"

"You should've thought of your family before you tanked up on that whiskey, Alex."

"Please, give me one more chance. I won't come to work with liquor in me ever again. I promise. Don't make me go home and tell Nellie and the kids I've been fired!"

Clayton Farley took a deep breath and let it out slowly as he rubbed the back of his neck. He glanced at Gil Harris's stony features and made a decision.

"All right, Alex," he said. "For the sake of your wife and children, I'll give you one more chance."

A smile broke across Alex's thin lips. "Oh, thank you, sir. Thank you."

From the corner of his eye, Farley noticed the two army officers looking on just outside the door. To Alex he said sternly, "I mean it, mister. You mess up just once more, and you're through workin' for me. Understand?"

"Yes, sir," Patterson said humbly. "You have my word on it, Mr. Farley. I'll never come to work with whiskey in me again. And no beer or wine."

"Okay, I'll take your word on it. Now apologize to your foreman for the grief you've given him."

Patterson blinked and swallowed hard. But he turned to Harris and said, "Gil, I'm sorry for comin' to work when I've been drinkin'. And...and I'm sorry for the grief I've caused you."

Farley looked at his foreman expectantly.

Harris finally nodded. "All right, Alex. I accept your apology. Let's get back to work."

Satisfied that the episode was over, Clayton Farley walked toward the army officers. "Sorry for the interruption, gentlemen."

"That's all right," Colonel Bateman said, stroking his silver mustache. "Do we get our tour now?"

"Sure. Let me take you upstairs and show you the living quarters first."

When the tour was finished, he stepped out front with

them, where the young man had left the sign to dry.

"I hope this Alex Patterson keeps his promise to you, Clayton," Bateman said.

"Yes, he's sort of a strange one," Crawley said.

Farley nodded. "Alex is a rather slow-moving, down-on-his-luck veteran of the War. He's from Alabama...fought on the Confederate side, of course. I understand he was wounded at Gettysburg. Don't know any more than that, but his wife has told some folks around town that something else happened to him in the War that changed his personality. As you gentlemen know, a lot of men were affected mentally."

Bateman and Crawley nodded.

Farley pulled at his ear in frustration. "This isn't the first time I've gone easy on him, as you may have picked up. I do it not only because of what he suffered in the War, but for the sake of his wife and children. Nellie's a fine woman, and those three bright-eyed youngun's are good kids. Nellie works hard. She takes in washing to help make ends meet. She even does washing for some of the single soldiers at the fort.

"And those kids work hard, too. They live in a small tumble-down shack about a mile east of town. They have a small barn and a chicken shed behind the house. They raise chickens as part of the family income. Sell eggs, and sell chickens for meat, too. The kids do most of the work with the chickens."

The soldiers seemed genuinely interested in hearing about the Patterson family, so Farley continued to speak.

"I understand Alex gets pretty cantankerous with Nellie and the kids at times. Only real friend he's got in town is Les Coggins over there at the Rusty Lantern Saloon. And that's only because Alex spends so much money there. Most of the people hereabouts don't like Alex because they know how he treats his family. And he isn't too nice to folks around town, either."

"Too bad," said Crawley. "I hate to see war mess up a man's mind."

Farley sighed. "Yeah. I don't know if it was the War that did it or not, but Alex is down on women, too, and makes no bones about it. He believes they're inferior to men in every way, and their only purpose is to be housewives and mothers. Any woman who works in a store or an office, as far as Alex is concerned, is out of line."

"Must be a miserable man," Colonel Bateman said.

"That he is," Farley said. "And to make it even worse, Alex hates anyone who had anything to do with the Union side in the War."

Bateman chuckled. "Well, he should stay away from the men in the fort then. About 80 percent of them are Union veterans."

Farley shrugged. "All I can say about that is, if Alex hasn't any better sense than to start trouble with one of the soldiers, he'll just have to suffer the consequences."

Bateman glanced at the major. "We'd better get back to the fort. Thanks for the tour, Clayton. You're doing a splendid job on the store. I know Solomon and Hannah will be pleased."

"I hope so. I heard Judge Carter say that Cooper was a captain under you in the War, Colonel Bateman."

"Yes. He and Crawley were both captains in my regiment. I couldn't have asked for better officers."

"You'll like Solomon, Clayton," Crawley said. "Great guy. One of the bravest soldiers I've ever seen on a battlefield. He got a Presidential Commendation from Abraham Lincoln for his bravery on the battlefield at Shiloh."

Farley nodded. "And the judge said it was you, Colonel, who talked Cooper into leaving his store in Independence and coming here."

Bateman chuckled. "Well, it was both of us. We stopped in Independence on our way here from Fort Benton and spent some time with Sol and his family. They were already thinking about coming west. All it took was a little gentle persuasion to get them to agree that Fort Bridger would be the best place to come."

"From the talk I hear around town," said Farley, "folks are really happy about the new general store."

Crawley chuckled. "Well, I can tell you for sure that the folks in the fort are happy about it."

"Especially Judge Carter," said Bateman. "He's eager to turn the grocery business over to the Coopers."

"Boss, can I see you a minute?" came Gil Harris's voice from the front door. "Question about the counter in here."

"Sure," Farley said. "Be right there."

The army officers bid him good-bye and headed back to the fort.

The sun was dropping below the horizon as Alex Patterson left the general store building and headed down Fort Bridger's Main Street. He cursed Gil Harris under his breath; all day long Harris had found fault with his work.

He passed the blacksmith shop and looked through the open door where Abe Carver pounded a horseshoe on the anvil. He kept on walking, and muttered, "No black man has a right to own a business. Carver should still be a slave on a cotton plantation down South, sayin', 'Yassuh, boss' to the plantation owner."

Just as he was about to turn off Main Street and head east out of town, he saw Pastor Andy Kelly angling toward him from across the street.

Alex hated Christians, especially Bible-thumping preachers like Kelly. He hated church, he hated the Bible, and he hated the name of Jesus Christ. The farther he could stay away from all of that, the happier he would be.

"Alex!" came Kelly's friendly voice. "Wait up! I'd like to talk to you!"

Alex quickly turned the corner and didn't look back.

As he drew near the gate to his place, he saw his wife and children gathered at the chicken shed, which stood on the edge of a grassy brush-covered ravine. He wondered why they were bent over, looking at the ground. Even the family dog seemed entranced.

Suddenly the dog saw Alex and ran toward him. Shep was a long-haired black-and-white English sheepdog who had strayed onto the place two years before. The children had begged their father to keep the dog, and Nellie finally persuaded him to let the dog stay.

As Shep loped toward him, wagging his tail, Alex noticed blood on the dog's muzzle. "Whose blood is that, you dumb hound?" Alex said.

The dog trotted alongside Alex as he headed for the chicken shed and finally saw the bloody remains of four chickens.

"Looks like we've got another wolf or coyote again, Alex," Nellie said, brushing her long black hair away from her face.

"Shep found 'em, Pa," Luke said. "He came to the house barkin', wantin' to tell us the chickens had been killed."

Alex's features darkened. "Yeah? Or wantin' us to *think* a wolf or coyote did it."

"Pa," Willa said in a pained voice, "Shep didn't kill these chickens!"

"Then why's he got blood on his muzzle?"

"He was just sniffin' the chickens after he found 'em dead, Pa," Joshua said.

"Well, I didn't want that no-good dog in the first place! Wouldn't surprise me if it was him who killed the chickens."

"Honey," Nellie said, taking hold of her husband's arm. "You know it's natural for a dog to sniff something dead. Shep's never given us any reason to believe he would do something like this. It's got to be a wolf or a coyote."

"Well, it'd better be! 'Cause if I ever know for sure that no-good mutt killed one of our chickens, I'll shoot him!" He frowned at his boys. "Luke, you and Joshua bury what's left of these chickens." With that, he turned toward the house and growled, "I need a drink."

Chapter Six

On Sunday morning, September 11, the members of the Comstock wagon train gathered after breakfast to sing hymns and hear a brief Bible message by Tony Cuzak. Micah Comstock led in closing prayer, asking God to watch over them as they continued their journey, especially since they were now in hostile Indian country.

When Stuart Armstrong reached the Cooper wagon, Hannah was hoisting Patty Ruth onto the wagon seat. She smiled at him and said, "Stuart, you've been driving this wagon long enough. It's time I take the reins and let you drive your own wagon. I've kept you from Tracie too long as it is."

Deep lines furrowed Stuart's brow. "Are you sure you're up to it, ma'am? I'll be glad to drive you all the way to Fort Bridger if you need me to."

"Thank you, but I'll be fine. I'm sure Tracie could use a break. You've been so kind to help me all these miles. If I have a problem with driving, I'll let you know."

"Promise?"

"Promise."

Stuart grinned. "All right. I'll hold you to it. Just remember, I'm at your beck and call."

"I'll remember...and thank you."

Stuart waved and headed for his own wagon.

Hannah stood up on the wagon seat and looked back to

see if her drivers were ready. As usual, Tony Cuzak was in the wagon directly behind her, followed by Perry Norwood, Vanessa Tolliver, and Buck Mylan. Each waved to her, indicating they were ready.

Mary Beth and B. J. came on the run with Biggie. B. J. lifted the dog into the wagon, then helped his older sister up before climbing in behind her.

Mary Beth suddenly realized her mother was sitting on the driver's side of the seat. "Where's Stuart, Mama?"

"Driving his own wagon. I told him it was time I took the reins."

"Shouldn't you just let him keep driving?"

"No, honey. I'm fine."

Patty Ruth, who clutched Tony the Bear in her arms, said, "I'll drive if Mama gets tired."

B. J. stuck his head through the canvas opening. "Oh, sure, Patty Ruth. I can just see you drivin' them oxen."

"I could do it," the little redhead retorted.

"Yeah, right. I bet—"

"B. J., that's enough," Hannah said in a tone he understood.

He eased back and whispered in Biggie's ear, "Patty Ruth thinks she's so smart."

Biggie ejected a low whine, as if he would take Patty Ruth's part.

At the same moment, George Winters rushed up, holding his little daughter by the hand. "Mrs. Cooper, Polly wants to know if Patty Ruth can ride in our wagon."

Polly cocked her head, squinting against the morning sun. "Could she, please, Mrs. Cooper?"

"Well, how about *you* riding in *our* wagon, Polly? Would that be all right, George?"

"Sure, if you really don't mind."

"Glad to have her."

"She can ride here in the seat next to me, Mr. Winters,"

said Patty Ruth.

Winters lifted Polly up and sat her on the seat as Patty Ruth scooted over to make room. The wind plucked at his hat brim. "You be a good girl, Polly."

"I will, Daddy."

Chris reined in Buster beside the wagon. "Are you gonna drive today, Mama?"

"Sure am," she said, smiling at him. "It's time."

Chris grinned. "I'm glad you're up to it again."

Ezra led the train out with his familiar, "Wagons, ho-o-o-o!" and wheels began to roll.

After about an hour, Patty Ruth and Polly decided they would like to ride in the back with Mary Beth. At Hannah's request, B. J. left Biggie with the girls, crawled up front, and sat beside her on the seat.

It was just past midmorning when the smell of rain filled the air, and the travelers saw storm clouds building on the western horizon. Within an hour, the sky was almost covered with clouds, and by noon the sun was blotted out.

Soon the western sky flickered with lightning. Thunder rumbled like distant cannons firing on a battlefield, and the wind grew stronger.

Chris had decided to ride Buster beside the wagon on his mother's first day of driving alone. At the sound of thunder, Buster nickered, and Nipper, who was tied to the back of the wagon, answered in kind.

"Looks like we may get rained on, Mama," Chris said.

Hannah nodded, holding tightly to the reins. "Yes, and I'd like you to tie Buster back there with Nipper and get in the wagon."

Chris quickly obeyed, then climbed over the tailgate and patted a welcoming Biggie.

Just then Ezra rode up from behind and said, "Hannah, it looks like we're in for a bad storm. We're gonna make a circle in that wide spot on the trail by those tall cottonwoods."

Powerful western winds drove the black thunderheads closer, and just as the wagons finished circling, tiny drops of rain pattered down, a promise of heavier rain to come.

George Winters came to get Polly as Hannah and B. J. climbed inside the wagon and Chris started to close the canvas flaps.

Polly wanted to stay, but her father told her she had to come with him. As they hurried away, he promised her she could ride with the Coopers again tomorrow.

Suddenly the wind stopped. A hush fell over the Wyoming prairie as if all the creatures beneath the blackened sky were holding their breath. The lull was short-lived. Soon the wind swooped down again, gaining strength.

Inside the Cooper wagon, Patty Ruth clung to her mother with Tony the Bear firmly held against her chest. Mary Beth sat on Hannah's other side. B. J. was trying to calm a nervous Biggie, and Chris was at the tailgate, peering past the edge of the canvas flap and speaking in low tones to the nervous horses.

The nearby cottonwoods thrashed in the escalating wind, and bolts of lightning chased each other across the black sky. The rumble of thunder shook the wagons.

Suddenly the rain fell like a waterfall, drumming the canvas roof and the metal buckets hanging on the side of the wagon. The fierce wind sprayed water around the edges of the canvas.

"I'm scared, Mama," Patty Ruth said, gripping her mother tighter.

Chris left the nervous horses to put an arm around his little sister. "It'll be all right, Patty Ruth. The storm probably won't last much longer."

The lightning and thunder did only last another thirty minutes. But the rain went on and on.

It was late afternoon before the rain let up and Ezra could lead his wagon train westward once more. By sunset, the sky was almost clear, and the wind had died down to a cool breeze.

Patty Ruth sat beside her mama on the wagon seat and took a deep breath. "God uses the rain to wash the world when it gets dirty, doesn't He, Mama?"

Hannah smiled and patted the little girl's cheek. "That's right, sweetheart. He sure does."

After supper, Ezra called a meeting around the main campfire. "Folks, we had quite a rain today. Far as I know, nobody's wagon suffered any damage. At this point, we're about sixty miles from Fort Bridger. We've been making exceptionally good time, even in spite of having to stop today during the rainstorm. We'll reach the Green River about one o'clock tomorrow. It may be swollen some because of the rain, but it shouldn't be too hard to cross.

"The Green is fifty-two miles from Fort Bridger, so if all goes well, we'll arrive on the sixteenth—this coming Friday. That's a day earlier than I expected. Of course, over the whole length of the trip, we're running better than a week late because of the mishaps and all that took place in Nebraska and eastern Wyoming. By the way, it's a fork of the Green River that runs through Fort Bridger.

"Anyway, we've made up a little time during the past few days, so I thought you'd like to know."

Hannah whispered to her children, "Getting there a day earlier than we'd planned is all right by me. We'll just have a whole day longer in our new home."

The train pulled out the next morning under heavy rain showers that started to ease off about eleven o'clock.

Polly Winters rode in the Cooper wagon again, as her father had promised. Since it was raining, Chris stayed inside the wagon, entertaining the younger children. Mary Beth was riding on the seat, next to her mother. Both wore slickers and bonnets to stay as dry as possible.

By one o'clock, the sky cleared and the sun shone. Slickers and bonnets came off, and Chris opened the flaps at both ends of the wagon bed and hopped out, then swung aboard Nipper.

Tony Cuzak, who drove the wagon just behind the Coopers', called to him. "Hey Chris! How come you're riding Nipper?"

Chris held the horse in place until Tony was abreast, then said, "It's been awhile since he's carried a rider. I thought it would be good for him to be ridden."

"Beautiful animal," Tony said. "Do you think your mother would consider selling him to me? I mean, since you're the only rider in the family now, and you have Buster."

"I doubt it, Tony. He was Papa's horse."

"Oh, sure. I understand. Just a thought. Since I'm going back to court Amanda, I'll need to buy a horse in Fort Bridger. No doubt there's a hostler there who'll sell me a horse."

"I would sure think so," said Chris, as he touched Nipper's sides with his heels. "Talk to you later, Tony."

Hannah looked a little surprised when she saw her son on Nipper. "Well," she said, "what's Buster thinking with you riding Papa's horse, son?"

"He's probably glad for a rest," Chris said with a grin. He scanned the land ahead and saw it sloping gradually toward a raging river. "That must be the Green, Mama."

"Yes, and it looks like the rains have swollen it right up to its banks."

"Mama...Tony just asked me somethin'. He wanted to know if I thought you would sell Nipper to him. He'll need a horse to ride back to the Kline place. I told him I didn't think you would."

Hannah didn't answer right away. Her attention was on Ezra, who was galloping back toward the train after taking a look at the river. She noted that he stopped at the lead wagon and said something to Micah, then began moving from wagon to wagon.

When Ezra reached her, he said, "The river's worse than I thought. I'm taking a vote. We can either wait for it to go down, which will no doubt take a couple of days, or we can take the train across a wagon at a time. Of course, if we get more rain, we'll have to wait on this side even longer."

"You know best about it, Ezra," Hannah said. "What should we do?"

"Well, I think we can get the wagons across, all right. However, I can't guarantee we'll do it without some damage to some of 'em. It's just whether the folks want to chance it so's we can stay on schedule, or sit it out till it goes back to normal."

Hannah thought for a moment. "How have those ahead of me voted?"

"To go ahead and cross the river. Every one of 'em, so far."

"All right. That's how I vote, too."

"Okay. I'll move on and see what the rest of the folks think."

The lead wagon was just reaching the river bank when Ezra trotted by, heading for the front of the train. As he moved past the Cooper wagon, he called, "Hundred percent voted to go across now, Hannah! We'll have a meeting at the bank."

Ten minutes later, the travelers stood in the welcome sunshine beside the roaring Green. The dark waters lapped at the edge of the bank, and fallen trees and tangled brush and clumps of foreign matter floated downstream with the rushing current.

Ezra stood with his back to the river and lifted his voice to instruct the people. "I have a rope in the lead wagon for just such an occasion as this. It's about ninety feet to the other side. I'll ride across and tie the rope to that big cottonwood over there. One by one, we'll tie the other end of the rope to a wagon and take it across. That way the wagon can't be swept away with the current.

"When it's your turn to cross, be sure that everyone stays seated and hangs on—the swiftness of the current will probably cause the wagon to rock and sway. Micah will stay on this side and help each wagon get started. When everyone else has crossed, he'll bring the lead wagon over."

He paused, scanning their faces, then continued speaking. "I need one of you men with a saddle horse to bring one end of the rope back to this side after each wagon reaches the other bank."

"I'll do it, Ezra," Dave Croft said.

"Okay. Let's get your wagon across first, Dave. Tie your horse behind. I don't want Mary to try to handle the reins crossin' the river. I'll need men to drive Hannah's wagon across, too, and also the supply wagon Vanessa's driving. It's just a little too much for a lady to handle the animals in the river."

Stuart Armstrong volunteered to drive Hannah's wagon, saying he would ride one of the Cooper horses back so he could bring his own wagon across. Tony Cuzak volunteered to do the same and drive Vanessa's wagon.

Ezra tied one end of the long rope to the front axle of the Croft wagon, then mounted his horse and plunged into the river. When he reached the other side he tied the rope to the huge cottonwood and waved for Dave to bring the wagon across.

Mary Croft sat beside her husband, and Becky rode in the back. Mary's face was devoid of color and her knuckles showed white as she gripped the edge of the wagon seat.

Dave snapped the reins and shouted at the oxen team to

move them toward the river. The lead oxen balked when their front legs felt the swiftness of the current.

"Hyah! Hyah!" shouted Croft, popping a whip over their heads. The six frightened oxen lunged forward, straining into the harness and yokes. The wheels quit turning and the wagon swayed on the current.

Mary and Becky let out tiny shrieks, and Dave's face pinched tight, but he shouted reassurance above the roar, "It's okay! We'll be all right!"

It only took a few seconds for the wagon to float downstream and reach the length of rope, then start to fishtail. The gallant oxen held their heads high and paddled furiously. The horse tied to the tailgate did the same.

Soon the animals' hooves found solid ground, and the Croft wagon rolled up the bank toward a smiling wagon master.

One by one, the wagons repeated the scary plunge into the river, ending the drama as their wheels touched ground on the far bank.

When it was time for the Cooper wagon to cross, Polly Winters wanted to ride with them. Her father agreed, making her promise to stay seated and hang on.

Stuart Armstrong urged the oxen into the river, with Patty Ruth seated between him and her mother. In the back, Chris gathered Mary Beth, B. J., and Polly close to him and made them link arms. B. J. held Biggie under one arm.

The wagon rocked and swayed as it floated downstream, reached the length of the rope, then began to move slowly toward the west bank as the oxen paddled. The men on the opposite bank pulled on the rope to help draw the wagon ashore.

Biggie began to squirm in B. J.'s tight grasp. Suddenly the little dog got free and headed for the rear of the wagon.

"Biggie, come back here!" B. J. said sternly. "You'll fall in the river!"

Biggie, however, paid him no mind, and hopped up on a box next to the tailgate. The wagon rocked with the tide, and Biggie lost his footing. Polly, who was closest to him, instinctively let go of Chris's arm and reached for the dog.

"Sit down, Polly!" Chris commanded, and leaned to grab hold of her.

Suddenly a heavy chunk of debris slammed into the side of the wagon and whipped it to one side. Biggie staggered sideways and fell inside the wagon, but Polly slammed into the tailgate and peeled over it into the raging waters.

"Mama-a-a!" wailed Mary Beth. "Polly fell into the river!"

Chris was already pulling off his shoes and telling Mary Beth to get a good hold on B. J. as Hannah hipped around on the seat. She saw Polly surface in the wake of the wagon, her arms flailing wildly, and then go down again.

"No, Chris!" she cried. "Don't go after her! You'll drown!"

"Listen to your mother!" Stuart shouted. "She's right! You'll never make it against this river!"

Several people on shore saw Polly tumble into the water and began to shout. George and Gladys Winters stood frozen in terror when they saw their little daughter bob to the surface, arms flailing, then disappear.

George broke away and ran down the bank, yelling Polly's name, while Gladys stumbled after him.

Tony Cuzak had just tied Nipper's reins to the tailgate of Vanessa's wagon when he heard the shouting and saw little Polly come to the surface in the swift waters, then go under again. He ran down the bank in time to see Chris Cooper plunge into the river from the rear of his wagon.

George Winters had leaped into the river too, but in his haste to save his little girl, he misjudged the speed of the water.

Already she was too far ahead of him.

Tony ran along the bank until he was beyond Chris's bobbing head, then plunged in. When he came up, he saw a terrified Polly Winters bob to the surface again, with Chris twenty feet behind her, swimming for all he was worth.

Tony was far enough down river that he began swimming at an angle toward her. All of a sudden, a large clump of brush slammed into him, pulling him beneath the surface. He was under for several seconds before he could work loose from the brush.

When he finally surfaced and saw two heads about twenty yards downstream, he realized Chris had reached Polly and was holding her face out of the water as he struggled to work his way toward the west bank.

Polly's father swam to the bank and climbed out to stand beside his wife, who watched her daughter in mute anguish.

On the other side of the river the Cooper wagon rolled ashore. Stuart leaped off the seat to help Hannah down, while Mary Beth and B. J. scrambled over the tailgate and rushed to the edge of the river. They could see two heads bobbing together in the raging current and Tony swimming toward them as they moved further downstream with every passing second.

Hannah was breathless. She moved her lips in silent prayer.

Young Chris Cooper fought the rapids until his strength was almost gone, but still he couldn't get Polly and himself to the bank. He was exhausted and knew he had to get himself and Polly out of the water quickly or they would both drown.

Just then he felt something touch his shoulder and heard a voice say, "Relax, Chris! Don't fight me! Hold on to Polly and let me take you to shore!"

Chris nodded and took a firmer hold on the little girl, giving himself to Tony's strength.

All three were coughing and sputtering when they finally collapsed on dry land a few minutes later.

The reunion on the river bank was a sweet and joyous one. While Hannah clasped her gallant son in her arms, the Winters held Polly, and voices poured praise on Chris and Tony for risking their lives for the little girl.

Everyone cheered on both sides of the river to see Polly in her father's arms, alive and well, and just now beginning to cry.

By three-thirty, all the wagons were on the west side of the river. Before they moved on, Ezra Comstock publicly commended Chris and Tony for their heroism.

After the applause died down, Ezra said, "Christopher Cooper, I have something very special I want to say to you. We've all learned on this journey what a brave man your father was—when he fought on the battlefields in the Civil War and when he laid down his life to save his family.

"Young man, if your father were here with us now, he would be very, very proud of you. I'm sure your mother, brother, and sisters are feeling the same kind of pride. You're cut out of the same mold the Lord made your father with. God bless you, son. You've done his memory proud today."

The people applauded even louder this time, some with tears streaming down their cheeks. Polly Winters broke away from her parents to wrap her arms around Chris's neck when he lifted her up and held her tight.

The wagon train had a ways to go before they could stop for the day, and the rejoicing travelers climbed aboard their vehicles to follow their wagon master once more.

Two hours later, Ezra signaled the train to stop for the day.

Supper was over by sundown, and the weary people sat in a circle, talking about the river experience and Polly Winters's close call.

As the last light of day gave way to the first evening star, Ezra stood before the people and said, "Our crossing of the Green set us back some. As I figure it, we won't make it to Fort Bridger on Friday. But if we have no further delays, we'll get there on Saturday around noon. Each man here will take a turn on watch through the night. We must stay alert, because Indians are never far away in these parts."

When the meeting broke up, Hannah and her children huddled next to their wagon and talked for several minutes. Finally Hannah said, "Okay, we're in agreement. Chris, will you and B. J. find Tony, please? Don't give anything away; just tell him the Coopers want to meet with him."

Soon, Chris and B. J. returned with Tony, and Hannah invited him to sit down with them. Tony looked at each face curiously, seeking a clue to the reason for his summons. All he could see was an excited light dancing in the children's eyes.

Finally Hannah said, "Tony, as a family, we want to tell you what a wonderful thing you did today. Chris and Polly might well have drowned if it weren't for you."

Tony's features turned crimson. "I just did what needed to be done, ma'am."

"Yes," Hannah said, "and my children and I are just going to do what needs to be done, too."

Tony looked at her quizzically.

"We've discussed it, Tony, and we've come to a full agreement. Chris told me earlier that you were wondering if I would consider selling Nipper to you, since you will need a horse to make your return trip to visit—and no doubt, marry—Amanda."

"Yes, ma'am."

"Well, neither the children nor I can bring ourselves to sell Solomon's horse to you."

Disappointment flooded Tony's face. "I...I understand, ma'am. I—"

"But we *can* bring ourselves to *give* Nipper to you."

Tony's eyes popped. "Wha—?"

"We love you, and we're in agreement that we want to give Nipper to you."

Tears glistened in Tony's dark eyes. "Mrs. Cooper, I don't know what to say. I—"

"How about, 'Yes, Hannah, yes Chris, Mary Beth, B. J., and Patty Ruth—I will accept your gift and ride him to Amanda and have a happy life.'"

Tony nodded with a broad smile. "Yes, Hannah, Chris, Mary Beth, B. J., and Patty Ruth—I will accept your gift and ride him to Amanda...and have a happy life."

"Good!" Hannah said. "That's what we wanted to hear. As of this moment, Nipper belongs to you!"

Tony shook his head and brushed at the wetness around his eyes. "Ma'am, I am deeply honored to be given the magnificent horse of the man who led me to Christ."

Hannah leaned forward and patted his arm. "And if Solomon could speak to us from heaven, I know he would say he's honored to have the man who saved his son and Polly from drowning own his horse."

Later that night, Hannah lay in the dark, silently thanking the Lord for the lives of her son and Polly and Tony. When she finished praying, she let sweet memories of Solomon drift through her mind, and she soon grew drowsy. She was almost asleep when she heard a sniffle.

"Mary Beth, is that you?" She heard another sniffle. "Are you all right?"

"I would be, Mama, if I could fall asleep in your arms."

When Mary Beth was snug in her mother's embrace, Hannah whispered, "Still having a hard time missing your Papa?"

"Uh-huh."

"I've noticed tears in your eyes the last couple of nights when you were writing in your diary. Sweetie, you've got to let the Lord help you accept Papa's death. You can't go on grieving this way."

"I know. Would you pray with me again, Mama?"

"Of course."

Afterwards, they both fell asleep, resting in the Lord's loving arms.

Chapter Seven

As the first light of dawn crept over the land, Chris Cooper quietly slipped from the wagon, carrying his shoes.

His first duty in the mornings was to untether Buster and Nipper and take them to the nearest water for a good drink. Even though Nipper was now Tony's, Chris had told him he would take care of the horse until they reached Fort Bridger.

He looked around as he put on his shoes and noticed a couple of the men on late watch talking together on the other side of the circle. The grass was wet with dew as he passed between two wagons and headed for the spot where he'd tethered the animals just before supper the night before.

When he reached the place, his head bobbed in disbelief. The stakes were in place, but neither horse was in sight. He rushed to the stakes and found that the ropes had been cut.

Heart pounding, he ran to the lead wagon and found Ezra and Micah putting salve on their oxen where the yoke rubbed them raw.

"Mr. Comstock! Micah! Our horses are gone! Somebody stole them!"

"Gone? You talking about Nipper and Buster?"

"Yes!"

"You sure they didn't just get loose and wander off?" Micah asked.

"Positive! The stakes are still there, but the ropes have been cut clean through!"

"Let's take a look," said Ezra, setting the can of salve on a wagon wheel.

The two men on watch saw the Comstocks and Chris hurrying across the circle and joined them just as they bent down to examine the ropes.

"What's happened, Ezra?" Lafe Tolliver asked.

"Indians stole the Coopers' horses," Ezra said with a sigh.

Lafe gasped. "How could they have gotten this close? We've had men on watch all night!"

"They got this close because they're Indians," Ezra said.

Hannah Cooper appeared, pushing her hair back from her face. "What's wrong?" she asked, glancing at Chris's face, then settling her gaze on Ezra.

"Indians stole Buster and Nipper, Mama," Chris said before Ezra could get the words out.

"Indians!" she said. "Ezra...?"

"'Fraid so, Hannah. Only Indians could have slipped in here past our watchmen and taken those horses. Come on, let's look around."

It took Ezra only minutes to find the place some fifty yards upstream where a small group of unshod ponies had stood while two braves moved in and stole the horses.

Hannah put an arm around Chris, who was close to tears. "Ezra," she said, "is there anything we can do to get Nipper and Buster back?"

Ezra lifted his battered hat and scratched his thinning, uncombed hair. "Humanly speakin', Hannah, no. Only God Himself can do that. If we'd track those savages and try to get the horses back, we'd just get ourselves massacred."

Hannah breathed in deeply and let it out slowly. "All right, then, we'll just ask God to bring the horses back to us."

Micah's jaw slacked. "Miss Hannah, ma'am...do you really

think the Lord has time to work on bringing back your horses?"

"Of course He does," she said. "The Bible says, 'Be careful for nothing; but in every thing by prayer and supplication with thanksgiving let your requests be made known unto God.' *Everything,* Micah. Our Lord is concerned about anything and everything that touches our lives. So we're going to have a prayer meeting. We're going to ask God to bring Nipper and Buster back to us."

As they walked back into the circle of wagons, Hannah kept her arm around Chris. She knew how much he loved his horse, and she knew how happy Tony had been to receive Nipper as his own. She was already praying that the Lord would act.

Word spread quickly about the theft and about Hannah's planned prayer meeting. Before breakfast fires were burning, the Christians in the wagon train collected beside the Cooper wagon, along with a few other interested parties. People throughout the wagon train were troubled that the Indians could so easily slip by the watchmen.

Hannah broke the news to Tony before most of the group arrived. Tony was dismayed to learn that Nipper had been stolen, but he joined the others in prayer and asked God to bring the horses back.

Later, while they were all eating breakfast, Patty Ruth patted Chris's hand and said, "Don't worry, Chris. Jesus will bring Buster back to you."

Chris's lower lip began to quiver and tears filled his eyes.

"You must have faith, Chris," Hannah said. "Jesus said that if we have enough faith, we can move mountains. Do you believe Jesus is powerful enough to make those Indians bring Buster and Nipper back?"

Chris nodded, his eyes downcast.

"Chris," B. J. said, "maybe Jesus will just let Buster and Nipper break away and come runnin' back to us."

Mary Beth seemed almost her old self when she said, "And God can do it any way He wants to, Chris."

Patty Ruth spoke again in her clear high voice. "I sure could tell that Mr. Tony believes Jesus is gonna bring the horses back. When he was prayin'—just like Mama—he was already thanking the Lord that He was gonna bring 'em back."

Hannah reached over and laid a hand on Chris's shoulder. "Let's trust Jesus to work it out, honey. All He asks is that when we pray, we believe He is able to do what we ask, and that He will answer in His own way, which is always best. You did pray with us, didn't you?"

"Yes, Mama."

"Well...?"

Chris raised his head and managed a weak smile. "I'm going to trust Jesus to do what's right."

"That's my boy!" Hannah said, patting his shoulder. "Now, let's just wait on the Lord and watch Him answer prayer."

When Chris learned the wagon train was going to pull out soon, he was in tears again. Hannah and Tony talked to him, telling him the Lord was not hindered by circumstances. He could bring the horses to them no matter where they were.

Chris climbed up in the lead wagon with Micah, and as the wagon train began to roll, Micah handed him the reins. "Here. You handle the oxen today."

The boy's countenance brightened. "All right!"

As the wagon rocked and swayed on the rough ground, Micah said, "Chris, you've got a wonderful mother. I think my own faith has been strengthened just listening to her pray."

"She's the best mother in all the world, Micah."

About an hour later, Ezra Comstock and Dave Croft were riding side by side, talking about the hardest part of the trip that still lay before them—the climb over the Sierra Nevada Mountains in California.

Neither man spoke for a moment, then Dave said, "It won't be the same when we lose the Coopers, Ezra. I'll miss them."

"Me, too. Those kids are real special. And Hannah...what a great lady!"

"I hope they find the happiness they deserve at Fort Bridger."

"They will. God's gonna bless 'em real good. I've got a feeling those folks at Fort Bridger are gonna be mighty glad to have Hannah and her brood in their town. They—"

Ezra's words were cut short as he saw a band of Indians riding toward them out of the dense forest to the north.

"We'd better form a circle quick!" Dave said.

Ezra squinted at the oncoming riders. "Wait a minute...I think it's Crows. We'll let 'em get a little closer before— It's okay, Dave. I can tell by the paint on their ponies. They're Crows."

He twisted around in the saddle and motioned for Chris to stop, even as he signaled that everything was all right.

As Chris pulled rein, Micah hopped from the wagon and ran along the line, telling everyone to haul up. Friendly Indians were coming. The travelers complied, then climbed from their wagons to watch the oncoming riders, whose copper-colored bodies shone in the sun.

As the Indians drew nearer, the one in full headdress waved. Ezra said, "It's my friend, Two Moons. Wonder what he and his braves are doin' this far from home."

Two Moons and his band of braves drew up in a cloud of dust. Ezra and Dave had already dismounted, and Micah joined them, leaving Chris at the lead wagon sixty yards away.

The morning breeze lifted the brightly colored feathers in the chief's headdress as he slid from the pinto's back.

Dave Croft did a quick study of the twenty-one solemn-faced braves and felt a small flicker of relief when he saw Ezra and the stalwart young chief clasp forearms in greeting.

"Ezra Comstock, my good friend! So good to see your face!"

"Yours too, my friend." Ezra was grinning from ear to ear. He turned and gestured toward Micah. "You remember my nephew, don't you, Two Moons?"

"Of course." The dark-eyed chief extended his arm for the Indian-style handshake. "It is good to see your face too, Micah Comstock."

Ezra turned to Dave. "Two Moons, this is Dave Croft. He and his family are travelin' with us to California."

Dave felt the power in Two Moons's hand and arm as they shook hands.

"I am happy to meet you, Dave Croft," the chief said with a smile.

"Likewise," Dave said.

Two Moons ran his gaze to the long line of wagons. Noting the crowd of people who looked on, he said, "They do know we are friends, yes?"

"They do," Ezra assured him. "Have you moved your village, Chief?"

"No. We still in same place." He pointed and said, "Our scouts report large herd of buffalo many miles to southeast. We go on hunting trip."

"Oh, I see. Well, I hope you find 'em and get a good kill."

The chief nodded.

"How are Sweet Blossom and Broken Wing?"

"Broken Wing is growing tall. Soon be as tall as Two Moons."

Ezra grinned. "I'm sure he'll be a great hunter and warrior like his father." Then he lifted his hat, scratched his balding head, and said, "Say, Two Moons, we...uh...we got a problem."

The chief's eyebrows arched. "Is there something Two Moons can do?"

Ezra dropped his battered hat back in place. "Well, you just might be able to."

"Speak."

Ezra told Two Moons about the Coopers' stolen horses and that it had to have been Indians who took them, for the band of thieves rode unshod horses. He then gave a description of Buster and Nipper.

"How many thieves?" Two Moons said.

"By what I could read in the grass, I'd say there were seven or eight of 'em."

Suddenly Two Moons stood even straighter and his dark eyes flamed. His mouth turned down as he said, "Two Moons and braves go to place where wagon train camped and find trail of thieves. We track them, Ezra Comstock. If we can, we bring horses back."

Vanessa and Lafe Tolliver were standing with Hannah Cooper and her children and the three young men who drove the Cooper supply wagons.

Buck Mylan turned to Tony Cuzak. "Did you tell Mrs. Cooper what we talked about before bedding down last night?"

"No, I didn't," Tony said, snapping his fingers.

Hannah looked at him. "Tell me what?"

"Buck and Perry and I got to talking, ma'am, and we decided we'd like to stay at Fort Bridger long enough to unload these supply wagons and stock the shelves in the store for you."

"Why, that would be wonderful!" Hannah said. "It sure

would save us a lot of work. But that would hold up the wagon train for probably three or four hours. I don't know if Ezra—"

"We already talked to him, ma'am," Perry Norwood said. "He said he'd be glad to give us whatever time we needed to do that for you."

"Well, bless his bones," she said with a chuckle. "Gentlemen, you've been such a help already—and you too, Vanessa—just by driving the wagons. But if you gentlemen really want to help me unload the wagons and stock the shelves, I'll sure let you!"

Tony grinned. "Then it's all set."

Patty Ruth had been studying the Indians with apprehension. "Mama..." she said.

"Yes, honey?"

"Are those In'ians gonna masker us?"

"Sweetheart, the word is *massacre*, but no, they aren't going to do that. They're friendly Indians. They won't harm us."

"Oh. I sure am glad."

"We all are, Patty Ruth," said Vanessa, stroking the little girl's cheek. "Soon you'll be safe in Fort Bridger, and you won't have to worry about Indians."

"Mama, look!" said B. J., pointing. "They're comin' this way!"

All eyes in the wagon train were fixed on the Crows as they galloped east along the line of wagons, their horses' hooves sounding like thunder. Patty Ruth, still a bit uneasy, gripped her mother's hand as they passed by.

As the Indians galloped away, Micah ran to the lead wagon. "Could you hear what was being said, Chris?"

"No, you were too far away."

"Well, those are Crow Indians. The one in the headdress is

my uncle's friend, Chief Two Moons. Uncle Ezra told him about Buster and Nipper. Two Moons is taking his braves to track them down!"

Chris's pulse quickened. "You mean they're going after the thieves so they can bring back Buster and Nipper?"

"That's it!"

"Oh, hallelujah!" shouted Chris, swinging his fist through the air.

Ezra drew rein at the Cooper wagon. "Hannah, that was my good friend, Two Moons. When I told him some Indians stole your horses, it made him mad. He's gonna track 'em and get your animals back for you!"

Hannah's features crumpled and tears filled her eyes. "Oh, praise the Lord!" was all she could say.

"See, Mama," Patty Ruth said, clutching Tony the Bear to her breast, "Jesus sent them In'ians 'cause you prayed!"

"He sure did, baby," Hannah said. "He sure did!"

It took Two Moons and his braves only a few moments to study the spot where the Cooper horses were stolen and see that the thieves had headed due north.

Three hours later, as they topped a ridge, Two Moons saw the band of thieves about a half-mile ahead, moving slowly northward. Two Moons and his braves recognized the seven riders as Teton Sioux from a village some ten to twelve miles farther north. The stolen horses were in their possession.

Two Moons gave a signal and led his riders into a thick stand of oaks and cottonwoods. He quickly organized them and ordered six braves to stay in low areas and ride hard to move ahead of the Sioux. He sent five more to the left, and five to the right. He and several braves would close in from behind.

Sioux sub-chief Tall Tree and his six warriors rode leisurely with the two white men's horses in tow. They had scouted the wagon train for several miles and spotted the two fine animals tied behind a wagon. Chief Strong Bull and his young warrior son, Sky Hawk, would be much pleased with the horses.

"Chief Strong Bull will like the horses, but even more, he will like how we got them," Tall Tree said to the others.

Owl Eyes, the brave riding next to him, chortled and said, "White men are thick in the head. We could steal fire, leave smoke...they would wonder where the fire went!"

The others laughed.

Suddenly there was a rumble of hoofbeats behind them. As they turned and looked toward the dark shadows of the forest just east of the trail, a tongue of orange-red flame stabbed from the shadows, accompanied by the sharp crack of a rifle. The bullet zinged over their heads.

Six Crows broke from the forest, galloping hard toward them.

The Sioux raised their rifles, preparing for a fight, when they heard more thundering hooves. Tall Tree's head whipped around, and he saw stern-faced Crows closing in from the other three sides. He shouted to his warriors, "Do not fire! They are more than us!"

As the Crows closed in, the Sioux raised their rifles above their heads with both hands.

Two Moons guided his pinto toward the sub-chief's horse until the animals were nose to nose. He looked at the sub-chief fiercely and said, "Tall Tree made big mistake. Steal horses of Two Moons's friends."

He instructed seven of his braves to relieve the Sioux of their rifles and knives, then turned back to the sub-chief and said, "It is best if you not steal from white men. You and your people must learn that white eyes have great numbers. Indians fight them, they come like snowflakes in winter wind, wipe us out. We do not like them to take our land, even as you, but when we show kindness and friendship, they treat us well."

Tall Tree's jaw jutted and hatred shone from his eyes, but he said nothing.

"We take white men's horses back now," Two Moons said. "We throw your rifles and knives on ground near Cold Creek by Big Bear Rock." With that, the Crows rode away.

Though no one said it, Tall Tree and his braves were glad to be alive.

As the Crows headed back on the trail of the wagon train, the youngest brave among them guided his horse up beside Two Moons. "Little Elk would ask something of Two Moons," he said.

"Yes, Little Elk?"

"You are great friend of Ezra Comstock. It is in my mind to know why."

The chief smiled and said, "Many grasses ago, maybe six or seven, Two Moons was young warrior. Fight in battle with Sioux war party toward sunset, on this trail, near Fort Bridger.

"Sioux have many more warriors than Crow. They shoot all of us down with arrows, ride away, think we are all dead. Two Moons lay on ground with arrow in chest, pretend dead. Rest of Crow indeed dead. Two Moons not live long. Soon Ezra Comstock come, leading wagon train. Ezra Comstock stop wagon train, remove arrow from Two Moons's chest, bandage him good, carry him to our village north of Fort Bridger. Two

Moons alive today only because of Ezra Comstock."

The young warrior nodded. "Little Elk understood now. Ezra Comstock good friend. This warrior very happy Two Moons not die that day."

Ezra Comstock and Dave Croft rode a mile or so ahead of the wagon train, admiring the flaming sunset as they scouted a spot to camp for the night.

Once again, Chris rode with Micah in the lead wagon. Periodically throughout the day he had stood up on the wagon seat and looked back for any sign of Two Moons and his braves.

He had just sat down again when he heard a man's voice from the rear of the train cry out, "The Crows are coming!" He leaped up to see them trotting over a grassy knoll toward the wagons.

"Micah! They've got Buster and Nipper!"

Micah shook his head in amazement and said under his breath, "Lord, give me the kind of faith Hannah Cooper has!"

Chris hopped out of the wagon and ran for all he was worth, shouting, "Mama! It's Buster and Nipper! They're back!"

Ezra and Dave had spotted the returning Crows and were galloping back toward the wagon train. Ezra waved his dirty old hat, shouting, "Ya-a-a-h-o-o-o!"

The entire group of travelers gathered around as Ezra introduced Hannah to Two Moons and his braves, and she expressed her gratitude, as did Chris.

"We do not want you to leave yet, Chief," Hannah said, "but we must pause right now and thank our Lord Jesus Christ for sending you and your men to us just when we needed you."

The Crows knew the name of Jesus Christ, for Ezra had talked to them. Though he had gotten nowhere with them, they held deep respect for the white man's God.

Chapter Eight

The children had been dismissed from school for the day, and schoolmarm Sundi Lindgren was closing up her desk when Alex Patterson stormed through the door and pointed an accusing finger at her.

"I told you never to stuff your rotten religion down my children's throats, woman! But I know you're doin' it, 'cause I overheard Luke and Willa talkin' to Joshua about this Jesus stuff!"

He moved toward her, and Sundi backed up until her back was against the blackboard. Her throat felt dry as she said, "I have prayer in class every morning, Mr. Patterson, but I have not spoken to your children personally about Jesus, because you told me not to. What I believe is not religion. I have the *Person,* Jesus Christ, in my heart and life. He gives salvation. Religion does not."

Patterson's eyes looked demonic. He sprayed saliva as he yelled, "I don't want you prayin' in my children's presence, woman, do you hear me? And don't be quotin' that Bible in class! Keep that religion stuff for church! My kids come here for an education, not to be fed a bunch of ancient superstitions!"

Anger took the place of Sundi's fear. Her chest tightened with emotion and the blood rose in her cheeks as she snapped, "Get out of here, Mr. Patterson! All the other parents like what I'm doing with the children, and you're not going to tell me how to do my job!"

Patterson's eyes drilled into Sundi as he pulled a long-bladed knife from under his belt and snarled, "You die!"

She screamed in terror as the knife pierced her chest...

"Sundi! Sundi, wake up!"

"Wha—?"

"Honey, you were having a bad dream."

Sundi woke, trembling and in a cold sweat, to see her sister, Heidi, bending over her.

"Oh-h-h-h, Heidi, it was awful! I was dreaming that Alex Patterson had me pinned against the blackboard as he railed at me for praying in class and referring to the Bible."

"You mean, like he's actually done before."

"Yes. But in my dream, his eyes were like the devil's. And he stabbed me with a knife!"

"Oh, how awful. Thank the Lord it was only a dream. It's over now. Try to go back to sleep."

Sundi lifted a shaky hand to her forehead. "What time is it?"

Heidi reached for the clock on the bed stand and angled it toward the moonlit window. "It's almost two-thirty."

Sundi threw back the covers and padded across the room to the water bucket and took a long drink from the dipper.

"Sundi, has Alex been giving you problems again?"

"No more than usual—just every time I see him. How about you?"

"The same. I avoid him when I can, but it's not always possible." Heidi paused, then said, "Has he been on you again about his kids?"

"Mm-hmm. He thinks I'm trying to get them saved. As much as I'd love to talk to those precious kids about Jesus, I haven't done it. Alex might *really* put a knife in me if I did.

They're getting some gospel when I pray in class every morning, and when I quote Scripture during a lesson now and then. None of the other parents has objected to prayer and bringing Bible truths into the lessons."

Heidi nodded sympathetically. "I'm sure Nellie Patterson isn't a Christian, but she wouldn't object like her husband does."

"Oh, Sis, my heart is so heavy for Nellie and those children! I'm sure we could lead them to the Lord if it wasn't for Alex."

"Well, honey, we're just going to have to get Alex saved first. Then we can reach his family."

Sundi let out a huge sigh. "Talk about a challenge!"

"All we can do is keep praying and let the Lord do His work."

"You're right about that. Well, we'd better get back to bed. Sorry to have awakened you."

"I'll survive," Heidi said, kissing her sister's cheek.

The next morning, the Lindgren sisters got up at the usual time and dressed for the day. Sundi put finishing touches on her long, sun-streaked hair, and went to prepare breakfast, while Heidi finished dressing.

Both girls were blonde and petite—full-blooded Swedes—and had come to Fort Bridger only a few months previously from a Swedish settlement in Minnesota.

Sundi had sky-blue eyes that twinkled with enthusiasm for life. Although Heidi was a year older, Sundi made most of the family decisions and had a more outgoing personality, which perfectly suited the job of schoolteacher.

Heidi was quieter and more serious, and was quite content in her profession as a seamstress and proprietor of her own dress shop. Her hazel eyes and dark-blonde hair with red-gold highlights presented a quieter beauty than her sister's.

After breakfast, Heidi and Sundi read the Bible together and took turns praying for Alex Patterson and his family. They yearned to see the whole family saved. But Alex made life miserable for his wife and children, and had forbidden them to go to church.

It was just past eight o'clock when Heidi hugged her sister good-bye and headed up Main Street to her shop. Heidi made beautiful dresses, and stayed quite busy. All the army wives in the fort, as well as many women from the town and surrounding ranch communities, were regular customers. On a normal day, there were always a few women waiting for her to arrive and open the shop at 8:30. Times were changing; women who had made their own dresses for years now wanted them made for them.

Heidi had reached Sixth Street when she heard hoofbeats behind her and turned to see Fort Bridger's town marshal.

"Good morning, Miss Heidi," said Marshal Lance Mangum, tipping his hat.

"And a good morning to you, Marshal."

"Looks like it's going to be a nice day, ma'am."

"Sure does. I've had enough rain to do me for a while."

"Me, too. As far as I'm concerned, it can stay like this till next April, then turn off nice."

Heidi laughed.

"I'll see you later; I have to get to the office." Lance tipped his hat and nudged the horse to a faster pace.

Heidi exchanged greetings with the few people she met. When she crossed Fourth Street into the block where her shop was located, she saw Alex Patterson coming into town. *He's probably heading for the construction site of the new general store,* she thought.

She hurried toward her shop to avoid any confrontation

and fumbled with the door key. She could hear his footsteps on the boardwalk. Before she could get the door open, Patterson drew up and scowled at her.

"I see you're still in business," he said.

Heidi turned the key, twisted the knob, and pushed open the door. She turned to look him in the eye and said, "Yes, and the business is doing quite well, thank you."

"I'm sorry to hear that. You ought to get married—"

"I know...stay home, have babies, and let my husband make the living," she finished for him. "Mr. Patterson, it is not my desire to be unkind to you, but let me say it as plainly as I can. What I do is none of your business. As long as I'm single, I have to eat to stay alive, just like you do. So I must provide myself a living."

Patterson's mouth turned down in a bitter curve. "There are plenty of single men around," he said. "Especially in the fort. You're better lookin' than the average woman around here. You could find a man to marry, if you tried."

Heidi forced herself to keep her temper in check, and said, "You wouldn't understand, Mr. Patterson, but since I'm a Christian, I'm waiting for the Lord to send the Christian man of His choice into my life. I'm not on the block to be taken by just any man who comes along."

Alex stiffened and blew out a hard breath. "Little Miss High and Mighty, ain'tcha? Well, let me tell you somethin'. You—"

"I said it a moment ago, Mr. Patterson, and I'll say it again. What I do is none of your business." Pastor Andy Kelly eased his horse up to the hitch rail as Heidi continued to speak. "If I choose to marry only a Christian, that's my business, not yours. And what's more, there's nothing wrong with my owning this shop and making a living for myself."

"You shouldn't be makin' dresses at all!" Alex said. "Every woman should make her own dresses at home, like *my* wife does! If I had my way, I'd burn this shop of yours to the ground! Women like you—"

"Hey!" cut in Kelly. "What's going on here, Alex? Why are you speaking to Miss Heidi in such an ungentlemanly manner?"

"Well...well, she oughtta close down this shop and be a housewife and mother. I was just makin' it plain."

"From what I heard, Miss Heidi was making it plain that what she does with her life, and how she makes a living, is none of your business, Alex. And she's right."

Patterson gritted his teeth. "The whole world's goin' to the dogs because of women like her, Kelly! She's stickin' her nose in where it don't belong. She oughtta be married, keepin' house, and raisin' kids!"

Kelly's features darkened. "It's *you* who are sticking your nose in where it doesn't belong, Alex! You have no call to talk to her this way!"

Patterson thought about punching Kelly in spite of the man's muscular build. Instead, he said, "She shouldn't be runnin' this dress shop, Kelly...and her sister shouldn't be teachin' school. There should be a man teachin' the students, not a woman! If you knew your Bible, you'd know that even God says women should stay home and have babies!"

"Maybe you need to do a little Bible study, Alex. There were godly women in Bible days who had to make a living for themselves *until* they married, and *after* their husbands died. And something else. Godly women often help their husbands run businesses, and there's nothing wrong with it."

Alex started to retort, but Kelly cut him off. "We've got a fine Christian couple coming to this town to run the general store. I've met them. Hannah Cooper is a sweet, godly lady, and she's in submission to her husband, but she will also be helping him run the store, just as she did in Independence."

A heavy frown ridged Patterson's brow. "A man oughtta run his business by himself," he mumbled, "and if it's too much, he should hire a man to help him. His wife should stay home, keep house, and be a mother to her children like my Nellie."

Patterson walked away, mumbling something about being late for work.

Kelly watched him for a few seconds, then turned back to Heidi. "Don't pay any attention to him, Miss Heidi. You're doing a commendable thing to operate your own business so you can make yourself an honest living."

Heidi looked toward her feet for a moment, then looked him in the eye. "Thank you, Pastor."

Kelly smiled. "See you in church tonight."

Heidi waited at the door, watching as he swung into the saddle. Before he turned the animal to ride away, he said, "I want you to know that I'm very glad to have a godly young lady like your sister teaching in the school, too. When Rebecca and I have children, I hope Miss Sundi is still here to teach them."

"I'll tell her you said that," Heidi said, smiling for the first time since Alex Patterson had accosted her. "That will make her feel real good."

Kelly nodded good-bye and rode away.

Sundi Lindgren stood on the front porch of the one-room schoolhouse, watching the children play during midmorning recess, when her attention was drawn to the road. She recognized Julie Powell, pulling a small wagon carrying her two children—Casey, three, and Carrie, nineteen months.

Sundi waved, and Julie headed toward the porch. "Recess just getting started, or is it about over?" she asked.

"Just getting started. We've got about twenty-five minutes. Nice to see you, Julie."

Sundi liked Julie and her husband, Justin. They had come to Fort Bridger about two weeks after the Lindgren sisters, and were fine Christians and good workers in the church. They owned few possessions and lived in a small rented house that needed extensive repairs. The owner of the house had agreed to let Justin make the repairs as time allowed and deduct his work from the rent.

During the day, Justin worked as a clerk at Swensen's Gun Shop and Hardware Store. Owners Hans and Greta Swensen were unable to pay Justin much, but they promised to pay him more as soon as the town's population grew and their business increased.

Julie let Casey get out of the wagon, instructing him to stay close by, and then glanced at the laughing children at recess. "Sundi, I don't know how you do it. How many students do you have? At least forty, isn't it?"

"Forty-two between the ages of six and seventeen," Sundi said. "Twenty-six of the children are from the town and surrounding ranches, and sixteen are from the fort."

Sundi kissed little Carrie's cheek and sighed as she said, "It's proven to be a heavier load than I realized when I agreed to leave Minnesota and come here as the schoolteacher. I've considered making a request of the town council to bring in another teacher, but I'm a bit hesitant, since this is the first year the town has had a school."

Julie scanned the playground. "But the town council should be able to see that this is too heavy a load."

"Well, even if they gave me an assistant to monitor the smaller children, it would help. I think I'll give it a little more time, then ask for a helper."

"You do that, Sundi. They owe you that much." Julie reached for her daughter and said, "All right, Carrie, time to go. Miss Sundi has to keep an eye on the children."

Sundi thanked Julie for stopping by, kissed Carrie and

Casey good-bye, and turned her attention toward her students. Some of the teenage boys were seeing who could jump the farthest after a forty-foot run. The older girls stood by, watching the boys and cheering them on.

Just as Sundi turned her attention in that direction, Luke Patterson sailed through the air. When he landed, his left foot twisted beneath him, and the ankle made a snapping sound. He fell to the ground, howling, and grabbed his ankle.

Sundi picked up her skirts and started to run, but several of Luke's schoolmates reached him first. Sundi pushed her way through the small knot of boys and knelt beside Luke, who was trying hard not to cry.

"Here, Luke," she said, "let me look at it."

The boy sucked air through gritted teeth as his teacher removed his high-top shoe and rolled down his sock.

"I'm afraid it may be broken, Luke," Sundi said. "Will you boys help me get him inside the schoolhouse?"

Moments later, Luke sat on a straight-backed wooden chair next to Sundi's desk. Sundi turned to Jim Summers, a rancher's son, and said, "Would you run over to Dr. O'Brien's office and see if he can come and look at Luke's ankle?"

"Yes, ma'am!"

As Jim headed for the door, Sundi said, "Tell Dr. O'Brien I think it's broken."

Jim nodded and was gone.

Sundi did what she could to ease the boy's pain until the doctor arrived fifteen minutes later.

Frank O'Brien, who was a retired army doctor, had come to Fort Bridger three years previously to go into private practice. He was short and stocky, with a thick head of silver hair and bushy eyebrows. His twinkling blue eyes had the unmistakable Irish droop at the corners.

O'Brien had a way about him that instilled confidence in his patients. As he knelt before Luke, he smiled and said, "Now, son, I may have to hurt you just a little in order to know what we've got here. You're a tough guy, aren't you?"

"Sometimes," Luke said, licking his lips. "I know you have to do it, Doctor, so go ahead."

The kindly doctor checked Luke's foot and ankle, feeling for telltale evidence of a break. Luke sucked in his breath and let out a tiny whine.

O'Brien nodded to himself. "It's broken, son. We'll need to get you over to the office so I can set it and put a splint on it."

"Donnie and I will carry him, Miss Lindgren," Jim Summers said.

Sundi nodded. "I wish I could go along, Luke, but I have to stay here with the others."

"Yes, ma'am," Luke said, trying to smile. "I understand."

As Jim and Donnie picked him up, Sundi noticed Willa and Joshua Patterson standing at the door, worry evident on their young faces. She hurried over to them and put an arm around each child. "Your brother has broken his ankle, but Dr. O'Brien is going to set it and put a splint on it at his office."

"Miss Lindgren," Willa said, "could Josh and I go with Luke?"

Sundi turned to the physician. "Dr. O'Brien, would it be all right if Luke's sister and brother went along?"

"Certainly," he replied. "If it's all right with you, I'll take them home with Luke after I put the splint on him."

Edith O'Brien was her husband's right hand at the office. She was short and on the portly side, and always dressed neatly, with every hair in place. She had no formal training as a nurse, but she'd been well trained by her husband to assist him. And her winsome smile and brisk efficiency were a good combination when it came to treating patients.

After Jim and Donnie carried Luke to the clinic, then left to go back to school, Edith directed Willa and Joshua to the waiting room, telling them they need not worry about their big brother. His ankle would heal in a few weeks, and he would be fine.

While the doctor prepared a splint, Edith administered a small dose of laudanum to ease Luke's pain. When it had taken effect, the doctor quickly set the ankle and splinted it. Luke looked a bit peaked but insisted he was all right, and Edith brought Willa and Joshua in to see him.

"Are you all right, Luke?" Willa asked, almost in tears.

"Oh, not bad. It hurts a little, but I'll be all right."

Dr. O'Brien stood over Luke and said, "You'll have to be on crutches for several weeks while the ankle heals. I have some that will fit you."

"Thank you, Doctor." Luke paused, swallowing hard. "Will I be able to do my work at home?"

The physician stroked his mustache. "Well, it will be much harder to do your chores. It'll take longer, and there'll probably be some things you won't be able to do until the splint is off and you're back to normal."

Luke tried to push down his anxiety.

O'Brien frowned. "What's the matter, Luke?"

A shuddering breath passed the boy's lips, and fear showed in his eyes. "It…it's my father, sir. H-he will really be mad if I can't do my work like usual."

"I see," said the doctor, running his gaze to the other children. "Tell you what. After I take you three home to your mother, I'll go to the construction site and talk to your father."

"Thank you, Doctor," Luke said.

The doctor smiled at him and nodded, observing that fear hadn't left the boy's eyes.

CHAPTER NINE

Clayton Farley watched his work crew apply finishing touches to the ground floor of the general store. He was pleased that the roof was finished and all the glass panes had been installed in the windows on both floors.

The outside had been given two coats of white paint. There were dark green shutters flanking the upstairs windows, and a small balcony with a wooden railing ran the width of the building.

The large sign: *COOPER'S GENERAL STORE—Solomon Cooper, Prop.* hung in place above the porch roof.

Inside, the wooden floor was completely finished. Three men were installing the shelves, while Gil Harris and Alex Patterson did touch-up work on the long counter.

When the front door opened, Farley looked up to see Colonel Ross Bateman and a uniformed man wearing a captain's insignia enter the store.

"Gentlemen," Bateman said, "I'd like to introduce Captain Errol Stanford. He's just arrived from Fort Hall, Idaho, to be one of my officers. I wanted to show him the new store."

Gil Harris welcomed Stanford, as did the other men. Alex Patterson ignored the visitors and continued to work on the counter.

"I first met Captain Stanford in Virginia back in 1862,"

said Bateman, "when he was a lieutenant serving under General Ambrose Burnside."

Alex's head snapped around and his eyes flashed. Farley moved close to Patterson and said, "Get hold of yourself, Alex."

Colonel Bateman glanced at Patterson, then turned to Farley. "What's wrong?" he asked.

Alex's eyes burned with hatred as he hissed, "Fredericksburg was my home town! It was Burnside and his filthy scumbucket Yankees who burned my house to the ground! My wife and children were forced to evacuate. What kind of lowdown scum would burn a man's house down and leave his family with no place to live? In the dead of winter, too!"

Captain Stanford felt his nerves tighten and his muscles bunch. He forced himself to remain calm, and spoke in a low tone. "I'm sorry for what happened to your home, but war is war."

Patterson's jaw clenched as he ground out his response. "There was no reason to burn people's homes, Yankee!"

"The South fired the first shot in the War, you know," Stanford said.

Alex leaped the counter and swung a haymaker. Stanford dodged the blow. Before Bateman and Farley could get between them, Stanford unleashed a right and then a left with lightning speed, causing Patterson to stagger back against the counter. Alex raised his fists to fight back, but Stanford batted them aside and drove a punch to his nose, splitting the skin. Alex slid to the floor in a sitting position.

Stanford looked at his commandant. "I'm sorry, Colonel, but he came after me."

"I saw it, Captain," said Bateman, "and so did these men. You had to defend yourself."

Clayton Farley bent down in front of Patterson, whose eyes were a bit dazed. "Alex, that temper of yours is going to get you in deep trouble one of these days. Captain Stanford didn't personally burn down your house! Now go to Doc O'Brien and get that cut stitched up."

Patterson nodded and slowly got to his feet. He pressed his hand against his nose to staunch the flow of blood. "I'll be back, boss, as soon as I get this taken care of." He gave Stanford a fierce glance and went out the front door.

Edith O'Brien was at the desk in the reception and waiting room when Alex Patterson came through the door, cupping his nose.

"Oh, my, Alex!" she said, rising from the chair. "That looks bad!"

"It's more than a nosebleed!" he said sharply.

"How did it happen?"

"Let me see Doc right now!"

"He isn't here. Come with me. Let's get you on the examining table. I'll put a compress on that cut and stop the bleeding. Doctor will stitch it up as soon as he arrives."

Alex followed her and lay down on the examining table. As Edith bustled around, gathering supplies, she said, "I asked how this happened, Alex."

"I...ah...got into a fight."

"With whom?"

"New captain at the fort. Name's Stanford."

"I suppose he fought on the Union side in the War?"

"Yeah."

"What's *he* look like? Will he be coming in for treatment, too?"

Alex cleared his throat. "No. He just got in a couple of lucky punches, that's all."

Edith held the compress above her patient, and said, "All right, move your hands." She pressed it over his nose and held it down. "I'll just keep this on till Doctor comes back."

"Where is the doc?"

"He's at *your* house," she said.

"My house? What for?"

"Well, Luke broke his ankle at school today, and—"

Alex's eyes widened. "How'd he do that?"

"It was a simple mishap during recess. The older boys were playing a run-and-jump game. Luke came down wrong on his left ankle."

"It's that new teacher's fault! She ought to be supervisin' the kids when they play! It wouldn't have happened if she'd been payin' attention to 'em!"

"Alex, you don't know that Miss Sundi *wasn't* paying attention to them. Children get hurt quite often when they play."

"Luke never had a broken ankle when Nellie was teachin' 'em at home! So did Doc set the bone?"

"Yes. Willa and Joshua were here with Luke. Doc took all three children home. Luke will be on crutches for several weeks, Alex. Doc wanted to talk to you about it. He was planning on stopping by the general store on the way back from your place."

"Well, I wish he'd hurry up and get here," Patterson muttered.

Only a few minutes had passed when they heard the office door open.

"You lie still and hold the compress, Alex," Edith said. "I'll see who it is."

She was almost to the door when it opened. Doctor O'Brien glanced at Alex, then looked at his wife and smiled. "I went to the general store," he told her. "Clayton Farley told me Alex had come here. How's the nose?"

"He'll need stitches for sure, dear," Edith said, as they walked toward the examining table. "I've got a compress on it."

"Good girl," he said, meeting Patterson's steady gaze. "Alex, let me wash my hands and then I'll get right on it."

Thirty minutes later, the stitching job was done and the nose was bandaged.

"You're starting to turn purple around both eyes," said the doctor. "Goes with getting punched in the nose."

"Yeah," said Patterson, sitting up. "What about Luke's ankle, and why did you want to talk to me about it?"

"It's a clean break, and it'll heal *if* he stays on the crutches I loaned him."

Alex stared at him blankly. "So?"

Doc sighed. "So...it's no secret that you work your kids pretty hard with all those chickens on your place. You're going to have to go easy on Luke. He won't be able to do everything he normally does, and even for a while after the splint comes off."

"Okay. So we'll spread the work around amongst the rest of us."

"You do that, Alex. And don't be rough on the boy."

"Don't fret yourself, Doc," Alex said, sliding off the table to a standing position. "I guess I owe you for takin' care of Luke's ankle, and for takin' care of my nose."

O'Brien cocked his head and squinted at him. "Clayton told me you started the fight with that new captain. That so?"

Patterson jutted his jaw. "Yeah."

"Well, I know you're having a hard time with your finances, Alex. So I'll not charge you for tending to Luke. But you owe me three dollars for the nose work. You can pay it a dollar at a time over the next three weeks, or you can pay me in chickens."

"I'll pay it in money. A dollar a week."

"All right."

As Alex headed for the door, O'Brien called after him, "Do go easy on Luke. He's a fine boy. He shouldn't have to be fearful of you for something that wasn't his fault."

Alex nodded and left the clinic.

Sundi Lindgren wrote the name *Betsy Ross* on the blackboard.

"Now, children," she said, "those of you in second grade and up had an assignment last week. You were to read in your history book about Betsy Ross. Can anyone tell me what her real name was?"

A hand went up in the back of the room.

"Yes, Clarence?"

"Her name was Elizabeth Griscom Ross, Miss Lindgren."

"Correct. Can anyone tell me where she was born, and in what year? Yes, Hattie?"

"Betsy Ross was born in Philadelphia, Pennsylvania, in 1752."

"Correct. And what was she known for? Tommy?"

"Betsy Ross made the very first American flag!"

All over the room heads shook in disagreement.

"What's wrong with Tommy's statement?" Sundi asked. "Yes, Jim?"

"Mrs. Ross made many American flags during the American Revolution, but even though legend says she made the first one, there's no historical record to prove it."

Sundi was about to commend Jim for his answer when the door at the back of the room swung open, and a hard-eyed Alex Patterson barged in. "I want to talk to you, woman!"

The children watched him with wide eyes. The man who had a reputation for being mean looked even more so with the white bandage on his nose and the purple circles around his eyes.

Sundi's heart began to pound. "Mr. Patterson," she said, "if you will come back after school, I'll be glad to talk to you."

Patterson moved closer, his head thrust forward. "You'll talk to me now!"

"Mr. Patterson, if it's about Luke's accident—"

"There wouldn't have *been* any accident if you were any kind of teacher! What were you doin' when Luke broke his ankle? Were you supervisin' your students? It's your fault my son's ankle is broken! This is the school's first year of operation, and already someone's hurt."

At the back row of desks, Jim Summers stood up and said, "Mr. Patterson, you have no call to talk to Miss Lindgren like that. She—"

"You sit down and shut up, kid!" Patterson yelled, pointing a stiff finger at him.

Jim's face reddened as four husky farm boys stood up, fixing the angry man with steady eyes. One of them said, "As Miss Lindgren told you, Mr. Patterson, you can come back after school and talk to her. However, the five of us will be here when you do."

"That's right," spoke up another. "You need to leave now. You're frightening these children."

Alex stiffened at this unexpected opposition and blinked his eyes in disbelief.

"Mr. Patterson," Sundi Lindgren said, "I was right there on the playground with the children during recess. The older boys asked if it was all right to play the run-and-jump game. I told them they could. I'm aware, as I'm certain you are, that they've played the same game around town for a long time."

Alex took a deep breath, scrubbed a hand across his mouth, and said, "You should have been watchin' 'em closer! I still say it's your fault that Luke's ankle is broken!"

"I'm sorry Luke's ankle got broken," Sundi said, "but it's not my fault. The children need to play at recess and burn off some of their energy. Running and jumping is something boys just naturally do." As she spoke, Sundi asked the Lord to help her keep her testimony before Alex Patterson.

He drew his lips into a firm line. "Tell you what, woman, I'm takin' my kids out of this school before one of 'em gets hurt real bad."

"Mr. Patterson, you're making a mountain out of a molehill. It isn't right to take them out of school. They need what I can teach them, and they need to be with other children. You mustn't do it."

Patterson threw back his head defiantly. "Don't tell me what my kids need, woman! I'll do with 'em as I please!"

The five teenage boys began to move toward the man. As he turned to look at them, Jim Summers pointed to the back of the schoolroom and said, "You found the door to get in here, mister, you can find it to get out."

Alex pointed a stiff finger at Jim, shouting, "You hooligans stay where you are! This is none of your business!"

"It's our business when you talk to our teacher this way!" Donnie Parks said.

Marshal Lance Mangum was riding his horse past the school and heard loud voices coming through the open door. He quickly swung his mount into the schoolyard, dismounted, and hurried into the building. He came up behind Patterson, who was still shouting threats, and laid a hand on his shoulder telling him to calm down. Patterson whirled around and swung his fist.

Mangum ducked, then sent a hard right to Patterson's jaw and followed it with a smashing left. Patterson went down in a heap, unconscious.

The marshal stood over Alex Patterson and ran his gaze from the five teenage boys to the teacher. "What's this all about, ma'am?"

"Luke got his ankle broken today at recess. Alex came here to let me know that he blamed me."

"Mm-hmm," Mangum said, leaning over to pick up the

limp form. “Sounds like him.” With a grunt, he hoisted Patterson over his shoulder. “I'll just let Mr. Hothead, here, cool off in a cell. He's going to learn to control his temper one way or another.”

Alex Patterson paced back and forth in his cell, cursing the marshal under his breath, when he heard the office door open, then close after a few seconds. He looked toward the hallway and saw Nellie coming in with the marshal at her side. Nellie shook her head at the sight of him. Not only did he have the bandage on his nose and both eyes purpled, but there were bruises where the marshal had punched him.

She moved up to the bars. “Why, Alex? Why?”

Nellie Patterson looked older than her thirty-five years. There were lines of worry and hardship on her kind face, and her dark hair was already streaked with strands of gray.

“Why, Alex?” she repeated.

Patterson glared at his wife but remained silent, watching the marshal from the corner of his eye.

Tears surfaced in Nellie's eyes. “Alex,” she said shakily, “one of these days you're going to do something really bad! Something you'll be very sorry for.”

The sound of footsteps in the office echoed down the hall. “Be back in a minute,” said Mangum.

Nellie wiped the tears from her cheeks. “Is this kind of thing going to just go on and on, Alex?”

“I want you to plead with Mangum to let me outta here. Use those tears on him, and tell him I can't make a livin' for my family if I'm behind bars.”

“I won't use tears on him,” she said, “but I'll try to reason with him. But I think he's just about run out of patience with you, Alex. I doubt he'll listen to me.”

There were two sets of footsteps and the sound of muffled voices, then the marshal appeared with Clayton Farley.

Alex's face flushed as Farley stepped up to the bars. Farley greeted Nellie then turned back to Alex and said, "So, what's this? You were supposed to come back to work after you got your nose sewn up. You know we're already behind schedule on the store."

Alex cleared his throat nervously. "Well, I...uh...I had to talk to the teacher about Luke's ankle gettin' busted."

"*Talk* to the teacher? From what Marshal Mangum told me, it was an all-out verbal assault."

Alex sent a hot look toward Mangum.

"Don't look at the marshal that way," Farley said. "He came to the store to let me know you wouldn't be coming back to work. Said he had to cold-cock you when you swung at him. You were frightening the children, Alex. What's the matter with you? Haven't you got any sense at all?"

Alex gripped the bars till his knuckles turned white. Under Nellie's gaze, he dropped his head and stared at the floor for a few seconds, then looked up but avoided his boss's eyes. "I...uh...I'm sorry. It's just been a bad day."

"We all have a bad day now and then, Alex," said Mangum. "That's no excuse for acting like a madman in front of a bunch of school children, nor for being unkind to Miss Sundi."

"Nor is it an excuse for taking a swing at the marshal," put in Farley.

"I didn't know it was him," Alex said. "Those boys were hollerin' at me. I heard a voice from behind tell me to shut up, and a hand touched my shoulder. I was mad. So I turned around swingin'."

"And because you were mad and swung at the marshal, you got yourself knocked cold and locked up in jail. Seems you made your own bad day," Farley said.

Alex let go of the bars and looked at Mangum. "Marshal, I'm sorry. I wasn't thinkin'. I just went kinda crazy. Really. I'm sorry I swung at you. I apologize."

Mangum held his gaze and was about to reply when Alex looked at Farley and said, "Boss, I'm sorry for this whole mess. I know you're behind on gettin' the general store done, and you need me there workin'. When I learned about Luke's broken ankle, I figured it wouldn't have happened if that new schoolmarm had been watchin' the kids like she should."

"Kids get hurt at recess quite often, honey," said Nellie. "It wasn't Miss Sundi's fault."

"I know, I know." He turned to face her. "How's Luke doin'?"

"He's all right as far as the splint and crutches are concerned. Right now he's living in fear of what you're going to say when you get home."

"Marshal," said Farley, "how long are you going to keep Alex in jail?"

Mangum thought for a moment. "Tell you what. If Alex will agree to go immediately and apologize to Miss Sundi and admit to her what he just admitted to Nellie, that it wasn't Miss Sundi's fault, I'll let him out right now."

Fresh tears welled up in Nellie's eyes.

"Sure, Marshal," said Alex. "I'll do that."

"Okay," Mangum said with a nod, taking a key ring from his belt. As he opened the cell door, he warned, "You'd better get that temper of yours in control."

Alex nodded silently.

"Okay, let's go to the schoolhouse," said the marshal. "I want you to apologize to Miss Sundi in front of the children. And I want you to apologize to the children for your tirade on their teacher."

Alex felt a wave of rebellion wash over him, but he knew that if he refused to make the apologies, he would be right back in the cell.

"Alex," Farley said, "there'll still be a couple of hours or so of work time left when you get through at the school. I'll be expecting you at the store."

Chapter Ten

Sundi Lindgren stood at the door of the schoolhouse as the children came in from afternoon recess. The last to come in were the boys who had stood up to Alex Patterson, and as each one entered, she thanked him for standing by her. She was about to close the door when she saw three people walking up the road from town. It was Alex Patterson, flanked by the marshal and Nellie Patterson.

Sundi stepped inside the schoolroom and said, "Everybody sit quietly at your desks. I'll return shortly."

The children craned their necks to see who or what had claimed their teacher's attention.

Sundi watched the trio, praying in her heart, *Lord, give me wisdom to deal with whatever is coming.*

Nellie smiled and said, "Good afternoon, Miss Sundi."

Sundi nodded and smiled at her warmly.

Lance Mangum indicated the man beside him and said, "Miss Sundi, Alex wants to say something to you and the children."

"Oh! All right...come in." She walked up the narrow aisle between the desks with Alex and the marshal following her.

Nellie waited at the back of the room, ignoring the curious eyes of the children who turned to look at her.

"Boys and girls...Miss Lindgren," began the marshal, "you saw me subdue Mr. Patterson a little while ago. I locked him up in jail because of the way he talked to Miss Lindgren, and because of the way he acted in front of you children. He wants to say something to you."

Alex, who seemed to have a hard time getting started with his apology, told Sundi and the class that he was sorry for the way he had spoken and acted that morning, and asked their forgiveness.

"Especially you, Miss Sundi," he said humbly. "I was very rude and unfair. I know Luke's getting hurt was not your fault. Please forgive me."

Sundi smiled and said, "I forgive you, Mr. Patterson."

"Well, I wouldn't blame you if you didn't."

"I'm glad to forgive you," she said. "The Bible teaches us that we're to forgive offenses to one another when asked. The Lord Jesus so graciously forgave me of all my sins, surely it's a small thing for me to forgive you for what happened here this morning."

Alex felt his insides squeeze down tight at the mention of Jesus and the Bible, but he painted a smile on his face and said, "Thank you, ma'am."

Sundi looked at Alex compassionately as she said, "I do forgive you, and I accept your thanks."

Sundi ran her gaze over her students' faces and said, "Mr. Patterson has asked for your forgiveness, boys and girls. What do you say?"

There was a jumble of words, assuring the man he was forgiven. However, the teenage boys on the back row were not as warm toward him as some of the others.

Sundi looked at Nellie. "Mrs. Patterson, how is Luke doing?"

"Dr. O'Brien says he'll have to use crutches for several weeks, but the break will heal all right. Luke will be back to school tomorrow, Miss Sundi."

"Wonderful! I'm so sorry it happened, Mrs. Patterson."

"I am too, Miss Sundi, but it wasn't your fault."

"Miss Sundi," Alex said, "let me say again that I know it wasn't your fault."

Sundi smiled at him. "You can be a nice man when you want to, Mr. Patterson."

The children laughed, and the marshal grinned. Alex felt embarrassed, and had nothing more to say.

"We'll be going now, Miss Sundi," Marshal Mangum said.

When the trio stepped off the porch, Alex mumbled a hasty good-bye and headed back to work.

At sundown, Alex Patterson entered his yard and saw his family gathered near the chicken shed again. Willa and Joshua carried dead chickens toward the crest of the ravine. Most of the two to three hundred chickens the Pattersons owned were moving about, clucking and scratching the ground to pick up the grain Luke had thrown there for their evening meal.

"Okay, what was it this time?" Alex asked.

"Probably the same coyote or wolf," said Nellie.

Alex watched Willa and Joshua as they dropped the dead chickens into a shallow hole halfway down the slope of the ravine. Then he turned to look at the dog. "That mongrel has blood on his face again! He's the one that's doin' it! Luke, go get my rifle!"

Shep went down on his haunches and laid back his ears and lowered his head, a whine in his throat.

"Papa, Shep didn't kill the chickens!" Luke said, hopping on his crutches toward the dog. "Please don't shoot him!"

Alex looked at his family accusingly and said, "I'm gonna find the dirty animal who's killin' the chickens! If I find out it's Shep, I *will* shoot him!" He glanced into the ravine where Willa and Joshua were finishing the burial. "How many this time?"

"Five," Joshua said.

"Looks like we're gonna have to build some kind of pen to keep the chickens in and the coyote, or *dog*, out."

"Yes, a pen would keep the chickens safe," Nellie said hastily.

"I won't be able to build one till I have more time to be home. Right now, Farley's got plenty of work for me." Alex turned to his eldest son. "So you busted your ankle jumpin', eh?"

"Yes, sir," Luke said, fear rising in his eyes. "I'm sorry, Pa. I'll do my chores as best I can."

Nellie moved closer to the boy. "Your father knows you will, honey. And until your ankle's healed, the rest of us will pitch in and do the work you can't. Right, dear?"

Alex stared at her for a moment, then said, "Yeah, that's what we'll do."

On Friday afternoon, September 16, Lieutenant Judd Stoddard was leading his scout unit toward Fort Bridger after a five-day routine patrol on the border of Utah Territory.

As the column of fourteen men drew near the Oregon Trail, Sergeant Bill McGraw pointed east. "There's a wagon train coming our way, Lieutenant."

"So there is," Stoddard said, raising his hand to halt the column. He pulled binoculars from a saddlebag, raised them to his eyes, and focused on the two horsemen who rode ahead of the train. After a few seconds, he said, "It's the Comstock train. I recognize Ezra out front with another man."

"Must've run into some kind of trouble along the way," said McGraw. "They were late getting to Fort Bridger before we even left on this patrol."

"You're right," agreed Stoddard. "Colonel Bateman said

Solomon Cooper wired him from Independence to say they expected to get here the last week of August."

He studied the wagon train with his binoculars for a few more moments, then said, "I'll alert the colonel that Comstock's wagon train is close. Probably just a day out at the rate they're moving."

"Sure can tell we're gettin' close to fall," Ezra Comstock said to Jock Weathers. "The last few days haven't been nearly so hot."

"I'll take the cool weather," Weathers said with a chuckle. "Don't like the heat."

"I don't either. Of course, I'm not too crazy about sub-zero temperatures, ice and snow, either. It gets into my bones and—" Ezra cut off his words as he stared at the rolling land to the southwest.

"What're you lookin' at?" Jock asked.

"Think I see some riders over that way. A few more minutes, and I'll be able to tell for sure."

Both men kept an eye on the hills for several minutes, then Ezra said, "Okay, Jock, it's an army patrol. See 'em?"

"You've got better eyes than me. I can make out somethin' movin', but I still can't tell what it is."

"Prob'ly a patrol out of Fort Bridger," Comstock said, rubbing his bristly jaw. He twisted around in the saddle and waved at his nephew. "Hey, Micah! See the army patrol?"

Chris Cooper was riding alongside the lead wagon, and focused on the army patrol as Micah called back, "Yeah, I see 'em! Probably from Fort Bridger!"

"Be back in a minute, Micah," Chris said. "I want to tell my mother about the patrol."

Hannah was talking with Patty Ruth when Chris rode up.

"Mama," he said, "Ezra just spotted an army patrol out of

Fort Bridger. It's off to our left at an angle toward those mountains in the distance."

"Really?" Hannah craned her neck to see beyond the wagons in front of her.

"Yes'm. We've got to be getting close now."

"Will we get there today, Mama?" Patty Ruth asked.

"No, honey. But I'm sure we'll get there tomorrow."

"I can't wait!" Chris said.

Jock Weathers galloped back toward the wagons, calling out that they'd just spotted an army patrol.

Hannah breathed a sigh of relief. It would be good to get to their destination. She missed Solomon more each day and felt that once the tiresome journey was over, she and the children could at last settle into their new life and feel some permanence and security.

Sol, darling, we're almost home...almost to that place you pointed out under the distant sky.

Late that afternoon, Ezra guided the wagon train to a spot near a huge rock formation with a brook running through it. Giant boulders were piled one upon another, spread over an area the size of two acres.

As soon as the wagons formed their circle, Ezra called the people together and said, "Folks, I stopped a little early today because this is the last stream before we reach Fort Bridger, which is about eight or nine miles due west beyond those hills. We'll arrive there sometime in early afternoon tomorrow and then rest the remainder of the day. We'll pull out for California on Sunday mornin'."

While the smell of cooking food filled the air, the children explored the base of the rock formation. During supper, they asked their parents if they could climb the big rocks before darkness fell. Because the boulders were well rounded, and the ones on the perimeter of the formation were not too high, the children were allowed this adventure.

Hannah gave B. J. and Patty Ruth permission to climb the low rocks. Chris and Mary Beth felt they were too old for such frolicking, but they went along with their mother to watch the younger children play. The sun was setting, leaving a fiery fan-shaped spray of orange light in the western sky.

"Hey, Patty Ruth," B. J. said. "I'll race you to the top of that boulder over there!"

The little redhead laughed. "You'll wish you hadn't ast me, B. J., 'cause I'll beat ya!"

"Oh, yeah? Let's see you do it!"

Patty Ruth handed Tony the Bear to Hannah. "Will you please hold Tony till I get back, Mama?"

"Of course," Hannah said with a smile.

"Okay, Patty Ruth," said B. J. scuffing the soles of his shoes like a bull ready to charge. "Let's go!"

"Not yet!" his little sister said. "Somebody has to say, "One, two, three...go!"

"I'll do it," Chris said. "Both of you line up side by side right here." As he spoke, Chris drew a line in the dirt with the toe of his shoe.

"Remember, you two," Hannah said "only to the top of that boulder, and no higher."

Both children nodded, their minds on the race.

"Okay," said Chris. "Ready? On your mark! Get set! One, two, three...go!"

Brother and sister sprang forward, and within three strides, B. J. was out ahead. He reached the boulder, bounded upward, and made his way to the top. When his little sister came puffing up behind him, he crowed, "I beatcha!"

A flush of color brightened the little redhead's cheeks. "You cheated, B. J.!"

"I did not! I beat you fair and square!"

"Liar!" screamed Patty Ruth. "You got a head start!"

"I did not!"

"Did so!"

"Hey, hey, hey!" came Hannah's voice. "What're you fighting about?"

"B. J. cheated!" announced Patty Ruth.

"Now, Patty Ruth," said Hannah, "I was watching when you started. You both started at the same time."

The little girl's lower lip protruded, and she said more softly, "Huh-uh. He cheated."

"Sweetheart," Hannah said, "B. J. didn't cheat. You must keep in mind that he's bigger than you. Not only that, but it's easier to run in pants than in a dress. You shouldn't feel bad that he beat you."

Patty Ruth glared at B. J. and said, "See there? You only beat me 'cause I'm a woman!"

Hannah stifled the laugh that bubbled up within her. "Come on, honey," she said softly, "let's go over here and sit on one of these rocks by the stream and watch the others climb."

Chris joined Mary Beth and Becky Croft while Hannah and Patty Ruth sat down. When Hannah placed the stuffed bear in Patty Ruth's hands, the little redhead said, "Just be glad you're a boy bear, Tony. Bein' a woman's really tough."

Hannah hugged Patty Ruth, then let her eyes roam the boulders for a glimpse of B. J.

"What'sa matter, Mama?"

"I don't see B. J. Do you see him?"

"Nope. He's prob'ly hidin' his face somewhere for cheatin' on me."

Hannah twisted around and looked toward the wagons. No B. J. The last time she saw him, he was standing near the base of the boulder he and Patty Ruth had climbed. She glanced toward her older children. "Chris!"

The boy started toward her. "Yes, Mama?"

"I can't see B. J. anywhere. Would you climb up and see where he is?"

"Sure, Mama."

Chris had started in that direction when a familiar voice called, "Hey, Mama!"

Hannah sucked in her breath when she saw B. J. atop one of the higher boulders, waving at her.

She leapt to her feet and shouted, "Brett Jonathan Cooper! You come down from there immediately! I told you not to climb the high rocks!"

"I didn't climb very high! There's lots of rocks higher than this!"

"You come down here right now!"

"First he cheats, and then he disobeys," Patty Ruth said in a half whisper.

"Right now!" Hannah repeated.

B. J. nodded and started down. Suddenly, he let out a fearful yelp and fell from sight.

Dave Croft and Curtis Holden were standing near Hannah, and had taken in the scene. As she started toward the rocks, Dave said, "Mrs. Cooper, Curtis and I will find B. J. You wait here."

The two men bounded over the lower boulders and climbed toward the place where B. J. had fallen. Seconds later, they dropped out of sight.

It was a quiet and chastened group of children who were called from the boulders as a result of B. J.'s fall.

Soon, others in the train gathered around Hannah and watched for Dave and Curtis to reappear. Ezra had just learned of it, and approached the nervous mother, saying, "You hold on, Hannah. Those crevices aren't real deep. They'll get him out."

Even as he spoke, the two men appeared just ahead of

where B. J. had fallen. Curtis had the boy cradled in his arms, and people cheered and applauded.

Hannah's hand flew to her mouth and her knees almost buckled when she saw blood on B. J's sleeve. He was in obvious pain, but was trying not to cry. She hurried to the base of the closest boulder and waited.

Dave Croft climbed down ahead of Curtis and told Hannah, "He skinned his left arm when he fell, but it doesn't look like anything is broken."

Tears filmed B. J.'s eyes as Curtis brought him to his mother, and his lower lip quivered. "I'm sorry, Mama. I did wrong."

Hannah's face showed both relief and concern as she said, "Curtis, please take him to our wagon. I'll have to get him cleaned up and stop the bleeding."

Ezra followed the small party to the Cooper wagon, where Chris hurriedly let down the tailgate and Curtis laid B. J. on it. The short chains held it level like a table.

B. J.'s siblings stood by, as did several others, while Hannah washed the skinned arm in cold water and got the bleeding stopped. As she smeared it with salve and began wrapping it with gauze, she said, "Ezra, I assume there's a doctor at the army fort?"

"Yes, but there's also a doctor in town to care for the civilians. His name's Frank O'Brien. He used to be an army doctor, but he left the service to go back into private practice. He's a good one."

"That's a relief," Hannah said with a sigh. "The scrape is pretty deep in a couple of places. He'll need a doctor's care."

"We'll have him to Fort Bridger by midday tomorrow," said Ezra, patting her shoulder.

That evening the Cooper children were inside the wagon and in their bedclothes early. Hannah gathered them around her and opened her Bible.

"B. J.," she said, "you admitted you did wrong by climbing high when I told you not to."

"Yes, ma'am. I'm sorry, Mama."

"I'm glad you are. Now, the rest of you think about this while I read you a familiar verse in the Bible."

"I know what it is," said Mary Beth. "At least, it's one of two verses."

"All right," said Hannah, "tell us."

"Well, it's either Colossians 1:20, 'Children, obey your parents in all things: for this is well pleasing unto the Lord.' Or it's Ephesians 6:1, 'Children, obey your parents in the Lord: for this is right.'"

Hannah smiled. "I was thinking of Ephesians 6:1, honey. It's good that we also take note from Colossians 1:20 that it is *well pleasing* to the Lord when children obey their parents in *all things.*"

As Hannah looked at her eight-year-old son, she could see guilt written all over his face.

"B. J.," she said, "was it well pleasing to the Lord when you climbed to that high rock against my command?"

"No, ma'am."

"And you got hurt as a result of your disobedience, didn't you?"

"Yes, ma'am."

"Does it say in Ephesians 6:1, 'Children, obey your parents when you think they are right'?"

B. J. shook his head no.

Hannah looked at her other children. "Chris?"

"No, Mama. It says we're to obey you because it's right to obey you."

"Mary Beth?"

"No, Mama. Chris is right."

"Patty Ruth?"

"We're s'posed to obey our mother and father always. An' since Papa wen' to heaven, we're still s'posed to obey *you* all the time."

"And what usually happens when you don't obey?"

"We get hurt," said Patty Ruth.

"And all four of you can recall several times in the past when you disobeyed Papa or me, and you got hurt. Right? So, let's take a lesson from B. J.'s disobedience today. He's suffering because he disobeyed me. This is the way it is when we go against the Scripture. Do you all understand?"

Four heads nodded yes.

"All right. Let's pray."

After a few minutes of prayer, she kissed each child goodnight and watched them crawl into their beds.

As she pulled back her own bedcovers, B. J. said, "Mama, please forgive me for disobeying you."

"You're forgiven, sweet boy," she said, and kissed him again.

"You owe me an apology too, B. J.," Patty Ruth piped up, "for cheatin' in the race by gettin' a head start."

"Patty Ruth," Hannah said, leaning over her, "B. J. did not get a head start. I saw both of you leave on Chris's count of three. Now, let it go."

Patty Ruth said no more aloud. But to herself, she said, *He got hurt 'cause he cheated!*

Hannah bid them all goodnight again, snuffed the lantern, and crawled into bed. She lay in the darkness, anticipating what the next day would bring, then let her mind drift to Solomon. Suddenly she heard sniffling.

"Mary Beth?" Hannah whispered.

"Yes, Mama?"

"Are you all right?"

There was a pause, then, "I just miss Papa so much."

"I know, sweetheart. So do I."

"Could I come and sleep in your arms again, Mama?"

"Of course."

With Mary Beth snuggled next to her, Hannah prayed

silently, *Please, God. Help this sweet girl adjust to her father's death. If there's anything else I can do to help her, please show me.*

CHAPTER ELEVEN

Venus twinkled in the darkening sky to the west as Lieutenant Judd Stoddard dismounted in front of Colonel Bateman's two-story frame house. A kerosene lantern burned on the porch. He mounted the porch, knocked on the door, and heard quick, light footsteps, and then the door opened to reveal a genteel lady.

"Hello, Lieutenant," said Sylvia Bateman. "My guess is, you're here to see my husband."

The lieutenant bowed slightly. "Yes, ma'am."

"Please come in. The colonel is upstairs and will be down in a moment. I'm about to feed him supper."

"I'm sorry to show up at such an inopportune time, Mrs. Bateman," Stoddard said, "but I have some very good news for the colonel, and I believe he'd want to hear it immediately. My patrol and I just arrived a few minutes ago."

"Don't apologize, my boy," Sylvia said, smiling at him. "It's no problem. Let me call him." She went to the bottom of the staircase. "Ross!"

Bateman's voice came from a distant room. "I'll be there in a couple of minutes, dearest. Go ahead and pour the coffee."

"You have a visitor! Lieutenant Stoddard is back and wants to see you!"

"Oh! All right! Be right there!"

Sylvia turned to Stoddard. "I'd invite you to sit down, but

by the time you got settled you'd be on your feet again. When my husband says he'll be right here, he means it."

They heard footsteps at the top of the staircase and saw the fort's commandant descending the stairs. "Welcome back, Lieutenant," Bateman said, clasping the man's hand in a hearty handshake.

"Thank you, sir."

"Patrol go all right?"

"Yes, sir."

"No Indian trouble?"

"No, sir. We sighted two Arapaho war parties, but both times they were going away from us."

"So, what can I do for you?"

"Actually, sir, I have some very good news."

"Now that's the only kind of news I like," the colonel said. "Let's hear it."

"Well, sir, you've been expecting your old friend Solomon Cooper and his family to arrive with the Comstock wagon train—"

"Are they here?" Bateman cut in.

"Not quite, sir. We spotted them late this afternoon from a distance. I used my binoculars and recognized Ezra riding his horse in the lead."

"You didn't meet up with them then?"

"No, sir. You know how slowly a wagon train moves, and the men were anxious to get home. It would have delayed us considerably to swing off course to meet them."

"Mm-hmm. So when would you estimate their arrival?"

"I'd say definitely tomorrow, sir. If Ezra moves his train out early in the morning, they'll probably arrive here about noon, or not too long after that."

"Wonderful! You hear that, Sylvia? Solomon and Hannah will be here tomorrow!"

Sylvia's face lit up with excitement. "Oh, it seems so long

since we saw them in Independence! I can't wait to have my little chats with Hannah like we used to during the War when you men were on the battlefields. She's such a dear!"

Bateman turned to the lieutenant. "Stoddard, I need you to go to the hotel and tell Clayton what you just told me. He needs to know so he can finish any last-minute preparations on the store before then."

"Yes, sir."

"Then, please let Pastor Kelly know, and ask him if he will inform the rest of the town—especially those who are preparing the big reception."

"All right, sir. Anything else?"

"Oh, yes. Stop by the hotel and give the Williamses fair warning in case there are any last-minute things they might want to do with the rooms they've reserved for the Coopers."

"Lieutenant..." Sylvia said.

"Yes, ma'am?"

"What about supper? With all these errands, are you going to get a chance to eat?"

"Well, I'll find something at the fort kitchen later."

"Nonsense! I'll put an extra plate on the table." She turned to her husband. "He'll have plenty of time after supper to do your errands, won't he, dear?"

"Why, of course!" said Bateman. "That all right with you, Lieutenant?"

"Sure is, sir! I've heard about your wife's cooking. Won't disappoint me to pass on that army food!"

It was going on eight o'clock when Lieutenant Stoddard entered the lobby of the Uintah Hotel. Night clerk Derek Kendall looked up from a stack of papers and smiled at Stoddard, whom he knew well.

"Hello, Lieutenant. Officers' quarters full tonight? Need a room?"

Stoddard laughed. "Not exactly, Derek. I need to see Clayton Farley. Do you know if he's in his room?"

"Yes he is...number twelve upstairs."

"Thank you. I also need to see Mr. Williams. I realize he could be at home or at the café—"

"He's in his office with Pastor Kelly," Kendall said, throwing a thumb over his shoulder.

"Oh, good. I need to talk to Pastor Kelly, too. Do you think they'll both be here for a while?"

"Don't know what their plans are, but I'll tell them you're here. Will you be with Mr. Farley very long?"

"Should only take a few minutes. I'll be right back."

"Okay. I'll make sure Mr. Williams and the preacher wait for you."

When Lieutenant Stoddard descended the stairs a few minutes later, he saw Gary Williams and Andy Kelly waiting at the counter in the lobby.

"We hear you're looking for us, Lieutenant," Williams said.

"Did we do something wrong?" Kelly asked with a chuckle.

Stoddard grinned. "Not exactly, Reverend. The colonel wanted me to tell you the wagon train bearing Solomon Cooper and his family will be here tomorrow around noon."

"Great!" Kelly said.

"The colonel wanted to know if you would spread the word around town, Reverend. Make sure everybody knows. We'll take care of the fort."

"I sure will! We'll be ready for the Coopers, I guarantee it!"

"I'd better go tell Glenda," said Williams. "We've kept the

rooms reserved for the Coopers, but she'll no doubt want to freshen them up."

Gary Williams found his wife in the kitchen of Glenda's Place, helping their Chinese cook, Ming Yang, clean up after a busy day. Glenda was just drying her hands when she saw her husband enter the restaurant.

"Look, Ming Yang," she said. "My husband has come to walk me home!"

The Chinese man stood with her in the kitchen doorway, showing his teeth in a big smile. "Ah! Is good, Miss Glenda! Is good! How you tonight, Mister Gary?"

"Just fine, Ming." Gary set his gaze on Glenda and said, "Lieutenant Stoddard just told me the Comstock wagon train is less than a day out. Should pull in here around noon tomorrow."

"Oh! Let's go check the rooms and make sure everything's all right!"

At ten o'clock the next morning, barber Cade Samuels, town council chairman, held a meeting at the town hall with everyone who had a part in the organized welcoming of Solomon and Hannah Cooper to Fort Bridger.

"Let's go over our plans so there'll be no hitch when the Coopers arrive today," he said. "I direct your attention first of all to the banner I've made."

FORT BRIDGER WELCOMES
SOLOMON & HANNAH COOPER & CHILDREN!
Hurrah for the new General Store!

"Looks great, Cade," said Ray Noble, owner of the town's livery stable.

Everyone murmured agreement.

"Now, Colonel Bateman," Samuels said, "you are set to make a welcoming speech, representing the fort, just as we discussed?"

"I am. And since Major and Mrs. Crawley are also friends of the Coopers, they will be at my side, along with Mrs. Bateman, of course."

"Good," Samuels said. "And as chairman of the town council, I'll welcome them to the town. And, Colonel, is the fort's brass band ready?"

"They'll be on the front porch of the new store building, ready to play, once they've been told the wagon train is in sight."

"And Ray will see to that," Samuels said. "You all know, I'm sure, that I've appointed Ray to meet the wagon train on horseback and guide it up Main Street to the new general store, where everyone will be gathered."

Heads nodded.

Samuels then turned his attention to Pastor and Mrs. Kelly. "Pastor, once the colonel and I have made our brief speeches, I want you and Rebecca to give them a personal welcome, since you already know them."

"Be glad to," Kelly said. "Rebecca and I are very excited about seeing them again."

Samuels looked at Judge William Carter, whose wife, Mary, sat beside him. "Judge, I've asked you to approach the Coopers once the formalities are over and give them your welcome and let them know you're happy to pass the sutler business to their general store."

"Gladly!" the judge said, making everyone laugh.

Samuels held up his hands for silence. "My good friend and president of the Fort Bridger Bank, Lloyd Dawson, has volunteered to foot the bill for a big cookout supper this evening as part of the festivities."

Everyone applauded and whistled.

Dawson rose to his feet. "Lois and I are privileged to pay for the festivities, and we've invited everyone in town and in the fort to attend the cookout. We hope everyone will come."

Colonel Bateman lifted his hand.

"Yes, Colonel?"

"Just so you know, we have four patrols out at any given time. This means that about fifty of my men will not be here for the supper. Otherwise, you can count on every man, woman, and child from the fort to attend. That is, except for the four sentries on duty."

"We can have someone carry food from the cookout to them," Sylvia Bateman said.

"Now, why didn't I think of that?" the colonel said.

"You're merely the commandant, dear," Sylvia quipped.

A ripple of laughter moved through the group.

Lloyd Dawson looked at the young black woman who sat next to Heidi and Sundi Lindgren, and a pretty redhead on the third row. "All of us know that our own Mandy Carver is the best cook in Fort Bridger."

"Amen to that!" said Ray Noble, who was a bachelor and had eaten at the blacksmith's home on many occasions. "God really blessed Abe Carver when He gave him Mandy!"

Mandy lowered her head, embarrassed by the acclaim.

Dawson continued speaking. "Mandy has agreed to be head cook at the supper tonight. She has...how many helpers, Mandy?"

"Seventy-two ladies have volunteered to help me, Mister Dawson—from the fort, the town, an' the ranches 'round the area. These folks here might like to know that Nellie Patterson is gonna be my 'sistant head cook. I promise we'll put on a feast that will honor the Coopers."

"I have no doubt of that," said Dawson with a broad smile. Then he set his attention on the Lindgren sisters and the redhead who sat with them, and said, "You'll all be happy to know that Heidi and Sundi and Lila Sparrow will provide music at the big supper. Lila's husband, Captain Jack Sparrow, and three other men from the fort will carry the pump organ to the grassy field just west of town where the supper will be held."

"Sounds like we've got the wheels rolling," said Cade Samuels. "Any questions?"

"Yes, Cade," said Ray Noble. "It's my understanding that the Coopers are to stay at the hotel until their living quarters are finished. Do the Williamses know the wagon train is near?"

"Yes," said Andy Kelly. "They found out last night."

"Anything else?" asked Samuels.

There were no more questions, and the meeting was dismissed. The people hurried away to make preparations for the big welcome.

It was almost noon when Ezra Comstock rode along the wagons, announcing they were five miles from Fort Bridger. Earlier that day, the Uintah Mountains to the southwest had come into view, and Ezra had pointed them out, saying they could be seen quite clearly from the town.

Another hour brought the uneven rooftops of Fort Bridger into sight. Hannah called all four children to the front of the wagon.

"Look, Mama!" Chris said, pointing between Hannah and Patty Ruth. "There's the town! We're home!"

A lump rose in Hannah's throat.

"I see the fort!" said B. J. "Do you see the flag on the pole, Chris?"

"I sure do! I can see the stockade fence, too!"

Patty Ruth clutched Tony the Bear to her chest and stood up on the wagon seat. She was so excited that she started bouncing up and down.

Mary Beth didn't say anything, though her eyes were fixed on the town and fort. Hannah watched her from the corner of her eye for a moment. The girl's outward facade didn't fool her mother. Mary Beth's heart was thumping with excitement just like everyone else's.

Hannah reached past a bouncing Patty Ruth and took hold of Mary Beth's hand. "Everything's going to be all right," she said.

Mary Beth nodded silently.

Biggie stood between the boys, wagging his tail, as they told him his new home lay ahead.

Patty Ruth stopped bouncing around and sat down. She leaned forward to look into her mother's eyes, and said, "Are you scared, Mama?"

Hannah forced a smile and looked down at her. "Not scared, honey. Just a bit nervous. We're about to enter the town where we'll live from now on. Except for the Kellys, the Batemans, and the Crawleys, we don't know anyone. Everyone else will be strangers."

Chris leaned close to his mother. "Mama, I heard Grandma Singleton say once that everybody is a stranger to us when we first meet them. So if we're going to have friends, they must be strangers first."

Hannah let a giggle escape her lips. "Christopher Cooper, you'd make a good teacher or preacher."

The boy laughed. "That's not for me! I'm going to be a soldier!"

"Yes, I know...like Papa."

"Right. I'll let B. J. be the preacher, and Mary Beth will be the teacher."

"Okay, Chris," Patty Ruth said, "so you're gonna be a so'jer, B. J.'s gonna be a preacher, an' Mary Beth's gonna be a teacher. What am I gonna be when I grow up?"

"Probably an old maid," Chris said with a snicker.

The little redhead glared at him, then turned to Hannah and said, "Mama, what's a ol' maid?"

Hannah gave Chris a mock severe look and said, "Chris was only kidding, honey."

Patty Ruth fixed her oldest brother with cold eyes. "*Were* you jus' kiddin'?"

"Yes, little sister. I was just kidding."

"All right," said Patty Ruth, closing her eyes and nodding. Then to her mother, "Mama, what is it?"

"What?"

"A ol' maid?"

"Well, honey, it's...it's a sweet lady who isn't married."

"Oh. So since I don't have a husbin', I mus' be a *young* maid?"

"Yes. That's it," said Hannah.

"So I'm a sweet *young* lady who don't have a husbin'."

"That's what Chris was saying, honey. He thinks you're sweet."

Patty Ruth gave him a loving look. "Thank you, Chris."

B. J. elbowed Chris in the side.

Chris's mention of his maternal grandmother a few minutes before brought the faces of Hannah's parents to mind. She missed them terribly. She longed to see her mother and father and hold them in her arms. She wondered if she would ever see them again on this earth.

Hannah's thoughts were interrupted when Chris peered around her and said, "I wonder if Fort Bridger has any pretty girls my age."

"I would think so," Hannah said, "what with the fort there, and all."

"Well, if there *are* any pretty girls in Fort Bridger," put in Patty Ruth, turning to look at Chris, "they won't be interested in a funny-lookin' boy from Missouri."

Chris gave her a dead-eye look, and Patty Ruth returned a sly grin.

The sun was starting its downward slant in the sky when the wagon train drew close enough to Fort Bridger that they could see people along its eastern edge.

The crouching green hills surrounding the town were showing a slight touch of tawny grass on the high spots. Autumn was coming to Wyoming.

The river fork that wended its way southwest across rolling plains, and ran through the town, glittered in the sunlight like a crystalline serpent. It twisted its way from the distant Green River until it visited Fort Bridger, then vanished far out in the muted, shimmering green and buff of the plains that spread toward the Uintah Mountains.

When Hannah saw a lone rider gallop out of town toward Ezra Comstock, she swallowed hard. Her mind went to Solomon's words the day they pulled out of Independence: *"Out there, Hannah, under the distant sky, is our new home and our new life."*

And now, without Solomon, Hannah Cooper had reached her new home.

Chapter Twelve

Nellie Patterson followed on her husband's heels as he went out the back door, carrying his rifle.

"Come with us, Alex," she said. "The whole town will be there."

"I told you. I'm stayin' here to see if I can catch that varmint who's been killin' the chickens. Or the *dog* that's been doin' it."

"Please, Alex," she said. "We'll be doing business with the Coopers at the general store. We need to show them, along with everyone else, that they're welcome."

"Hah! They wouldn't pay us any mind, Nellie. And for that matter, I can tell you two other people who won't be there—Les and Wanda Coggins."

They drew up to the shed and stopped. The chickens were moving around, clucking.

"Why aren't they coming?" she asked.

"Les heard that the Coopers are Christians. Since he owns the saloon, he figures they wouldn't approve of the way he makes his livin', so he and Wanda ain't goin'."

As Alex opened the shed door, Nellie said, "Aren't you even coming to the cookout?"

He gave her a sour look and mumbled, "I would, but not with you and that—that *slave* woman workin' together." With that, Alex closed the door in her face.

❦ ❦ ❦

Ezra Comstock was riding four or five wagon-lengths ahead of the train when he saw a lone rider galloping toward him.

"Looks like we got company, Uncle Ezra!" called Micah.

"More like a welcomin' committee of one," the wagon master called back. "It's Ray Noble."

"Why would he come out here?"

"Don't know, but he's smilin' from ear to ear, so he must be glad to see us. Big smile like that makes a man feel welcome."

Ezra removed his tattered old hat and waved it at Noble. The livery stable owner lifted his hat and waved in return.

When Noble came within thirty yards, he drew rein and wheeled his horse around, then swung his arm in a forward motion and headed back toward town.

"Hey, Ray!" Ezra shouted. "What's goin' on?"

Noble halted his horse, looked back, and without a word swung his arm forward again. At the same time, he nudged his horse away from the wagon train.

"What's he doing, Uncle Ezra?" called Micah.

"I haven't the slightest idea. He wants us to follow him, so we'll do it. We were goin' into Fort Bridger anyhow."

The wagon master rode closer to the lead wagon and said, "When we get to town, Micah, we'll make a circle at the west edge like we've done in the past, and take the rest of the day off. We'll load up with supplies at the sutler's store while Hannah's drivers get her stuff unloaded and on the shelves in the new store. They should have enough daylight left to get it all done. We'll pull out at sunrise in the mornin'. I'll ride back now and tell everybody the plan."

As Ezra stopped at each wagon, the people asked what the rider's strange behavior was all about. Ezra told them he didn't know, but he knew the man, so everything was all right.

The army brass band waited on the porch of the general store, their instruments glistening in the sun. A crowd of several hundred people were gathered in the street—every man, woman, and child from the town and surrounding ranches were there to greet the Coopers.

Clayton Farley stood with his building crew. He'd asked Gary and Glenda Williams to stay close by. He wanted them near when he told the Coopers that their living quarters weren't quite finished and explained about the hotel arrangements.

All the inhabitants of the fort were on hand, too, except for the sentries and the fifty-odd men who made up the Indian patrols. Included in the army crowd was the fort physician, young Dr. Robert Blayney, and his wife, Ruth, who stood with Dr. and Mrs. Frank O'Brien.

The welcoming committee was a combination of fort and town people, who now stood together in a small group on the boardwalk in front of the store.

A slight breeze blew across the town, causing the large banner stretched across Main Street to lightly bounce and sway. There was a noticeable touch of fall in the air, which had become more apparent during the last few days. The sun was shining out of a cloudless blue sky, and the trees in and around the fort and town had begun their usual display of reds, golds, and russets. The willows were beginning to droop some, and they swayed in the soft breeze that caused the yellowing aspen leaves to shimmer and dance.

At the sound of hoofbeats, all heads turned to the east end of town. Everyone recognized Justin Powell galloping in. He was employed at Swensen's Gun Shop and Hardware Store. But since all the town's stores were closed for this occasion, he had ridden out with Ray Noble to scout the wagon train.

"Get ready, everybody!" Justin shouted, reining in his

mount, "The wagon train will be here in a few minutes! You'll know the Coopers because Ray's fixing it so their wagon will be in the lead when it reaches this point!"

The director of the army band pulled his baton from a small leather case, and the band members made ready.

Hannah saw Ray Noble finally stop and let Ezra catch up to him. He said a few words to the wagon master, who nodded and then rode to Micah and said something to him. She watched Ezra trot to the next wagon, the next, the next, and the next. When he finished talking to the driver of the wagon directly in front of her, he started to ride back to the front.

"Ezra-a-a!" she called.

Comstock drew rein and turned in the saddle. "Yes'm?"

"What's going on?"

"Oh, just a little adjustment that'll take place in wagon order. Won't affect you. Just follow me!"

Hannah shrugged her shoulders and urged the oxen ahead as the other wagons began to move.

Justin Powell sat his horse in the middle of the street on the east edge of the crowd, watching for the wagons. Those who had the same view of the street peered eastward with anticipation.

Suddenly Justin called out, "Okay, Ralph! Strike up the band! They're here!"

Patty Ruth was the first to hear the strange sound. "Mama, what's that?" she asked. She tucked her knees under her on the seat and cocked her head to listen.

At the same moment Hannah and her other children recognized the music.

"It's a military marching band, Patty Ruth," said Chris.

"Why's a band playing, Mama?" asked Mary Beth.

"I have no idea, honey. Apparently the fort has a band, and they must be practicing."

"Look, Mama," B. J. said, "Micah's pullin' his wagon over to the other side of the street."

"The others are doing the same," said Chris.

Hannah started to follow, but Ezra appeared on his horse and said above the ever-increasing volume of the band, "Hannah, you follow me."

When the wagon in front of Hannah cleared the way, she saw the huge crowd gathered in the street. Then her attention was drawn to the large white banner stretched across the street.

A lump rose in her throat and tears filmed her eyes as she read the bright red letters.

The crowd began to cheer and applaud, the din mingling with the blare of the band.

When Mary Beth saw her father's name on the banner, she burst into tears. Chris felt a wave of emotion rise within him, and B. J. held Biggie close, crying into his fur. The dog whined, realizing something was awry.

Patty Ruth looked at her mother's tears, and turned to her sister and brothers. "Mama, what's wrong? Why are you and Mary Beth and B. J. and Chris cryin'?"

Chris leaned close so she could hear him above the noise. "Papa's name's up there on that banner, along with Mama's, Patty Ruth. The people don't know Papa died on the trail."

Ezra Comstock signaled for Hannah to stop in front of the brand-new, glistering white store building. When he looked back, he saw her looking up at something and weeping. His eyes followed her line of sight to the sign above the porch roof.

COOPER'S GENERAL STORE
Solomon Cooper, Prop.

The smiling, cheering crowd assumed she was simply overcome by the warm welcome and continued to applaud and wave at the Coopers, and shout words of welcome.

"Oh, Solomon," Hannah said between sobs, "I know you're looking down on this."

The people from the wagon train had parked their wagons outside of town and were just now arriving on foot.

Ezra dismounted to go to Hannah, but when he saw the commandant step off the boardwalk and head toward her, he rushed toward the officer.

"You're Colonel Bateman, I assume, sir," said Ezra as they both came to a halt, facing each other.

"Yes, and you must be Ezra Comstock."

"Yes, sir. I need to talk to Mrs. Cooper first, if you don't mind, Colonel. Privately, I mean."

Bateman's eyebrows arched. "Well, all right. I'll wait right here."

The din of welcome continued as Ezra hurried to the Cooper wagon and said, "I'm sorry about this, Hannah. I only learned about the reception just before we came into town. I didn't know about the banner or the sign on the store, but you understand these good people had no way of knowing."

Hannah wiped at her tears and choked out, "I know. What they're doing is wonderful. It's just that—"

"I understand. As you can see, Colonel Bateman is here and wants to talk to you. He's probably gonna make some kind of welcome speech. Do you want me to tell him about Solomon?"

Hannah pulled a hanky from her skirt pocket and dabbed at her eyes and nose. "No. I should be the one to tell him. Please ask him to step over here."

Ezra motioned to Bateman. The colonel hastened toward the wagon with his wife, Sylvia, just behind him. Cade and Regina Samuels, the Crawleys, and the Kellys followed.

When the crowd saw the commandant and the others moving toward the wagon, the cheering and applause trailed off, as did the band music.

Colonel Bateman looked up and said, "Welcome, Hannah...children. I guess this is quite a surprise to you."

Hannah tried to smile. "Yes, Colonel. And such a kind thing for all of you to do. I—" Her throat tightened, and she swallowed with difficulty.

Bateman ran his gaze around the wagon, looking for the Civil War hero who had served under his command. "Where's Solomon?"

Chris reached a hand toward his mother as she struggled to regain her composure. By this time, the crowd had gone totally quiet.

Andy and Rebecca Kelly moved up close to the wagon. "Mrs. Cooper," said the preacher, "is there anything I can do for you?"

Hannah sniffed and drew in a deep breath, then said in a quavering voice, "Hello, Pastor. No, thank you. I...I just need to explain to everyone that...that Solomon is dead."

A shock wave went over the front edge of the crowd, and the news quickly reached the others.

Kelly turned to Bateman and said, "Colonel, we need to call this reception off. This dear lady and her children are in no frame of mind to—"

"No, please," said Hannah. "It's all right, Pastor. Let me tell you gentlemen and all these sweet, kind people what happened."

"All right," Kelly said, taking a step back.

Hannah rose to her feet in the wagon box and ran her gaze to the white structure before her. "Before I do that, let me say that the store is beautiful."

"The contractor who built it is in the crowd, Hannah," said Bateman.

"Over here, Mrs. Cooper!" called out Clayton Farley, from where he and the Williamses stood near the porch. "I'll see you when the reception is over."

Hannah smiled at him and nodded. She drew another deep breath and spoke loudly so all could hear, telling them how Solomon had died as a hero on the trail, giving his life to save her and the children.

A sorrowful silence prevailed as the crowd stood listening.

When Hannah finished the story, she looked out over the crowd and said, "What you've done here is appreciated more than my children and I could ever tell you. We never expected such a warm and wonderful reception. I...I never dreamed there would be any kind of a formal welcome at all. I know we're going to be very happy as citizens of Fort Bridger."

The crowd cheered and broke into applause.

"I'd like to introduce my children to you," she said.

When she got to Patty Ruth, the little redhead said in a low tone, "Mama...Biggie!"

"Oh, of course," said Hannah, grinning. She picked up the little black-and-white rat terrier. "This, folks, is our family pet, Mr. Big Enough. He is known as Biggie for short."

Biggie got his applause too.

Pastor Kelly stepped forward. "Mrs. Cooper, may I help you down?"

The children followed their mother as Kelly helped her from the wagon seat. When Hannah's feet touched ground, Rebecca Kelly hugged her, then hugged each of the children while Sylvia Bateman embraced Hannah. Christel Crawley followed suit, and the major and the colonel expressed their words of welcome to the entire family.

Cade Samuels stepped up with Regina by his side, and Colonel Bateman introduced them to Hannah, explaining that in addition to being the town's barber, Cade was the town council chairman.

"Mrs. Cooper," said Samuels, "I'd like for you and the children to step up on the porch of your new store building."

Hannah led her children onto the porch and quietly told them to turn and face the people. Patty Ruth leaned against her mother's leg, holding on to Tony the Bear.

Samuels gestured toward the crowd and said, "Mrs. Cooper, I'm sure all these people will want to know, as I do, are you planning to go ahead and operate the general store?"

"Why, of course," Hannah said.

The crowd cheered.

One man called out, "God bless you, Mrs. Cooper! This town needs a good general store!"

The cheering grew louder.

When it died down, Hannah said, "Ladies and gentlemen, if you will look across the street, you'll see the wagon train. Among those wagons are four supply vehicles that are carrying goods to stock my shelves so I can open up for business in a day or so."

There were more cheers and applause.

At Cade Samuels's signal, Judge William Carter stepped up on the porch with Mary beside him. "Mrs. Cooper," Samuels said, "this is Judge William Carter."

Hannah did a slight curtsy. "I know who you are, sir, and I'm very happy to meet you."

"This is my wife, Mary," he said, then, "Mrs. Cooper, let me say right here in front of everybody that I'm very glad you're going to stay and run the store."

"Thank you, Judge." Hannah turned to face the crowd. "I will do my very best to serve the people of the town, the fort, and the surrounding area, even as Judge Carter has done with the sutler's store."

Cade Samuels put his hand on Chris's shoulder. "Mrs. Cooper...children," he said, "we all want you to know that we're superbly happy to have you in our town. And just to underscore it, we have a big cookout planned this evening in honor of your arrival. Our town's banker, Lloyd Dawson, is providing the food, and I'm sure he won't mind if I invite all of your friends from the wagon train to join us."

"That's right!" came Dawson's voice from the edge of the porch.

Samuels seemed to pull himself up with a jerk and said, "Oh, my! I almost forgot our formal welcome for the Coopers."

Bateman stepped forward and addressed the Cooper family, welcoming them in the name of the army fort and all its inhabitants. Cade Samuels then gave his brief speech, welcoming them in the name of the town of Fort Bridger and its surrounding farms and ranches.

Hannah's voice broke a little as she said, "My children and I want to thank all of you for this magnificent reception, and for your warmth and kindness. We're looking forward to knowing each one of you."

After more applause and cheering, Samuels said, "Mrs. Cooper, these great people want to come by and introduce themselves briefly. Are you and the children up to it?"

"Of course," Hannah said. "These are our people now, and we want to meet them."

As a long line began to form, Hannah led the children off the porch to street level, and began greeting the people.

The travelers returned to their wagons so Micah Comstock could lead them outside of town to form the circle. Vanessa Tolliver, Perry Norwood, Buck Mylan, and Tony Cuzak returned to the Cooper supply wagons and drove them into the alley behind the store for unloading.

The line of people moved slowly as they passed by Hannah and her children. Several families and individuals had come and gone when Hannah set eyes on a sweet-looking, elderly couple in front of her.

"Hello!" she said warmly, thinking of her parents.

"Mrs. Cooper," said the small man with twinkling eyes and bushy brows, "I'm Dr. Frank O'Brien, and this is my wife, Edie. Well, her name's actually Edith, but I call her Edie."

Edie O'Brien moved toward Hannah and wrapped her arms around her, saying, "We're so glad you've come to our town, honey."

"Me, too," said Hannah, hugging her tight, and catching a whiff of lavender perfume.

"And these children!" said Edie. "I must hug *them!*"

"While you're doing that," said the doctor, "I'll just avail myself of a hug from their beautiful mother!"

The rest of the people in line waited patiently while the O'Briens paid attention to each of the Cooper children.

When Frank O'Brien got to Patty Ruth, he chuckled and said, "That's some bear you have, little lady! What's his name?"

Patty Ruth thought the O'Briens seemed almost like her own grandparents back in Independence. She grinned at him, and said, "His name's Tony Cooper."

The doctor laughed heartily. "Tony Cooper! Hey, I like that!"

"Doctor," said Hannah, "Ezra Comstock told me about you. My son, B. J., here, fell and skinned his left arm yesterday. It really needs your attention. Could I bring him to your office yet today?"

O'Brien looked at the eight-year-old. "I thought you winced a bit, son, when I hugged you."

"Yes, sir," B. J said with a nod.

O'Brien turned back to Hannah. "Tell you what, Mrs. Cooper. Edie and I will take him to the office right now. We sure don't want him getting blood poisoning from that scrape. I hate to take him away from this nice reception, but if it's that bad, it better be attended to right away."

"Oh, thank you," she said, relief showing in her dark brown eyes. Then to B. J., "Honey, it's best that you go with Dr.

O'Brien right now. When I'm finished here, I'll come to the office and get you."

"Okay, Mama," B. J. said.

"My office is in the next block north on the other side of the street," said the doctor. "You can't miss it."

"I'll find it," Hannah said.

"I'll go with him, Mama," said Chris.

Hannah watched her sons walk away with the O'Briens and noticed with gratitude that Edie had a boy on each side of her, with her arms draped around their shoulders.

Thank You, Lord, she said in her heart. *We're going to be very happy here.*

Chapter Thirteen

Mary Beth glanced up at the street banner again and fixed her eyes on her father's name. "Papa," she said under her breath, "if you're looking down from heaven, you can see what kind of a welcome they planned for you. These seem to be such nice people. I'm sure you would have liked them."

Her attention was drawn to the man who stepped up in line after her brothers and the O'Briens walked away. The sun glinted off his badge.

"Howdy, Mrs. Cooper," he said, smiling. "I'm the law around here. My name's Lance Mangum."

Hannah read the badge and said, "Marshal Mangum, I'm happy to meet you."

The marshal turned toward the girls. "So this is Mary Beth and Patty Ann."

"No, sir, Mister Marshal. My name's Patty *Ruth.*"

"Oh! I'm sorry. Your mother did tell us it was Patty Ruth. And your doggie there in the wagon. What's his name?"

"Big Enough Cooper. But we mostly call him Biggie."

"And what's your bear's name?"

"Tony Cooper. I use to have a bear named Ulysses Cooper, but I gave him to a little boy who didn' have no toys."

"Didn't have *any* toys, honey," Hannah said.

"Mm-hmm. Matthew didn' have no toys."

Mangum grinned at Hannah, who shook her head and looked at the sky.

"Mrs. Cooper," said Mangum, "I want you to feel free to call on me anytime you have a need of any kind."

"Thank you. I'll remember that."

Next were pharmacist Eugene Thurman, his wife, Dora, and their two teenage sons, Eugene Jr. and Harold, who both had eyes for Mary Beth.

When they walked away, Patty Ruth poked her sister. "Those boys think you're cute," she said.

"They don't either," said Mary Beth, blushing.

Little sister giggled and said to her bear, "Tony, they *do* think Mary Beth's cute, don't they?"

She made Tony's head nod, and said in a low voice. "Yes, Patty Ruth. Those boys think Mary Beth is the cutest girl in all the world."

Hannah chuckled and turned her eyes to the next couple in line. "Hello, Mrs. Cooper," said the pleasant-voiced man. "I'm Dan Bledsoe, and this is my wife, Carlene. You may have noticed the sign on the store next door. We own Bledsoe's Family Clothing Store."

"Oh, of course!" said Hannah. "I did notice the sign when we first pulled up in the wagon. So you're our neighbors."

"Well, with the business, anyway. Our house is a couple of blocks east. We understand you'll be living above the store."

"Yes," said Hannah.

Other merchants followed the Bledsoes and made themselves known. As each family passed by, Hannah realized what a friendly place they had come to. She knew the next two young women had to be sisters.

"Hello," said the shorter one, "I'm Sundi Lindgren, and this is my sister, Heidi."

"Are you married?" Patty Ruth blurted.

Sundi looked down at the little redhead and grinned. "Not yet, honey."

Patty Ruth thought about Sundi's answer for a moment. "Mama," she said, eyeing the sisters, "I didn' know *old* maids were so pretty!"

"What's that?" asked Heidi.

"Recent family subject," said Hannah, shaking her head.

"Oh," Heidi replied. "Well, Mrs. Cooper, if you ever need dresses made, I'm at your service. I own Heidi's Dress Shop down the street."

"Thank you," Hannah said. "And what does your sister do?"

"I'm Fort Bridger's old maid schoolmarm," Sundi said with a giggle.

Mary Beth's eyes lit up.

"What grades do you teach?" Hannah asked.

"All of them."

"All *twelve?*"

"Yes'm. I have forty-two students, and it looks like I'll soon have forty-five."

Hannah turned to her oldest daughter. "Hear that, Mary Beth? This is your teacher."

"Yes, I heard," Mary Beth said, observing that she was almost as tall as her teacher. "Miss Lindgren, I'm planning on being a teacher someday, too."

"Oh, really? Well, wonderful. We'll get along real well. And I'll do everything I can to help you achieve your goal."

"Thank you," Mary Beth said with a big smile.

Sundi turned to Hannah. "Your children will have a little catching up to do, Mrs. Cooper, since school has already started. But I'll work with them."

"I appreciate that," Hannah said warmly.

"Can the children start school on Monday?"

"I'm planning on it."

Sundi leaned down to Hannah's youngest. "How old are you, Patty Ruth?"

"Five."

"So you won't be coming to school until you're six, right?"

"Mm-hmm. Can Tony come to school?"

"Who's Tony?"

Patty Ruth lifted the stuffed bear toward Sundi's face. "This is Tony. Can he come to school?"

"Well, honey, I don't know. I'll have to give that some consideration."

"What's cons—consid—"

"Consideration means she'll think about it, sweetheart," said Hannah.

"Oh. Well, if Tony can't come to school, I guess I'll jus' have to stay home."

"Maybe Tony could come to my dress shop and stay with me during the day when you go to school, Patty Ruth," said Heidi. "Would you care if Tony stayed with me when you get old enough to go to school?"

"Well, I'll jus' have to give it some consi—consider—"

"Consideration," said Sundi.

"Yeah...that."

"Okay," Heidi said, laughing, as she cupped Patty Ruth's chin in her hand. "You give it some consideration between now and when you start to school."

The Lindgren sisters moved on and were followed by Abe and Mandy Carver and their three children, Tyrone, Leroy, and Annie Frances.

Hannah introduced her girls to the little boys, then picked up three-year-old Annie Frances and hugged her. "What great big eyes she has! Isn't she a doll?"

Annie Frances giggled.

"Miz Cooper," said Mandy, "I'm the head cook for the cookout. An' right behind us is my good friend, Nellie Patterson, who's my 'sistant head cook. I want you to meet her and her children."

Mandy gestured for Nellie to come close and introduced her to Hannah and the girls. Nellie introduced her children, Luke, Willa, and Joshua.

"We're so glad to meet you," Hannah said, smiling warmly. "Luke, what happened to your leg?"

"It's my ankle, ma'am. I broke it during recess at school when us boys were having a running and jumping contest."

"Oh, I see. Next time it might be one of *my* boys!"

Abe spoke up. "Miz Cooper, I noticed that you have two horses tied behin' your wagon. Any time they need new horseshoes, I'll make 'em an' put 'em on at no charge."

"Why, thank you, Mr. Carver," said Hannah.

"It's the least I can do for a sister in Christ, Miz Cooper."

"Oh, you're Christians!" Hannah said excitedly.

"Yes'm," Abe said, grinning broadly.

"We sure are," said Mandy. "I know you've met Pastor Kelly, but have you ever heard him preach?"

"No, but I'm told he's very good."

"You'll like him, I promise," said Mandy. "He really makes the Bible easy to understand."

"And he tells Bible stories by actin' 'em out," Abe said.

"Sounds wonderful," Hannah said.

"Well, Miz Cooper," said Abe, "we better be lettin' more folks meet you."

Hannah thanked them for coming by and did the same with Nellie and her children, noting a sad look in the woman's eyes.

When everyone had welcomed Hannah and the girls, Clayton Farley approached them with the Williamses.

"You already know who I am, Mrs. Cooper," he said. "I want you to meet Gary and Glenda Williams. They're the owners of the Uintah Hotel, and they also own the café attached to it, called Glenda's Place."

"Oh, yes, just in the next block," said Hannah. "I did notice the buildings. They look brand new."

"Almost," said Gary. "Mr. Farley built them, even as he's putting up every building and house under construction right now in this town."

"Well, I'm glad Colonel Bateman was able to engage you to build the store for us, Mr. Farley," she said.

"Ma'am, you might not be so glad when I tell you we're somewhat behind on the store building."

"Oh? It looks finished to me."

"The first floor is finished, ma'am—ready for you to move your goods in, stock the shelves, and open the doors for business. But the living quarters aren't yet ready for occupancy. It'll take about two more weeks to finish it."

Hannah was visibly disappointed, even as she struggled to hide her reaction.

"I'm really sorry it's not done, Mrs. Cooper," said Farley, "but I've had a hard time hiring enough men to stay on schedule. I brought my regular crew with me from Cheyenne City, expecting to be able to hire some local help. There were fewer men available than I thought."

Hannah managed a smile and said, "I guess we can live in the wagon for two weeks. We've lived in it for four-and-a-half months."

"Oh, you won't need to do that," Farley said hastily. "You see, I've made arrangements with Gary and Glenda for you to stay at the hotel."

"In the cellar," Gary said, chuckling. Glenda elbowed him in the ribs.

Hannah laughed. "The cellar, eh?"

Glenda's eyes shone as she said, "We have three rooms on the second floor of the hotel set aside for you, Mrs. Cooper." Compassion welled up in her heart, and she moved to Hannah and embraced her. "I'm so sorry for what happened to your husband. I know you have a lot of adjusting to do with this sudden change in your life. Please let me be your friend. Let me help you in any way I can."

Hannah blinked back tears, and said, "I'd love to have you for a friend. I sense something about you..."

"What's that?"

"That you're my sister in Christ."

"Yes!" Glenda said, hugging her again. "And as ornery as he is, my husband is your brother in Christ!"

Gary laughed. "I'm not ornery *all* the time, Mrs. Cooper."

"When he's asleep, he's pretty good," Glenda said, grinning at him.

Hannah and the girls laughed. Then Hannah said, "Please, you two, call me Hannah."

"And you can call me Patty Ruth!" spoke up the little redhead.

"All right, Patty Ruth," said Glenda.

"An' my sister's name is Mary Beth."

"Yes. Hello, Mary Beth."

"Hello, Mrs. Williams," Mary Beth said with a smile.

"You should know, Hannah, that Mr. Farley is paying for your rooms," Glenda said.

Hannah glanced at Clayton Farley. "Oh, that's not necessary. I can pay for the rooms."

"But you won't," Clayton said. "That's my responsibility. Your living quarters should have been done by now. And let me say, too, that the cost of the structure is turning out to be less than I had told Colonel Bateman, so you'll be getting some money back."

Hannah smiled and said, "Well, that's good news, Mr. Farley. But really, I can pay for the rooms."

"No, ma'am. I'm paying for them, and that's final."

"Then please accept our thanks."

"My pleasure."

"This may present one problem, Glenda," said Hannah.

"What's that?"

"Our dog. I don't think you'll want him in your hotel."

Glenda laughed. "That's no problem at all. Gary and I live in a house on the block right behind the hotel. We have a dog, too. The backyard is fenced, and you'll be able to see Biggie from your hotel room windows. He and Butch will have a good time together."

Tony Cuzak, Perry Norwood, and Buck Mylan appeared, coming around the store building. "Mrs. Cooper," said Tony, "we're ready to unload the supply wagons. Okay if we open up the back door and get started?"

Hannah looked at Farley.

"The first floor is ready to go," he said.

"You want us to put it on the shelves?" Tony asked.

"Well, I really need to see the inside of the store before I know just where I want everything. Why don't you stack the boxes inside, and I'll stock the shelves on Monday."

"You won't have to do it alone, Hannah," said Gary. "We'll put out the word that you need help, and you'll have plenty of volunteers. In fact, I volunteer Glenda to help you all day Monday."

Glenda elbowed him again. "Take care of your own volunteering, Mr. Williams!" she said with a laugh. Then to Hannah, "I'll help you till everything is ready for you to open the store."

"But the café," Hannah said. "Don't you have to work there?"

"Not really. I help out just because I enjoy it, but I have a sufficient crew."

"Well, we'll get busy, then," said Tony.

"Tell you what," said Farley. "If you'll wait until I show Mrs. Cooper the inside of the building, and the barn and corral out back, I'll round up some of my men to help you unload."

Tony nodded his thanks and left to tell the other drivers.

"Hannah," Gary said, "I'll find some men to help me get your personal things to the hotel if you'll show me what you want to go there."

"Certainly," Hannah said. Before she could turn back toward the wagon, Glenda put an arm around her and said, "All your meals will be free at the café while you're at the hotel, Hannah. And I expect you and the children to eat three meals a day."

"Glenda," Hannah argued, "there's no need for that. I can pay for our meals."

"Not while you're our guests, you can't," Glenda said firmly. "Well, I know Mr. Farley's eager to show you the inside of your store, so I'll get on back to the hotel."

"The girls and I will be going to Dr. O'Brien's office to see about the boys," said Hannah. "We'll come to the hotel from there."

"See you then," Glenda said, and hurried down the street.

"All right, Mr. Farley," Hannah said, turning to the building contractor. "This is the moment I've been waiting for. Let's see what our store looks like."

Clayton moved to the front door, paused, and said, "I'll have the sign redone, ma'am, and put your name as proprietor."

Hannah swallowed hard. "Yes, of course. Thank you."

Clayton held open the door for Hannah and the girls and then followed them inside. The sweet aroma of freshly cut wood, mixed with dried paint, filled the store. The workmen had already piled boxes in corners and other open spots, and were coming and going from the wagons at the back of the store, carrying more supplies.

Hannah gazed at the long counter, where wide-mouth jars would hold an array of penny candy. Behind that counter, she would take in the money six days a week to provide for her children.

She took in the well-built shelves behind the counter, as well as shelves along the other walls and in long rows throughout the store, except for the area around the black potbellied stove in the center. Solomon's sketch of the floor plan had made room for several chairs where customers could sit in the winter months, warm themselves, swap stories, and catch up on the latest news in Fort Bridger. There was also a spot for a small table with two chairs that would hold a checkerboard. In her mind's eye, she could already see the people sitting in the chairs chatting, and two men playing checkers.

"Mama!" Mary Beth said. "It's beautiful!"

Hannah drank it all in before turning to Clayton Farley. "You've done a superb job! I watched Solomon draw the plans, and you've followed them precisely."

"Thank you, ma'am. Even though it's not finished yet, I'd like to show you the living quarters."

"Oh, yes! Let's look at it."

As they stepped onto the back porch, Hannah's line of sight went to the barn and corral. "Oh, Mr. Farley, could we look inside the barn?"

"Sure. Come on."

They followed Clayton Farley across the forty-foot span to the barn. There was a normal-sized door facing the store, and a set of double doors that opened into the corral on the opposite side.

Hannah was pleased with the barn and corral, and surprised to see the haymow filled with hay. Mary Beth commented that Buster would like his new home.

Farley led them back to the outside staircase, eager for them to see the upstairs.

Patty Ruth clung to Tony the Bear and did a little extra hop on each step as they followed the builder up the stairs.

Inside Mary Beth looked around in wonder. "Mama!" she said. "Look at all the windows! It's so bright in here!"

"Yes! This is exactly how Papa drew the plans."

Farley led Hannah and her girls around sawdust piles and various lengths of wood to show them the kitchen and eating area, where a brand-new cookstove was in place. The counter and cabinets were about half finished. They took a look at the parlor, which had windows on two walls, then entered the bedrooms, where doors for rooms and closets leaned against the walls. Hannah pointed out which bedroom Solomon had chosen for his girls, and both were happy with its location.

As they headed toward the door, Hannah said, "Mr. Farley, you really have done a fabulous job. Thank you so much."

"I'm glad you're pleased, ma'am. I just wish it was finished."

"Don't feel bad. We'll make out fine at the hotel."

As they stepped onto the stair landing, they saw Tony, Buck, Perry, and Pastor Kelly carrying boxes into the store. Three other men were coming around the corner of the building, and Rebecca Kelly stood at the foot of the stairs, looking up at Hannah.

"Those three men have been working up here, Mrs. Cooper," Farley informed her. "Plus another man who should be here soon. We'll stay on it, and I'm sure we'll have the apartment finished in a couple of weeks."

Hannah nodded. "Fine," she said, smiling.

"I'll go collect some of my men to come and help get these supply wagons unloaded," Farley said.

"I very much appreciate it," Hannah said.

The three carpenters waited till Hannah, the girls, and the boss, descended the stairs, then bounded up to get back to work.

"Mrs. Cooper," Rebecca Kelly said, "I just wanted to tell you that I'll be here Monday morning to help you stock shelves."

"Wonderful! I'll take you up on it!"

"See you in church tomorrow!" Rebecca said, moving away.

"You sure will," Hannah called after her.

Hannah then went to the four men who were unloading the wagons to thank them and to say that she and the girls needed to get to the doctor's office to see about B. J. She'd see them at the cookout.

When Hannah and the girls reached the street, Ray Noble was coming down the boardwalk at a good clip. "Oh, there you are, Mrs. Cooper!"

Hannah stopped. "Yes, sir?"

"My name's Ray Noble, ma'am. I'm the town's hostler."

"Oh, yes. You're the man who met Ezra outside of town and set us up for the surprise."

"Yes, ma'am. I want to tell you that I'll sell your oxen and wagons for you, if you'd like."

"Oh, yes. The oxen and the wagons. I've wondered what I was going to do with them. I sure would like for you to sell them for me. I'll pay you whatever commission you say."

Noble smiled. "Oh, no, ma'am. There's no commission. It'll be my welcome gift to you."

Hannah Cooper was overwhelmed with the kindness and generosity this town had shown her. "I don't know how to sufficiently thank you, Mr. Noble."

"It's my pleasure, ma'am. If you're through with the wagons and the oxen by cookout time, you can let me know then."

"All right. We'll see how it goes. Once again, thank you."

As Hannah walked down the street with her daughters, a sense of joy welled up in her breast. *Thank You, Lord,* she said deep inside. *Thank You for bringing us to Fort Bridger and for giving us so many new friends already. We, indeed, are going to be very happy here!*

CHAPTER FOURTEEN

Luke Patterson guided the horse and buggy into the yard. As he turned the horse in the direction of the barn, Nellie looked toward the chicken shed, wondering if her husband was still out there. Her question was answered when the shed door opened, and Alex stepped out with his rifle in hand.

The family alighted from the buggy, and Nellie handed Luke his crutches as Alex came toward them and said, "Luke, you can unhitch the horse and put him in the corral. You hitched him up so you oughtta be able to unhitch him."

"Yes, Pa, I can handle it."

"Any sign of the coyote, Alex?" Nellie asked.

"Nah. Shep nosed around out here some, but that's all."

"The welcoming for the Coopers is over, Alex," said Nellie. "Mr. Farley is expecting you back to work on the Cooper building tomorrow."

Alex nodded. "So what do you think of the Cooper family?"

"They're a very brave family. Solomon, the head of the house, was killed on the trail."

"Oh? How'd that happen?"

"A rattlesnake bit him three times when he tried to keep it from biting any of his family as they slept."

"That's too bad."

"My heart goes out to Hannah. She's a very sweet person."

"They have nice children, too, Pa," said Luke. "Their oldest daughter is really pretty."

"Alex?" Nellie said timidly.

"Mmm?"

"Some people have volunteered to help Hannah get things set up in her store on Monday. I didn't say anything to her, since I needed to ask you first."

A scowl passed over Alex's face. "You mean that woman is gonna run the store anyhow, without her husband?"

"Yes."

"She's got no business operatin' a store! It's a *man's* job! She should stay home and take care of her children!"

"She can't stay home, Alex. She has to provide for her children."

"Then she oughtta take in washin' like you do, or find somethin' else to do at home to make her livin'!"

Irritation rose up in Nellie, and boldness with it. "That's easy for you to say, Alex. The poor woman has had her husband taken from her suddenly. Right now, she's needing someone to help her, and I'd like to be one of those who does."

Alex's eyes flared with anger. "You stay home and take care of your duties here!" Then he stomped away toward the chicken house.

Dr. O'Brien carefully wrapped gauze on B. J.'s arm while Edith held his hand and talked to him to keep his mind off the pain.

"B. J.," she said softly, stroking his hair, "I'm glad you want to call me Grandma. That pleases me very much."

"You're a lot like my Grandma Singleton," B. J. said, smiling in spite of the stinging in his arm. Dr. O'Brien had bathed it in alcohol before applying a healing salve and the gauze.

"Since your grandparents and our grandchildren are so far

away, we really need some grandchildren to adopt."

"How about us? Adopt us!" B. J. said.

"Our sisters will want you to adopt them too, when they get to know you," Chris said, looking up from the picture album he was holding.

"It will sure be wonderful if they do," said Edith.

Chris's eyes were devouring photographs from Dr. O'Brien's days as an army physician. Every page displayed pictures of soldiers, tents, rifles, cannons, cavalry horses, and the like. O'Brien, himself, was in most of the photographs.

"Wow!" Chris said, as he turned a page and saw a picture of a tall, gaunt man. "You've got a picture of President Lincoln!"

"Mm-hmm," the doctor said as he began tying the gauze on B. J.'s arm.

Chris studied the short, stocky man with coal-black hair standing next to Lincoln in the picture. "Grandpa? Is this *you* standing by Mr. Lincoln?"

"Sure is."

Chris's eyes bulged. "Wow! You knew Abraham Lincoln?"

"I did, Chris. That picture was taken in 1840 on the front porch of his house in Springfield, Illinois, when he was a lawyer. I went to the Lincoln home to treat Mrs. Lincoln, who had a severe case of influenza. I was their family physician until I became a U.S. Army doctor in 1847."

"Wow!" Chris said. "So did you work as an army doctor on battlefields in the War?"

"Yes."

Dr. O'Brien helped B. J. off the examining table to a chair beside Chris, then sat down on another chair, facing the boys. "B. J., I think it's best for you if we just wait till your mother comes to get you. You look a little peaked. Be best if you just sit and rest for a while."

"Yes, sir," said the eight-year-old.

"Now, Chris," O'Brien said, slapping his thigh. "Let me tell you about some of the battles, and some of my war experiences."

The doctor was still telling war stories when they heard the front door open. Edith rose from her chair and headed to the waiting area. She returned a few seconds later, leading Hannah and the girls.

Patty Ruth rushed to B. J., clutching Tony the Bear to her chest. "Does your arm hurt?" she asked.

"Not much. Grandpa fixed it up real good."

"Grandpa?" Hannah said.

"Me and Chris just adopted the O'Briens as our grandparents."

"Oh?"

"You know, Mama," spoke up Chris, "like we adopted Grandma and Grandpa Holden when we were traveling."

"But they're gonna go on to California," said B. J., "and they won't be our grandparents any more. So we adopted Grandma and Grandpa O'Brien. And they adopted us, too!"

Hannah exchanged an amused glance with the O'Briens and said, "I guess a lot has happened in the last couple of hours!"

"Our own grandchildren live in Illinois," Edith said. "We need grandchildren right here in Fort Bridger to love on." As she spoke, she went to Mary Beth and Patty Ruth and put her arms around them. "Could we adopt you precious girls, too?"

"Sure!" Mary Beth said. "You can adopt us, and we'll adopt you, too! Right, Patty Ruth?"

"Uh-huh," said the little redhead. "And how about Tony, Grandma?" she asked, holding up her stuffed bear. "Will you 'dopt him, too?"

"We sure will, honey, if Tony wants us as his grandparents."

Patty Ruth looked down at her bear. "You want them to be your grandma and grandpa, don't you, Tony?"

She dropped her voice as if Tony were speaking and said,

"Yes, Patty Ruth. I want to be their grandbear. Could I hug them?"

Both of the O'Briens hugged Tony, then Dr. O'Brien hugged the girls.

Edith turned to Hannah. "As long as all this adopting is going on, this makes you our daughter, and you may call us Mom and Dad."

Hannah's eyes misted. "You make me think of my parents, and how much I miss them. But since they're so far away, and you two are so sweet, I'll be your adopted daughter. Mom and Dad O'Brien, it is! Ezra Comstock told me you're Christians. That makes it even more wonderful!"

"Honey," said the doctor, "we've both known the Lord since just a week before we were married. Neither one of us went to church, but we wanted a church wedding. We came to this country from Ireland with our parents and lived in an Irish settlement at Braidwood, Illinois, where we met and were high school sweethearts."

"Frank had already finished medical school in Chicago," said Edith. "He was going to set up his practice in Springfield, so we decided to have our wedding there. We picked the first church we saw. We talked to the pastor about marrying us, and he wanted to know if we were Christians. We stammered a bit, not really knowing how to answer him."

Doc laughed. "So he opened his Bible and showed us how to be saved. We'd both heard it before but had paid little attention. This time we listened, and that preacher led us to Jesus."

"And how wonderful it's been ever since!" said Edith. "We were so glad when Pastor Kelly came here to start the church. Frank teaches the adult Sunday school class and loves it."

"And we were so glad when Pastor Kelly told us the Coopers were Christians and would be joining the church," said the doctor.

Edith clapped her hands. "Isn't the Lord good?"

"That He is," agreed Hannah. "He's such a wonderful, loving God." She turned to O'Brien. "So what about my boy's arm?"

"It's going to heal, all right, but it will be slightly scarred in a few places where the rock dug into the skin. If I can see him on Tuesday, I'll put on a clean bandage."

"Is after school all right?" asked Hannah, opening her purse. "I can have Chris bring him over."

"Sure. That'll be fine."

"How much do I owe you?"

Doc put an arm around B. J. "Tell you what, I'll just take the boy as payment."

Patty Ruth giggled. "You can have Chris too, Grandpa!"

Chris playfully punched her shoulder. "Well, he wouldn't want *you!* You aren't worth that much!"

"How about if I take Tony for payment?" said O'Brien, a twinkle in his eye.

Patty Ruth clutched the bear and shook her head. "Huh-uh! You can't have Tony! You'll just have to keep B. J."

"Seriously, Dad," said Hannah, "what's the charge?"

"There's no charge. You'll have many expenses getting settled. I'll take care of B. J. till the arm is healed, and there'll be no charge. It'll make Edie and me feel good to know we're helping you get settled."

Hannah's eyes teared for what seemed to her the hundredth time that day. "I...I don't know what to say. I'm overwhelmed at your kindness. This whole town—everybody's been so kind and so friendly. You've all made us feel so welcome."

"That's because you *are* welcome, dear," said Edith, hugging her.

"Thank you, Mom. You mentioned your grandchildren in Illinois. How many do you have?"

"Six—three boys and three girls. Our son, Fred, and his

wife have a boy and two girls. Our daughter, Evelyn, and her husband have a girl and two boys. They live near each other in Chicago and go to the same church. They've heard Dwight L. Moody preach many times."

"I'd love to hear him sometime," said Hannah. "It's good to know your children and their mates are dedicated Christians."

The merriment left Doc's face as he said, "We have another son—Patrick Michael. He's a medical doctor, and for that we are very proud of him. He's been working with two older doctors in a clinic in Fort Wayne, Indiana, since he graduated from medical school three years ago. Plans now are for Pat to come to Fort Bridger within a year or so and take over my practice."

"Oh, I see. Well, that'll be a blessing, I'm sure, to have your own son take over the practice. Is he married?"

"No."

Hannah's brow knitted. "Is there something wrong? You seem upset."

Edith's hand went to her mouth and deep lines formed on her brow as Doc said, "Our hearts are very heavy for Pat, Hannah. Though he's a Christian, his letters indicate that he's grown cold toward the Lord. He's not in church regularly. We can tell he's drifted from being the strong Christian he used to be."

"Oh, I'm so sorry," Hannah said. "I'll be praying for Patrick, that the Lord will work in his life."

"Thank you, dear," Edith said. "Our hearts are so burdened over him."

"God will do His work in Pat's life," Hannah said. "We'll just pray and believe Him for it." She turned to her children. "Guess we'd better get to the hotel and settle in as much as we can. Time for the cookout soon."

"We'll see you there," the O'Briens said.

As they walked down the street, Hannah said, "Boys, since we have to pass the store, we could take a few minutes and let you see inside."

When they reached the store, Clayton Farley was just closing up. His workers had gone for the day, and so had the men who had unloaded Hannah's supply wagons. Biggie was waiting for them on the front porch, wagging his tail, and Patty Ruth and B. J. ran to pet him.

Farley smiled at Hannah and said, "I'm thinking maybe the boys want to see the place, right?"

"Right," Hannah said, returning a smile.

"Ray Noble came and took your oxen and the four wagons, ma'am. What things were left in the family wagon are in the storage room at the back. All your supplies are now inside the store."

"Thank you, Mr. Farley."

He reached into his pocket. "I'll go ahead and give you a key, ma'am. Best that we lock the doors, now that all your supplies are in here. Just lock up when you leave. I'll see you at the cookout."

Hannah and the girls guided Chris and B. J. through the store with great excitement that soon turned to a keen sense of Solomon's absence. Everything was exactly as he had planned it.

Mary Beth's lips trembled as she looked around. "I wish Papa were here. He would have loved it."

Biggie ran around the store, smelling everything in sight.

Patty Ruth began to sniffle. "Mama, I miss Papa!"

Hannah reached for her hand and squeezed it. "We all do, sweetheart. All of this is such a part of him."

"Papa's looking down from heaven right now," Chris said. "I know he is. And he knows how much we miss him."

"Yes," Hannah said past the lump in her throat. "We miss him terribly."

B. J. sniffed and wiped tears.

"But Papa wants us to be happy," said Hannah. "He wants us to go on and fulfill his dream. And that's exactly what we're going to do! Come on, girls. Let's show the boys the barn and our apartment!"

Biggie followed as they examined the barn and corral, where they found Buster and Nipper chomping hay. Then they went upstairs to look through the unfinished apartment. The boys were pleased with their bedroom and its location.

As they reentered the store, Hannah closed and locked the back door. "Children, let's take just a few minutes and pray together. I want us to dedicate this store to the Lord."

"Yes, Mama," said Mary Beth in a half whisper, "we should do that."

Hannah and her children stood in a circle by the potbellied stove, holding hands. They prayed, dedicating the store to the Lord and asking for His blessing as they served Him in Fort Bridger.

The sun was sinking low when Hannah and the children left the Williams house with Glenda, having situated Biggie. He and Butch, who was a lovable mongrel, became instant friends.

The rooms at the hotel were warm and inviting. The windows were open slightly, allowing the cool afternoon air to enter. Fresh white ruffled curtains billowed gently in the breeze.

Bright patchwork quilts adorned the beds, and soft rag rugs made the floor attractive and comfortable. A white painted washstand in each room held a flowered water pitcher and washbowl.

"Glenda, these are the most beautiful hotel rooms I've ever seen!" Hannah said. "Are they all decorated like this?"

"Yes. Gary and I take pride in making each room as much like home as possible. We want people to be comfortable here...especially the Coopers."

Hannah's heart felt like it would swell up and burst. Her voice quivered as she took Glenda's hand and said, "I don't know how to thank you for making the children and me feel so welcome. This whole town has given us such a marvelous reception. I haven't seen one unfriendly face."

Glenda grinned. "How about that one?"

Hannah turned to see Gary Williams standing at the open door. "A bit ornery," she said, chuckling, "but not unfriendly."

"Well, at least you didn't say *ugly,*" he said, entering the room. "Seriously, Hannah, I'm glad everyone has made you feel so welcome."

"We feel at home already. The O'Briens have adopted my children as their grandchildren, and they even adopted me as their daughter."

Glenda smiled. "Doc and Edie are wonderful Christians."

"That's for sure," Gary said. "I don't know if half the people Doc treats pay him anything, they're both so generous.

"You talk about being happy here, Hannah," Gary went on, "and I'll guarantee you this: You're going to love the church. Pastor preaches the Word and pulls no punches when unsaved people come into the services. He lays out the truth about hell and judgment, but he does it in such a way that they know he loves them."

"And he comes down hard on sin in the lives of Christians," Glenda said. "But we always know that behind it is his love for us. He's a tremendous preacher and a wonderful pastor."

Gary pulled out his pocket watch. "Tell you what, folks, we'd better do what freshening up we're going to do. It'll be time to head for the cookout in about half an hour."

"And are you going to enjoy the food!" Glenda said. "We've got the best cook in town supervising the meal. We have a couple of great cooks at the café, but Mandy Carver is the best. You met the Carvers?"

"Yes. They're sweet people."

"And assisting Mandy is Nellie Patterson. She's just a half-notch under Mandy when it comes to cooking."

"Oh, yes. I remember Nellie and the children," said Hannah. She thought of the sad look on their faces but said nothing.

At the cookout that evening, before the meal, Hannah and her children mingled with their wagon train friends, feeling a touch of sadness that they would have to say good-bye in the morning. Hannah made sure she spent a little time with each family, letting them know she would never forget them. She then moved among the crowd, getting better acquainted with the folks of Fort Bridger.

Before Mandy, Nellie, and their helpers were ready to feed the crowd, the Lindgren sisters and Lila Sparrow gave a brief concert of gospel hymns. The Lindgren sisters played violins, and Lila accompanied them on the pump organ.

As twilight fell over the land, lanterns were lit and placed on every table.

When the meal was ready, Cade Samuels signaled to Pastor Kelly, who thanked the Lord for the food and also for sending the Coopers to Fort Bridger. There were many "Amens" to that, and then the people looked toward the magnificent spread of food.

Mandy Carver stood by the long food table formed by wooden planks across sawhorses. The planks were covered with snowy-white cloths and loaded with food.

"Folks," Mandy said, speaking loudly, "there's plenty of food for everybody. Our honored guests, Miz Hannah Cooper and her children, will come by and pick up their food first. Then you other folks at the head table come by. After that, it's everybody for hisself! We hope y'all enjoy the food!"

There was a round of applause, and Cade Samuels ushered

the Coopers to the long table.

The kids' eyes stared in amazement at the crispy fried chicken, succulent ham, and roast beef, several kinds of potatoes and other vegetables, along with salads and pickles, biscuits and homemade breads, and desserts of various descriptions. It was an array of food to tempt any palate.

After they took a little bit of everything, Hannah and the children sat at a special table with the Samuels, the Batemans, and the Kellys.

Chris Cooper was pleased to be positioned directly across the table from Colonel Bateman. He waited until everyone was eating before bringing up his favorite subject. "Colonel Bateman, I'm going to be a soldier when I grow up."

"Seems I recall hearing you say that when we visited you in Independence," the colonel said with a smile. "Are you planning on going to West Point?"

"Yes, sir. As you know, my father became an officer in the Civil War by earning it. But since the War's over, if a man's going to be an officer, he must get the right education."

"That's right."

Chris chewed a few bites, then said, "Colonel Bateman, the last time I was in a fort, I was too little to appreciate it."

"Oh, yes?"

"I was wondering, sir, if...well, if sometime I might be able to come inside the fort."

Bateman smiled at Hannah as she listened to her son. He set his gaze on the boy and said, "I believe that could be arranged. I could give you a personal tour of the fort sometime next week, Chris. Would that fit into your schedule?"

"Yes, *sir!* I could probably take some time off from school and—"

"The tour will have to be *after* school, Lieutenant Cooper," cut in Hannah, a wry smile on her lips.

Chris shrugged. "Okay. Could we make it after school, Colonel?"

"We can do that, son. I won't be able to do it this coming week, understand, but the one after that. I'll let you know when the time gets closer."

Chris was ecstatic. "Did you hear that? I'm going to take a tour of the fort with Colonel Bateman! Hallelujah!"

Chapter Fifteen

When the meal was over, the Lindgren sisters and Lila Sparrow provided music again, while people moved about, talking and laughing.

Hannah and her children stayed at their table as people came by to talk with them. She noticed a man in uniform with a captain's insignia on his shoulders walking toward the table with his wife and three children. She could not recall having seen them at the reception earlier in the day.

"Mrs. Cooper," the man said, "I am Captain John Fordham. This is my wife, Betsy, and our three children Ryan, Will, and Belinda."

Hannah got to her feet. "I'm happy to meet you. These are my children Chris, Mary Beth, B. J., and Patty Ruth."

"We weren't in town this afternoon, Mrs. Cooper," said the captain. "Sorry to have missed the big welcome, but we heard it went well."

"Yes," Hannah said, smiling happily. "It sure was a surprise, and we've found everyone to be so warm and friendly."

"We're glad you and the children have moved here," said Betsy. "Everybody's looking forward to having the general store." She paused, then patted Hannah's shoulder. "And let me also say how very sorry I am about the loss of your husband, Mrs. Cooper. If there's anything I can do to help you, please let me know. We live in one of the houses inside the fort. Anyone can tell you which one is ours."

"Thank you so much," said Hannah. "I appreciate your kindness."

"Captain Fordham…" Chris said.

"Yes?"

"I'm going to be a soldier when I grow up. My papa was a captain in the War. I'm going to go to West Point so I can be an officer. And you know what?"

"What?"

"I talked to Colonel Bateman, and he's going to take me on a tour of the fort in a few days!"

"Hey, that's great! I hope I'm there when you take the tour. If not, and you ever have any questions about the fort or the army, or even West Point, let me know. I'll be glad to answer them."

"Thank you, sir! I will!"

Hannah noticed little Belinda Fordham looking at the stuffed bear in Patty Ruth's arms.

Suddenly Belinda moved close to Patty Ruth and said, "Little girl, could I hold your bear for a minute?"

Hannah was pleased when she saw Patty Ruth smile and hand the bear to Belinda, saying, "Of course. Tony likes little girls. 'Specially me."

"I like you, too," said Belinda, holding Tony to her breast. "Could we be friends?"

"Sure," said the little redhead, keeping her eyes on the stuffed bear in Belinda's arms.

Belinda handed the bear back, and said, "Let's go play, little girl."

"My name's Patty Ruth," came the level reply, as they moved away from the table.

"Stay close by, girls," said Betsy.

"Yes, Patty Ruth," added Hannah.

B. J. Cooper and Will Fordham ran off to play near some cottonwood trees within sight of their mothers.

The music had stopped moments before, and as Sundi Lindgren put away her violin, she saw Mary Beth Cooper standing alone by her mother. She walked toward the girl and greeted her.

"Hi, Mary Beth. Get enough to eat?"

"I sure did, Miss Lindgren."

"Why don't we sit down at the end of the table and talk teacher talk?"

Mary Beth grinned. "I'd love it!"

Hannah glanced over to see her daughter in conversation with Sundi Lindgren and gave an inward sigh of relief. Maybe things were going to be all right with Mary Beth after all.

Hannah walked to the table where Mandy Carver and Nellie Patterson were finally partaking of their own cooking. "Ladies," she said, taking a seat beside Mandy, "that was a fantastic meal."

"Thank you, Miz Cooper," said Mandy, showing her a beautiful smile. "We had lots of help."

"Mrs. Cooper," Nellie said, "I know you need help stocking your shelves on Monday. I wish I could come and help you, but I won't be able to. Please understand that I would if I could."

"Thank you," Hannah said. "I appreciate your desire to help, believe me. But there is something you *can* do for me. You too, Mandy. Call me *Hannah*, will you? *Mrs. Cooper* sounds so formal. Friends call each other by their given names."

"I have an idea we're gonna be very good friends, Hannah," said Mandy.

"Yes," Nellie said with a nod.

That night after prayers, the four Cooper children snuggled down in their warm nests, very thankful to be in real beds once again.

When Hannah climbed into bed in her own room, the soft feather mattress felt so good to her tired body. Thoughts of Solomon washed over her anew, and she rolled onto her side, hugging the spare pillow to her breast, and cried.

When an hour had gone by and she was still wide awake, Hannah prayed, "Lord Jesus, I need to get to sleep. Tomorrow's church, and I want to be fresh. In Psalm 127:2, You said, 'he giveth his beloved sleep.' I claim it now, Lord. Because You saved me, I am accepted in the beloved. Please help me go to sleep."

Within a few minutes, her weary mind and body sank into the refreshing slumber she needed.

At the Williamses' house, Glenda had prepared a hearty breakfast at sunup for Hannah and the children. The Coopers needed to eat early so they would have time to tell their friends at the wagon train good-bye before church.

The table was set with brightly flowered dishes, and the delicious aroma of hot buttered biscuits, ham and eggs, and fried potatoes drew the hungry bunch to the table. Gary thanked the Lord for the food, and they dug in—all except Mary Beth, who made a weak attempt at eating, but mostly just pushed the food around on her plate.

After breakfast, Glenda whisked Hannah off to her sewing room on the pretense of showing her some new dress material she had bought recently. When they entered the room, Glenda put a finger on the material as it lay on a table, and said, "This really isn't why I brought you in here."

"Oh?" Hannah said, looking surprised.

"I want to know about Mary Beth. She seems so disconsolate."

Hannah nodded. "She's having an awful time handling Solomon's death. Solomon never showed any favoritism with his children, but he and Mary Beth were very, very close. She just can't seem to adjust to it."

"Bless her heart. I'll tell Gary, and we'll be praying for that sweet girl."

Hannah wrapped her arms around Glenda and hugged her tight. "Thank you, Glenda. You and Gary have shown us so many kindnesses. I appreciate them all."

The wagon train was almost ready to pull out when Hannah and her children appeared. Chris led Nipper, saddled and bridled to give to his new owner.

Many tears flowed as Ezra Comstock had the people make a circle around Hannah and the children and then led the crowd in prayer, asking the Lord's blessing on them as they began their new life in Fort Bridger. It was like family parting.

Ezra finally mounted his horse and took his position in front of the lead wagon. He thrust his arm forward and shouted, "Wagons ho-o-o-o!" and the wagon wheels began to roll.

Tony Cuzak stood with the Coopers watching the wagons move out.

When Micah Comstock's wagon moved forward, Chris struggled not to break down, but he couldn't quite keep some tears from slipping down his cheeks.

Patty Ruth hugged her big brother's waist and looked up at him, saying, "It'll be all right, Chris. Jesus will give you a new best friend."

Chris hugged her and wept for a brief moment before turning to Tony and handing him Nipper's reins.

Tony tied his gear behind the saddle, then turned to Hannah. "I'll never forget any of you," he said. "It was your husband who led me to the Lord. If I never see you again on this earth, at least I know I'll meet you in heaven."

Hannah embraced him and said, "I wish you all the best as you return to Amanda, Tony."

"I'll write you, and let you know when we get married."

"Please do that. And give Amanda my love."

"I will."

While Chris and B. J. were telling Nipper good-bye, Mary Beth hugged Tony and said in a strained voice, "Please take good care of my papa's horse."

"You can bank on that," Tony said.

Then he bent down and picked up Patty Ruth to hug her. When he lowered her to the ground, she said, "Thank you for giving me Tony, Mr. Tony. An' please tell Ulysses I still love him, an' I will never forget him."

"I'll tell him," Tony promised.

As the boys spoke with Tony, Hannah stepped close to Nipper and stroked his long face. She fought a lump in her throat as she told Solomon's horse good-bye.

Patty Ruth patted the horse's muzzle and said, "Mr. Tony will take good care of you, Nipper. An' someday when you die an' go to heaven, Papa can ride you up there."

Mary Beth rushed to her father's horse and threw her arms around his neck, sobbing. "Good-bye, Nipper. You always did good for my papa. I will never forget you."

Nipper bobbed his head gently and nickered. Mary Beth held onto his neck for a long moment, then stepped back.

Tony swung into the saddle and rode away, turning once to wave.

The town hall was full for church services. Dr. Frank O'Brien taught the adult Sunday school class, and Hannah enjoyed his teaching as she sat with Gary and Glenda Williams and Edie O'Brien.

The Cooper children liked their classes, too. Patty Ruth had Heidi Lindgren for her teacher, and Mary Beth was in Sundi's class. Justin Powell taught B. J.'s class, and Chris's teacher was Abe Carver.

In the preaching service, Hannah found that Pastor Andrew Kelly was an excellent preacher. She appreciated his clear presentation of the gospel and marveled at how eloquently he exalted the Lord Jesus Christ. A number of adults and young people responded to the invitation and opened their hearts to the Lord.

After the evening service, Hannah and the children walked to the hotel with Gary and Glenda. Hannah met several couples strolling home, and thought of Solomon and all the years they had gone to church together in Independence. She felt a strong wave of loneliness but concealed her feelings from her new friends and her children.

At bedtime, after praying with the children and tucking them in, Hannah went to her own room and flung herself across the bed, giving in to a good cry. Every fiber of her being longed for her husband. When she had gained control of her emotions, she rose from the bed and changed into her nightgown and then told the Lord, "I never knew it could be so hard to lose one's mate. Please give me the strength only You can give to get through this difficult time."

Hannah looked up from the bed to see Dr. O'Brien smiling down at her. "It's a boy, Hannah!" he said. "Strong and husky, too!"

"Well, where is he, Doctor?" she asked. "I want to see my baby!"

"Right over there," O'Brien said, indicating the other side of the bed.

Hannah turned her head on the pillow and saw Solomon, tall and ruggedly handsome, as he held a little blanketed bundle in his arms. He smiled from ear to ear and leaned close, exposing the fat little face. "Oh, darlin', you've given me another beautiful child! And he looks just like me!"

The weary mother felt warm tears moisten her cheeks as she took the bundle in her arms. Solomon leaned over and kissed her. "I love you, sweetheart," he said softly.

"I love you too, darling," she said, then looked down into the face of her newborn son. "And I love *you,* too— Oh, Sol, what are we going to name him?"

He cleared his throat gently and said, "Well, honey, I...ah...have been thinking about that. And now that I see how much he looks like me...you *do* see that, don't you?"

"Oh, yes! No question about it."

"I'd be honored if we could name him Solomon Edward Cooper Jr." He hastened to add, "But I don't want him to be called Junior. I'd like to call him Eddie."

Hannah's face was beaming. "Now isn't that something!"

"What?"

"I've been thinking *exactly* the same thing. But I didn't want to say anything until you brought up what name you had in mind."

Solomon grinned. "Really? The same thing?"

"Mm-hmm."

Solomon pulled the blanket away from his little son's face and said, "Hi, Eddie! You know who I am? I'm your papa! I love your brothers and sisters with all my heart. But you know what? There's plenty of room in my heart to love you just as much. And your beautiful mama feels the same way."

The baby made a tiny sound, wiggling his body.

"See, Hannah? He understands! He knows what I'm telling

him. He knows we're his parents, and that we love him. Oh, thank you, darling, for giving me my precious little Eddie! We're going to have such a wonderful time together as he grows up. And—"

Hannah's eyes snapped open and she sat up in the bed, hearing herself gasp. She looked around the moonlit room and drew in a sharp breath. She eased down on the feather mattress and touched her midsection where the baby was nestled, and cried herself to sleep.

When morning came, Hannah sat up in bed and reached for her Bible on the bed stand, holding it close to her heart as she bowed her head and said, "Good morning, dear God. I love You. I love You my precious Father. I love You my precious Lord Jesus. I love You my precious Holy Spirit. Speak to me now from Your Word. I need strength of soul, and I need direction. Give me what I need today to go on without Solomon."

Ever since she had become a Christian, Hannah had gone to the psalms when she needed strength and direction. As she opened the Bible now, she said, "Where today, Lord?" Her thumbs parted the pages and her eyes fell on Psalm 143. The opening words caught her attention:

> Hear my prayer, O Lord, give ear to my supplications: in thy faithfulness answer me...

"Oh, yes, dear God," she said in a half whisper, "hear my prayer. In Thy faithfulness, please answer me."

Hannah read slowly down the page, verse after verse, until verse 8 seemed to leap off the page at her:

> Cause me to hear thy lovingkindness in the morning; for in thee do I trust: cause me to know the way wherein I should walk; for I lift up my soul unto thee.

"Oh, yes!" Hannah said, tears filling her eyes. "Yes! Dear Lord, I need to hear your lovingkindness today—this very morning. I *do* lift up my soul to Thee. Show me the way wherein I should walk. Oh, thank You for speaking to me through Your Word!"

Today she would begin setting up the store for business. She struggled against the pain in her heart and told the Lord that she loved Him, and asked for wisdom to meet the day's challenges. She prayed for her children, her parents, Pastor and Mrs. Kelly, Tony Cuzak, Patrick O'Brien, the people in the wagon train, and her special new friends in Fort Bridger.

When Hannah finished praying, she read Psalm 143:8 again and thanked the Lord for that verse and the strength it had given her. As she laid the Bible on the bed stand, she decided to make this verse the first Scripture she would read every morning. Its words echoed through her mind again: *Cause me to hear thy lovingkindness in the morning.*

After a hearty breakfast with the Williamses, Hannah walked the children to school, since it was their first day. Sundi Lindgren met them at the door with a welcoming smile. She told Hannah she would come to the store that afternoon to help her.

Hannah met Glenda and Patty Ruth on the way back, and together they headed toward the store. When they arrived, Glenda said, "Well, honey, it looks like you're going to have plenty of help!"

Patty Ruth's eyes widened. "Look at all the ladies, Mama!"

Hannah was stunned to see ten women from the town and fort.

"Good mornin', boss," Mandy Carver said. "We're here to stock shelves and whatever else you tell us to do."

Hannah smiled broadly. "Thank you, ladies! I appreciate this more than you will ever know."

She lifted her eyes to the sign above the porch roof and read:

COOPER'S GENERAL STORE
Hannah Cooper, Prop.

The women were studying her reaction. She forced a smile and said, "Whoever made that sign did an excellent job."

Hannah felt Glenda's loving hand on her back and took strength from it.

"Well, ladies," Hannah said, taking a deep breath, "let's get to work!"

Betsy Fordham stepped forward, holding Belinda by the hand. "Hannah..."

"Yes, Betsy?"

"I know you've got a busy day ahead of you. What are you going to do with Patty Ruth?"

"I'm planning on keeping her here in the store. She'll have to find ways to amuse herself while I'm working."

Little Belinda smiled at Patty Ruth, who was clutching Tony the Bear to her chest.

"If you'd like, I'll take Patty Ruth home with me and keep her till you're through working this afternoon. I'll feed her lunch, and she and Belinda can play together."

Hannah smiled. "She wouldn't be in the way? I mean, seeing as how your house is inside the fort?"

"Of course not."

Hannah looked down at her daughter. "Honey, would you like to spend the day playing with Belinda?"

"Sure, Mama. I'd like that."

"All right, Betsy, and thank you. How do I find your house?"

"You won't need to. Just tell me what time you plan to quit, and I'll bring Patty Ruth here."

"Okay. I think five o'clock will do it."

"Then we'll come at five."

Hannah hugged her daughter and said, "You be a good girl, won't you?"

"Yes, Mama."

"See you this evening, then."

As Betsy walked away, holding the girls by the hand, Belinda looked past her mother at Patty Ruth and said, "I'm glad you're coming to my house, little girl."

"My name's Patty Ruth," the little redhead said.

Chapter Sixteen

While the women unpacked boxes and stocked shelves according to Hannah's directions, the sound of workmen's voices and hammering and sawing came from overhead.

Hannah worked at the counter, placing the wide-mouth jars of penny candy where she wanted them, and stocking the shelves behind the counter with the same items as the store in Independence. She looked at the cash drawer and smiled. It had been constructed exactly as Solomon had designed it, and would function even better than the one in their previous store.

Hannah listened happily to the women's excited comments about so many of the items they were unpacking that had not been stocked at the sutler's store.

She picked up a heavy box and felt a slight pang in her midsection. Her hand went to the spot, and she thought about last night's dream. It had seemed so real. Am I really carrying a boy? she wondered.

As Hannah finished emptying the box and was about to pick up another, she heard heavy footsteps on the back stairs, then Clayton Farley entered the rear door with two of his workers. Hannah recognized the men from Saturday's cookout.

"Good morning, ma'am," Clayton said.

Hannah smiled at him. "Good morning, Mr. Farley... gentlemen."

The workers returned her greeting, then Farley said, "I'm leaving one man upstairs to work on the kitchen cupboard, Mrs. Cooper. One of my new buildings down the street is at a point where the walls are framed and need to be raised and anchored in place. These fellas and I are going to help. We'll be back sometime in the early afternoon."

"Fine," said Hannah. "See you then."

The hours passed, and by noon, almost a quarter of the goods had been put on the shelves. The women stopped work to go home for lunch, and Hannah had several invitations. But she didn't feel hungry and politely declined.

As Hannah kept working, she could hear footsteps in the apartment above and the sounds of work. She paused before lifting another box onto the counter and ran her gaze over the store. It was looking more like "home" than it did early that morning. She made a mental note to talk with Judge Carter. It would be wise to contact the distributor in Cheyenne City and stay ahead on ordering goods.

She lifted another box, set it on the counter, and went to work on its contents. Her thoughts went to her three oldest children. She wondered how they were doing on their first day at school.

"Bless them, Lord," she said audibly. "And help my Mary Beth. She's having such a horrible time adapting to life without Solomon. I've asked You before, Lord, to please show me if there's something else I can do to help her."

Another pang shot across her abdomen. She wondered when she should tell the children they were going to have another brother...or sister. She decided to let them settle into their new life first. At least until after they moved into their living quarters upstairs.

She finished emptying the box and turned to skid another one toward the shelves when she saw a tall, dark figure standing in front of the counter.

"Oh! I didn't hear you come in."

The man didn't apologize for frightening her, but looked at her with dark hooded eyes, and said, "I'm workin' upstairs."

Hannah swallowed hard, her fluttering heart trying to settle, and forced a smile. "I...I'm Mrs. Cooper. And your name?"

"Alex."

Still smiling, she extended her right hand across the counter. "I'm glad to meet you, Alex."

When he ignored her hand, her smile faded. "Is there something I can do for you, Alex?"

"Mr. Farley told me to come down and ask you to look at the kitchen cupboard when I was finished with it. I'm finished. You want to come and see if you're satisfied?"

Hannah walked around the end of the counter. "Why... why, yes. I'll be glad to come up and look at it."

Without a word, the man headed for the back door. She hurried to catch up. As they climbed the stairs toward the apartment, Hannah said, "I don't recall seeing you at the cook-out. I thought all of Mr. Farley's men were there."

"I had more important things to do," Alex said.

"Do you have a family in Cheyenne City?"

They reached the top of the stairs, where the door was standing open. He stepped through first, not bothering to hold the door for her, and said over his shoulder, "I have a wife and three kids. Last name's Patterson. We live just outside of town."

"Oh, yes. I met your wife and children on Saturday." Hannah thought of Nellie Patterson's sad countenance.

Alex led her to the kitchen cupboard and said, "I suppose you saw the apartment on Saturday?"

"Yes."

"Cupboard was still pretty rough then. How's it look now?"

She ran her gaze over the cupboard and caressed the counter top with a palm. "Why, it's beautiful!"

"Makes a bright kitchen with the cupboard white."

"Yes, it looks fine."

When it was obvious Alex had no more to say, Hannah said, "Thank you for letting me see it," and headed for the door.

His voice cut across the room. "You really shouldn't do it, woman!"

Hannah jumped. She turned about slowly and said, "Pardon me?"

"You shouldn't be runnin' this store without your husband! Women were meant to work in the home, and nowhere else."

Hannah's eyes fluttered in disbelief. She cleared her throat and said, "Mr. Patterson, that's a bit cut and dried, isn't it? Some women have no choice but to work outside the home."

"Bah! Where there's a will, there's a way! This whole country of ours is goin' to the dogs because mothers are ignorin' their kids and workin' jobs. You've got no business ownin' and runnin' this store. You oughtta be takin' care of your home and your kids."

Hannah felt her temper rise. *How dare this man speak his mind to me about something that's none of his business?* She wanted to tell him off, but thought about her Christian testimony.

Alex's voice grated into her thoughts and across her nerves. "The only right thing for you to do is sell this store to some man and let him run it. No woman should be the proprietor of a store! Or even work in one, for that matter. Judge Carter's wife don't work at the sutler's store. And what's more, that Heidi Lindgren shouldn't be runnin' that dress shop! Women shouldn't be buyin' ready-made dresses, anyhow! They oughtta stay home and make their own, like my Nellie does."

"Mr. Patterson, I think you should get back to whatever you're being paid to do."

"And then there's that schoolmarm sister of hers," he said. "That Sundi oughtta resign and let a man take over the school!

Oughta be a man teachin' those kids!"

"Mr. Patterson—"

"And then there's Greta Swensen over there workin' with her husband at the gun shop and hardware store! She's got no business workin' in there! She oughta go home and tend to her house!"

The apartment door stood open, and two elderly women looked up toward the shadowed door, listening to Alex Patterson's verbal onslaught. Then they hurried away.

Hannah prayed silently for the Lord's help, then spoke softly. "Mr. Patterson, what women do, other than your wife, is really none of your business."

"Oh, yeah? Well—"

"And that goes for me, too. I have no animosity toward you, sir, but you shouldn't be telling me what I ought to do. My husband is dead. I have no choice but to go on with the store. I have four children to feed and clothe, and I must provide a roof over their heads."

"Well, you oughtta get married again and let your husband do the providin'."

Hannah's voice rose slightly as she countered, "Mr. Patterson, I just lost my husband—the love of my life and the father of my children! Do you think I can just put aside my grief with a snap of the fingers, let alone find some available man with a burning desire to marry a woman with four children and take on the responsibility of providing for them?"

"Well...it still ain't right for you to be runnin' this store."

"Oh, I see. So I'm supposed to take my children out and live in a field somewhere, am I? I'm supposed to let them go threadbare and hungry. Is that what I'm to do, Mr. Patterson?" The silence was so palpable Hannah felt she could whack it with a hammer. "Well, Mr. Patterson?"

Alex scowled and said, "I've been told your husband served under Colonel Ross Bateman in the War. Is that so?"

"You haven't answered my question," Hannah said.

"I want to know about your husband! Did he fight under Bateman?"

"Yes. Solomon was a captain in Colonel Bateman's regiment. Why?"

"Because all Union soldiers were vicious and bloodhungry, that's why! They ravaged our homes, killed innocent women and children, and pillaged our crops! They were nothin' but lowdown scum!"

Hannah knew if she stayed in the man's presence any longer, she'd lose control. "The cupboard's fine, Mr. Patterson, and this conversation is finished." She wheeled about and headed for the door.

Patterson's face turned crimson and a vein throbbed in his neck. He followed Hannah to the landing and stayed on her heels as she descended the stairs.

"Your Yankee soldiers wore blue in the War, woman," Alex blared, "but underneath that blue were yellow bellies and yellow stripes down their backs! They wouldn't fight us unless they outnumbered us! Well, we showed 'em more'n once who the real men were! Gutless wonders, those Yankees! Every one of 'em! Most of 'em didn't even know how to fight!"

Hannah whirled to face him. "If the majority of them didn't know how to fight, why did General Lee so readily sign the documents of surrender at Appomattox Courthouse? Tell me that. Why didn't he take brave men like you, who browbeat women, and wipe out Abraham Lincoln's yellow-bellied, yellow-backed armies?"

Patterson was stumped for a reply.

"Mr. Patterson," said Hannah, "I've tried to be nice to you, but you're making it next to impossible. Will you kindly get back to whatever you're supposed to be doing now that the cupboard is finished?"

"Not till I've had my say, woman!"

Suddenly a man's voice called out, "You've already said too much, Alex! Leave Mrs. Cooper alone!"

Hannah turned to see Pastor Kelly walking toward them. Two elderly women stood behind him.

Kelly fixed Patterson with fiery eyes and said, "Do as Mrs. Cooper said, Alex. Go!"

"Mind your own business, preacher boy!"

Kelly kept his voice low and level as he said, "It *is* my business when a lady is being mistreated by a man. Leave her alone."

"And what're you gonna do if I *don't* leave her alone, preacher boy?"

Kelly stepped to within an arm's reach of Alex. "I could punch you till you'd be glad to leave her alone, Alex, but I don't want to do that. You're wrong to speak to Mrs. Cooper in such a tone, and I heard enough to tell that you were wrong to launch a verbal attack on her. Why vent your hatred for the Union army on her? She wasn't a Yankee soldier."

"No, but her husband was! I hate all Yankees, alive or dead!"

A dark red flush crawled up the preacher's neck. He forced his voice to stay calm as he said, "Aren't you being paid by Clayton Farley to work?"

"I'll get to it," Alex said.

"Well, get to it *now.* Mrs. Cooper is through talking to you."

"You preachers!" Alex roared. "Always tryin' to run people's lives! Well, I resent you buttin' in and tellin' me what to do!" He put up his fists. "I oughta teach you a lesson right here and now!"

"Punching me isn't going to settle anything, Alex. You're being paid to work on that building, not to harass this dear lady. Now just remove yourself from Mrs. Cooper's presence before this gets any worse."

But Patterson was blind with anger and swung at Kelly. The preacher dodged the blow and grabbed Patterson in a bear hug, pinning his arms to his sides. "Listen to me, Alex! I don't want to fight you! Now calm down!"

The breath sawed in and out of Alex's mouth. "You ain't tellin' me what to do! Y'hear me?"

"Alex, either you tell me you're through acting like a madman, and that you're going back upstairs to work, or I'll squeeze you till you pass out."

Patterson's body relaxed, and he nodded. "Okay, all right. Let go of me. I won't do nothin' to you."

Hannah looked on intently as Kelly released Alex and took a step back. Alex abruptly planted his feet and swung at Kelly again. Kelly ducked and sent a blow to Alex's jaw, stopping him momentarily in his tracks. That was all Kelly needed. He moved with a quick left and a right to Patterson's midsection, then sent a solid right to the jaw that dropped Alex flat on his back, unconscious.

A few people had heard Patterson's angry voice and joined the elderly women near the store. Buster's head protruded over the split-rail corral fence next to the gate, and he nickered as he watched the scene.

Hannah bent over the unconscious man as Andy Kelly stepped close. "I'm sorry I had to do that, Hannah," he said, "but he didn't leave me any choice."

"That's right, Pastor," spoke up Justin Powell, who had come out the back door of Swensen's Gun Shop and Hardware Store with his boss. "He left you no choice at all."

"You pack a mean wallop, Preacher," Hans Swensen said with a chuckle. "Remind me to stay on your good side."

Kelly grinned. "No need to worry about that, Hans. I only use force when absolutely necessary."

Hannah headed for the corral gate.

"What are you doing, Hannah?" Kelly asked.

"Looks like it's going to take some water to bring Alex around," she said, stopping at the water trough.

"I'll get it for you," said Cade Samuels.

"Thank you, Cade. There's a small bucket hanging on the well pump."

Alex lay totally still while Samuels pumped the bucket of water and brought it back to Hannah. As she poured the cool water in his face, Alex groaned and began to stir, rolling his head back and forth.

"What's it about this time, Pastor Kelly?" Clayton Farley said as he rounded the back corner of the general store with Marshal Lance Mangum.

"I was just coming back into town after making some house calls," Kelly said, "when Mattie Freeman stopped me on the street and told me Alex was giving Mrs. Cooper a hard time. I found them back here. Alex was shooting off his mouth, and I tried to cool him down, but it didn't work. I had to subdue him the hard way."

"Isn't this guy ever going to learn?" said Mangum, shaking his head.

Patterson's eyes fluttered and he tried to sit up. Hannah leaned over and helped him to a sitting position. He looked into her face, attempting to focus on her. "You'll be all right in a minute or two, Mr. Patterson," she said.

Patterson shook his head and worked at getting up. Clayton Farley stepped forward and lifted him to his feet.

"Alex," he said, "you've pushed it too far. I've given you chance after chance to act like a decent human being, but you insist on causing trouble."

Patterson blinked and shook his head again.

"What were you giving Mrs. Cooper a hard time about?" demanded Farley.

"It's all right, Mr. Farley," Hannah said. "He just seemed to have some things bottled up inside. He let them out on me. I'm sure he'll be all right now."

"Things like what?"

"Oh...he feels that women shouldn't work outside the home."

"Was that the only subject, ma'am?"

"He...ah...he must've had some bad experiences with Yankee forces. From what he said, I take it he was in the Confederate army."

Farley nodded. "He's from Alabama." He fixed steely eyes on Alex and said, "I gave you your last chance when you tried to punch Marshal Mangum. I told you then to get that temper of yours under control. Apparently you don't care about working for me, or you'd have done something about it. You had no call to launch a tirade against this nice lady, did you?"

Alex remained silent.

"Well, *did* you? She didn't do anything to you, did she?"

There was a long silence, then, "No."

"I've had enough, Alex. You're fired. Get out of my sight!"

Patterson turned without another word and walked away, disappearing around a back corner of the store. Hannah bit her lip as she watched him till he was gone.

"Mrs. Cooper," Farley said, "I apologize for the conduct of my former employee. What he did was inexcusable. I have to get back to the other job, but I'll be back here in a little while."

"I have to get back to my office too," said Mangum, giving Hannah a lopsided grin. "See you later."

Hannah smiled and nodded.

As both men walked away, Hans Swensen came closer, with Justin Powell at his side, and said, "Pastor Kelly, I commend you for defending this lady. It's good to find a preacher who's also manly. My experience has been that most preachers are sissies."

Hannah smiled. "You're right, Mr. Swensen. A sissy this preacher is not!"

Justin spoke up. “I’ve told you before, boss, you need to come hear my pastor preach. He’s a man’s man, I guarantee you.”

Hannah turned to Kelly. “Thank you, Pastor, for coming to my rescue.”

“I’m glad I was here when you needed someone,” he said with a smile. He then excused himself and left.

Hannah went back inside the store. She looked at the clock and realized it was almost time for the ladies to return from lunch. As she began stocking shelves behind the counter, her heart was heavy for Alex Patterson.

“Lord,” she said, “please have mercy on Alex’s family. And please bring Alex to Yourself. A good dose of Calvary love would make him a new man.”

Chapter Seventeen

Hannah greeted the women returning from lunch and watched them settle into their work again. She turned to pick up more goods to shelve just as Glenda set a picnic basket on the counter.

"I figured you'd be hungry by now, so I brought you some goodies." She removed the checkered cloth. "There's some bread and cheese and—"

"Glenda," Hannah interrupted, eyeing the contents of the basket, "I can't eat all of that!"

"I won't let you eat it all," Glenda said with a chuckle. "I haven't eaten lunch yet, either. I thought we could eat together."

Hannah gave her a quick hug. "You're a case, Glenda Williams! What am I going to do with you?"

"Put up with me, I guess. Anyway, along with the bread and cheese, there's some cold fried chicken and some chocolate cake. And here's some lemonade."

"Let's get started," said Hannah. "Just looking at that food makes me hungry!"

Both women felt refreshed after the good meal and went back to work with renewed energy.

Soon Clayton Farley and two of his workers returned from another construction site. Clayton motioned for the workers to go on upstairs and then sought out Hannah.

"Are you all right, ma'am, after what happened this morning?" he asked.

"Well, it was a bit frightening, but yes, Mr. Farley, I'm fine. Thank you for asking."

Farley nodded to her and excused himself to check on the work in progress upstairs.

With the area around the front counter finished to Hannah's satisfaction, she began placing bolts of cloth on a specially built table near the front of the store. She'd been at it half an hour when the front door opened and Nellie Patterson entered.

Hannah noticed how drawn and pale the woman looked and tried to warm her with a smile. "Hello, Mrs. Patterson."

"Hello," said Nellie. "Mrs. Cooper, I...I just learned what happened here with Alex. I want to apologize for my husband's rudeness. I'm so sorry—" Her voice broke off.

"It's no fault of yours, Nellie. Did you also hear that Mr. Farley fired your husband?"

Nellie's shoulders seemed to droop even more. "Yes," she said, barely above a whisper.

"I'm so sorry. I wish Mr. Farley hadn't done that."

Nellie shrugged. "It's been coming, Mrs. Cooper. Mr. Farley has been very patient with Alex."

"You can call me Hannah—and may I call you Nellie?"

The woman nodded, blinking at her tears.

"Nellie...you seemed so sad when we met on Saturday. Is there anything I can do for you?"

Hannah watched her pull a hanky from her dress pocket and dab at her eyes, but all she said was, "There's nothing you can do, but thank you."

"Would it help just to talk about it?"

"Well, I—"

"Let's take a little walk."

"I don't know..."

"Just a moment," Hannah said. She walked over to the other women and told them she would be back in a few minutes, then left the store.

Nellie felt a comfort in Hannah's presence that she'd seldom experienced before. "You don't know what it means to have someone to talk to. I appreciate your willingness to take the time when you're so busy."

"It's my pleasure, Nellie."

"But here you are, a new widow, and you care enough to listen to my troubles!"

"The best way to help yourself is to help others. A person all wrapped up in herself is a pretty small package. I take it you haven't seen Alex since he was fired?"

Nellie shook her head no. "He probably went home. I'll have to face that episode when I get there." She gestured toward a bench on the boardwalk. "Maybe we could sit down here?"

"Sure," said Hannah.

"Please don't think I'm talking bad about Alex behind his back, Hannah, when I tell you some things. I simply want you to understand why he treated you the way he did."

"All right. But you don't seem the type to run down your husband behind his back."

"I love him, Hannah. With all my heart. You see...well... the War changed Alex. Before the War he was a kind and gentle man. Whatever happened to him on those battlefields changed his personality completely. He's never been the same since. Inside him there's a hatred toward Yankees that just festers. I've told him it will eat him like a cancer, but it does no good. He just hates and hates and hates anybody or anything that represents the Union army. One thing that embittered him so much was the Yankees burning our house in Fredericksburg. We lost everything."

"Oh, Nellie, I'm so sorry. I remember that General

Burnside's troops shelled the town and burned many houses and buildings."

Nellie nodded. "I was told that Alex unleashed on you for being the wife of a Union soldier."

"Yes. He did that."

"And they said he was in a tirade about women working outside the home, and he let you have it because you're going to be running the store."

Hannah nodded. "He did that, too."

"You see, Hannah, Alex was an only child. His parents were poor Alabama farmers. They had to eke out a living. When Alex was three years old, his father fell from the hayloft and broke both hips. He was able to get around somewhat after that, but not enough to keep up with the farm work as he had before.

"Alex's mother had to get a job to help make ends meet. She worked as a clerk at the local feed and grain supply. A neighboring farmer's wife watched Alex after school until he finished grammar school. All those years he used to cry and beg his mother to stay home, like the other children's mothers. He never understood why she worked, even though she tried to explain it to him. He just thought she didn't want to be a mother to him.

"When it was time for Alex to start seventh grade, he made a big scene over his mother working, and his father beat him. Alex ran away from home and never knew if his parents even tried to find him.

"He took a live-in job on a farm some twenty miles away, and learned a few months later that his mother had taken sick and died of pneumonia. He never saw his father again. A deep root of bitterness toward both parents has grown inside him. It's no excuse for the way he talked to you, Hannah, but maybe you can understand, at least, why he's like he is."

Hannah brushed a tear from her eye. "But even then,

Nellie, you said he was kind and gentle."

"Yes. He held his bitterness and hatred inside. He never took it out on others like he does now." She paused, as if deciding whether to go on with the story. "He...he began to take it out on the children and me first. Then he gradually started making life miserable for people around him, especially women who work outside the home and anyone connected to the Union side of the War.

"He still makes life miserable for us. Sometimes I think about packing up the children and leaving him. But we don't have anywhere to go. I love him, Hannah, but his cruelty is almost unbearable at times. I'm afraid that one of these days, Luke—our oldest son—will run away from home just like his father did."

Nellie broke down and sobbed. "Oh, Hannah, I don't know what to do! And on top of it all, Alex's job is gone!"

Hannah scooted closer to Nellie and put her arms around her. "I'm sorry life has dealt you so many heartaches, Nellie. I wish I could make everything all right for you."

Nellie clung to her. "Hannah, after the way my husband treated you, it's a wonder you don't hate him."

Hannah eased back so that she could look into Nellie's tear-blurred eyes. "Believe me, I probably would if it wasn't for Jesus, who lives in my heart. Before I was saved, I was pretty hard to live with. Jesus made me a brand-new person inside. Do you know what I'm talking about, Nellie?"

Nellie wiped her cheeks with the palm of her hand. "I've heard about being saved, Hannah, but that hasn't happened to me. Pastor Kelly came to our home and tried to explain the gospel to the family, but Alex cut him off and wouldn't let him talk. Alex was very rude to him on the first visit, but he came back and tried again, anyway. The second time, Alex told Pastor Kelly never to come back again—that he wasn't interested in anything to do with God or Jesus Christ or the Bible or church, and neither was his family."

"Is that true of you and the children?"

"No. We've begged Alex to let us go to church, but he won't hear of it. And now that Pastor Kelly got the best of him with his fists, it'll only be worse."

"Would you agree with me that the most important thing in this life is to be ready for the next one?" Hannah said. "I mean, since the next one is forever, and there are only two eternal destinations?"

Nellie nodded. "Yes, Hannah. And for sure, I don't want to go to hell."

"Then let me point out first that we are all sinners in need of salvation. God says in His Word that 'all have sinned and come short of the glory of God.' He also says—"

"Hannah!" came Sylvia Bateman's voice from up the street.

Hannah rose to her feet. "Yes, Sylvia?"

"We have some items we don't know where to put. Can you come help us?"

"All right. I'll be right there." Then to Nellie, "Can we talk about this again real soon?"

"Certainly," Nellie said, rising to her feet. "And I want to say again that I deeply appreciate your attitude toward Alex. If you're an example of what a real Christian is, I want to know more about being one too."

Hannah was still working with the women at 3:45 when Chris, Mary Beth, and B. J. arrived at the store, all smiles.

"Well, look at your children, Hannah!" said Glenda. "I think they must've enjoyed their first day of school."

The Cooper children had nothing but praise for Miss Lindgren. Mary Beth told Hannah she liked Miss Lindgren's teaching style even better than that of Miss Powers in

Independence. She now wanted to be just like Miss Lindgren when she became a teacher.

All three children excitedly told their mother how they'd made friends with the other children at school, most of whom had been at the cookout on Saturday night.

Hannah nodded happily, knowing in her heart that this was just one more confirmation that the Lord had led them to Fort Bridger.

At five o'clock, Hannah and her helpers had nearly half of the goods on shelves. The women said they would all return in the morning, and again on Wednesday, and stay until everything was in place.

Hannah's plan to open for business on Thursday was now a sure thing. She would tell as many people as she saw tomorrow and let them spread the word.

"Don't worry about the fort, Hannah," called Sylvia Bateman. "We'll help you get the word out there!"

As the women began to leave, Betsy Fordham arrived with Belinda and Patty Ruth. Hannah's youngest talked about her exciting day and how she had played with Belinda's kitten.

"We'll come by and get Patty Ruth again in the morning, Hannah," Betsy said.

"Betsy, are you sure you want to do this? I really don't want to make extra work for you."

"Of course I'm sure," said Betsy. "And besides, Patty Ruth doesn't make extra work. We just enjoy having her."

"That's right, Mrs. Cooper," Belinda said. "Me and your little girl like to play together."

"Well, it certainly is a help to me," Hannah said.

"Good," said Betsy. "See you in the morning then."

"'Bye, little girl," said Belinda. "See you in the morning."

"My name's Patty Ruth!"

Glenda Williams was one of the last women to file out the door. "Hannah," she said, "are you going to call it a day now?"

"I sort of wanted to get this one top shelf filled before I quit."

"Okay. How about I take your youngins with me? We'll have supper at our house."

"All right. I'll be there about six."

When Glenda and the children were gone, Hannah raised her eyes toward the ceiling of the store, listening to the sounds of the men still working. She bit her lip nervously, then went out the back door and climbed the stairs. Clayton Farley and his two men were just coming out the door as Hannah reached the landing.

"Oh, I'm glad you're still here, ma'am," said Farley. "In all the fuss with Alex, I didn't think to ask if you'd seen the kitchen cupboard."

"Yes," Hannah said. "It's looks fine. Could I talk with you privately, Mr. Farley?"

"Of course. See you fellas in the morning."

The two workers excused themselves and descended the stairs.

"What can I do for you, ma'am?"

"It's about Alex..."

"What about him?"

"I'd like you to give him his job back."

Farley's eyebrows arched. "After the way he treated you?"

"I'm thinking of his family, Mr. Farley. Nellie came here to apologize for the way Alex treated me. We had a little talk. Please understand that my asking you to give Alex his job back was *my* idea, not hers. I didn't even tell her I was going to talk to you about it. That poor woman has it hard enough. She certainly doesn't need the worry of where their next meal is coming from."

Clayton Farley rubbed his chin. "Well-l-l..."

"Please, Mr. Farley. For his family's sake."

"I've given him chance after chance to straighten up, Mrs. Cooper."

"I realize that. But should his wife and children suffer because of it?"

"No, they shouldn't, but—"

"Please, sir."

"Well...the man does do fine work. And I certainly feel sorry for Nellie and those kids. Okay. I'll let him stew in his own juice till this evening, then go over to his house and tell him I'm hiring him back."

"Oh, thank you, Mr. Farley! Thank you!"

Alex Patterson didn't go home after being fired. He walked the fields and forests around Fort Bridger, cursing Clayton Farley and the Yankee woman who owned the new general store. But his anger couldn't quite suppress a feeling of dread for the moment when he'd have to tell Nellie and the children he no longer had a job.

It was almost sunset when Alex finally turned off the road into his yard. Smoke coming from the kitchen chimney told him Nellie was cooking supper. He could hear the children laughing as he walked alongside the house toward the back porch.

They won't be laughing in a minute, he thought. And Nellie...this was going to devastate her. Well, he had to have his say, no matter what. A man can't keep a thing like that inside him.

Just as he reached the back porch, he looked toward the chicken shed and saw bloody, chewed-up carcasses and feathers scattered all around. This time the wolf or coyote had caught a great number of chickens outside the shed.

Alex's day had been bad enough, but this was the match that lit the fuse. He started to count the number of chickens he'd lost and then stopped in his tracks as Shep come over the crest of the ravine. The dog's face, mouth, and chest were covered with blood, and a thick sludge of crimson clung to his coat at the side of his neck.

Alex felt rage boil up within him. Just as he'd thought. It was Shep all the time! He felt an ache somewhere behind his right eye, and the pressure began to build, blurring his vision. "Shep!" he yelled! "You dirty chicken-killin' cur! I'll shoot you dead!"

The dog laid back his ears, tucked his tail between his legs, and went down on his belly.

Nellie and the children heard Alex yelling and came out the back door just as he came toward them at a run. They saw Shep on the ground and the blood on him.

"Alex! What happened?"

He barely broke stride as he said, "I knew it all the time! That filthy hound killed at least half the chickens! I'm gonna shoot 'im!" Even as he spoke, he dashed through the back door.

"Mom, don't let him kill Shep!" cried Willa.

Nellie and the children followed Alex into the kitchen where he was taking his rifle down from the wall.

"Alex, listen to me!" Nellie said. "I know what it looks like, but Shep wouldn't kill the chickens!"

Alex whirled around, his face beet red. "Don't give me that! He's got the evidence all over 'im!"

The children began weeping. Nellie jumped in front of Alex and grabbed his arms. "Listen to me!" she cried. "Get your temper under control! Shep is no chicken killer!"

"Get outta my way, woman!" Alex shoved Nellie aside and bolted out the door, working the lever of his Winchester .44.

Nellie ran after Alex, her breath coming in ragged gasps. Luke hopped after them on his crutches, trying to keep up, and the other children followed.

Somehow she managed to outrun her husband and place herself between him and the dog, crying, "No, Alex! No! Don't shoot him!"

Alex's eyes blazed with white-hot fury and his hands trembled as he gripped the rifle. "Outta my way! That dog dies, and he dies now!"

Shep was still on his belly, looking up at Alex with pitiful eyes.

"No!" Nellie screamed. "Alex, I'm telling you...don't do something you'll be sorry for!"

While her parents argued back and forth, Willa threaded her way through the dead chickens and looked down the slope of the ravine.

Alex had pushed Nellie aside and raised the rifle to his shoulder, sighting on Shep's head, when Willa's scream sliced through the air. "Pa-a-pa! Come look!"

Alex ignored her cry and lined the muzzle between the dog's eyes. Suddenly Nellie slammed him with her body, yelling for him to listen to Willa.

Alex stumbled and the rifle discharged, sending the bullet chewing into sod three feet from Shep's head. Alex swore at Nellie, who was already dashing toward Willa. A terrified Shep whined and remained where he was.

"Alex! Come here!" Nellie called.

When he reached the spot where Nellie and Willa stood, he looked over the edge of the ravine in disbelief. Halfway down the slope, lying against the trunk of a small tree, was a large wolf. Its coat was torn in several places, and its throat had been ripped open. Feathers were still stuck to its mouth.

They heard a low whine and turned to see Shep limping toward them.

"Oh, Shep!" cried Willa. "You killed the wolf, and you're hurt!"

Without a word, Alex knelt beside the dog and examined him.

"How bad is it?" Nellie asked.

Alex cleared his throat. "He's...he's been bitten on the right foreleg. And his coat is torn on the left side of his neck. He's still bleedin'."

Luke hobbled up close to his father. "See, Papa? Mama was right. Shep wouldn't hurt the chickens. He caught that chicken-killing wolf in the act and killed him."

Shep whined again as all three children petted him.

Alex handed his rifle to Nellie and said, "I'll carry Shep into the house. We've got to stop the bleeding."

As the family headed toward the house, Nellie said, "I'll save you the trouble of telling me you were fired by Mr. Farley today. I found out when I was at the sutler's store. I've told the children."

Alex nodded grimly. "I was dreadin' tellin' you. I'll try to find another job tomorrow."

"Alex," Nellie said, her voice strained with emotion, "I'm not rubbing salt in your wounds, but don't you think it's time you did something about your anger?"

He didn't answer.

They entered the house, and Nellie found, upon closer examination, that she could take care of Shep's wounds. When she'd finished bandaging him, she fed him, then the family sat down to an overcooked supper.

Nellie looked across the table at her husband. "So where are you going to look for a job?"

"Well, I—" Alex was spared a reply when a knock came at the front door.

"I'll get it," said Willa, shoving back her chair.

The family sat in silence as Willa opened the door. "Oh, hello Mr. Farley," she said.

Farley's voice filtered to the kitchen. "Is your father here, Willa?"

"Yes. We're having sort of a late supper. Please come in."

"I can come back later."

"Oh, that won't be necessary, Mr. Farley. I'm sure Papa will want to see you now."

Alex mouthed silently to Nellie: *I wonder what he wants?* then rose to his feet as Willa ushered the building contractor into the kitchen.

"Hello, Mrs. Patterson...children," said Farley.

"Good evening," replied Nellie. "Won't you please sit down?"

"No need for that, thank you," he said. Then to Alex, "I came to tell you that you can have your job back if you want it."

"Well, yes, sir," Alex gasped, tears welling in his eyes. "I would like that. But...but what changed your mind, Mr. Farley?"

"Not *what,* Alex, *who.*"

"Pardon me, sir?"

"It was Hannah Cooper who changed my mind."

Patterson's eyes blinked in disbelief. "What did you say?"

"You heard me right. Mrs. Cooper came to me just as my men and I were quitting for the day and pleaded with me to give you back your job. Because of her, I'm offering you a job."

Tears spilled over onto his cheeks as he gripped Farley's hand. "Thank you, sir."

"Don't thank me," Farley said. "Thank Hannah Cooper."

"Oh, he will, Mr. Farley," Nellie said.

Farley nodded, then set steady eyes on Alex. "If anything like what happened today ever happens again, I'm telling you straight out, even Hannah Cooper won't be able to salvage your job. You've got to get a grip on that temper."

Alex glanced at Nellie, then said quietly, "I'll work on it, sir."

Farley bid the family good evening and departed.

Nellie turned to her husband. "I hope you'll think over what Mr. Farley just said, Alex. And I hope you'll remember what that temper almost caused you to do to Shep."

Alex took a deep breath and nodded.

"*And* first thing tomorrow morning, you must thank Hannah for getting you your job back."

Chapter Eighteen

Hannah awakened on Tuesday morning with Solomon on her mind. She sat up in the bed and glanced at the growing light of dawn filtering through the curtains. Then she flipped the pillow against the headboard and scooted back against it. She picked up her Bible from the bed stand and turned to Psalm 143:8: "Cause me to hear thy lovingkindness in the morning; for in thee do I trust: cause me to know the way wherein I should walk: for I lift up my soul to thee."

She bowed her head. "Good morning, Lord. I sure could use an easier day emotionally than I had yesterday."

She prayed for her children, her parents, her new friends in Fort Bridger, and for Nellie Patterson, that she might be saved. Then she read a chapter from the Old Testament and one from the New.

After breakfast with the Williamses, the oldest Cooper children headed for school and Gary went to the hotel. Hannah, Patty Ruth, and Glenda headed for the store. As they met people on the street, they told them the grand opening would be at nine o'clock Thursday morning, and to please spread the word.

When they arrived at the store, Betsy Fordham and little Belinda were on the front porch, as were most of the women who had helped Hannah stock shelves the day before.

Betsy greeted Hannah and Glenda, then tugged on one of

Patty Ruth's pigtails and said, "You ready to go to our house again, sweetie?"

"Sure am. I like it inside the fort. An' I like to play with Belinda."

"I like to play with you too, little girl."

Patty Ruth gave her friend a level look and opened her mouth to speak.

Belinda beat her to it. "I know your name's Patty Ruth, but I like to call you little girl."

Patty Ruth shrugged. "Okay."

Betsy laughed and said, "We'll have Patty Ruth back at five again, if that's all right, Hannah."

"That'll be perfect."

Glenda led the rest of the volunteer helpers inside. Hannah hugged Patty Ruth and watched them walk away. She turned to enter the store and saw Alex Patterson coming down the street toward her. At the same time, Clayton Farley and two other workers were approaching from the opposite direction.

Alex hastened his pace, raised a hand, and called, "Mrs. Cooper, I need to talk to you a moment."

"Certainly," she said. She wondered if Farley had done as he said he would.

When Alex drew up, he looked past Hannah. "I'll be up in a minute, Mr. Farley." Then he said to her, "From what I was told by the boss man at my house last night, you asked him to rehire me."

"Why, yes. Yes, I did."

"I want to thank you. I don't know why you went to the trouble to talk to Mr. Farley on my behalf, but thanks." Alex then hurried past her toward the corner of the building, where his boss and coworkers had gone moments before.

Hannah smiled to herself. "Mr. Patterson!" she called after him.

He turned around. "Yeah?"

She walked toward him. "I'd like to tell you why I went to the trouble to talk with Mr. Farley. You see, Mr. Patterson, I'm a Christian, and—"

"I'm not interested, ma'am," Alex said. "I don't want anything to do with Christianity. Excuse me. I've got to go to work."

Hannah watched him walk away and murmured, "He's not running from me, Lord, he's running from You. Please do whatever it takes, but bring Alex and his family to Yourself."

As Hannah entered the store, Glenda said, "I couldn't help but hear it, Hannah. The man actually thanked you for getting his job back. But he sure didn't want to hear anything about the Lord, did he?"

"No, he didn't. Oh, Glenda, I'm so burdened for Alex and his family. I talked to Nellie yesterday afternoon about the gospel. She really seems interested, but I think she's afraid of Alex—of what he might do if she got saved."

"What did she say?"

"Nothing, really. I just detected some fear there. I believe she can be reached, but it probably would be easier if Alex got saved first."

"That would take a miracle," Glenda said.

Hannah looked deep into her friend's eyes and said, "Our Lord is the God of miracles, isn't He?"

"That He is," Glenda said, hugging her. "And He can save Alex Patterson. I know it!"

"And I know it, too. I'm praying that whatever it takes, the Lord will bring Alex to Himself."

That evening when Alex Patterson arrived home, he found Luke and Joshua sitting on the back porch with Shep.

"Your ma got supper ready?"

"Real close, Alex," came Nellie's voice through the kitchen door. "Did you see Hannah?"

"Yep, and I thanked her to, just like you told me," he said, brushing past her into the kitchen. "I'm hungry. Let's eat."

When the Pattersons had been eating for a few minutes, Nellie said, "I'm real proud of you, Alex. I know it wasn't easy for you to thank Hannah for getting your job back."

He scowled at her from the other end of the table. "When I thanked her, she couldn't leave it at that. She started preachin' at me!"

"She just cares about us, Alex. You can't fault her for that."

Alex's jaw hardened. "I can fault her for bein' one of them I'm-gonna-push-my-religion-down-your-throat types."

"I don't think she's pushy, Alex. She just cares—"

"Wait a minute! Have *you* been talkin' to 'er?"

"Well...yes. Yes I have," Nellie stammered.

"When?"

"Yesterday."

"What for?"

Nellie fidgeted on her chair. "If you must know, I went to the general store after I learned at the sutler's about your being fired. I was ashamed of the way you'd treated Hannah, and I went there to apologize."

The children watched their father with a feeling of dread.

"And I suppose that's when she tried to shove her religion down your throat!"

"She talked to me about salvation, Alex," Nellie said. "She didn't try to shove anything down my throat."

"I'm tellin' you right now, woman, you ain't makin' friends with that fanatic! You hear me?"

Nellie glanced at the children, then met her husband's piercing gaze. "I hear you, Alex."

"The only time you're to go near her is when you're buyin' stuff from the store. That's all! And when you're in there, don't you be makin' friends with her. Is that clear?"

"I can't be unfriendly," Nellie said.

"No, but you don't have to get chummy, and you sure don't have to listen to all that Bible stuff! All I need is to have my wife become one of those Andrew Kelly, Bible-thumpin', you-gotta-git-borned-again fanatics."

Nellie was quiet for a long moment, then said, "I'm holding off getting some things I need from the sutler's so I can buy them on Thursday at Hannah's grand opening. Is that all right?"

"Has to be, doesn't it? Sure, I could stop you from goin' to the grand openin', but we still need groceries and the like from here on out, so why should I stop you? The main thing is that you do your buyin' and get out. I don't want anyone in this family buildin' friendships with Christians."

When Hannah and her children arrived at the Williamses' home for supper, they made over Biggie, who had not had much attention from them lately. Glenda explained that Gary had some important business at the hotel and would grab a bite at the café.

After supper, Hannah and her girls helped with the dishes and cleaned up the kitchen. As they were heading for the door, Glenda said, "I'll just walk over to the hotel with you. Probably ought to check up on my husband."

Hannah laughed. "If anybody needs checking up on, it's Gary!"

Moments later, they rounded the corner on Main Street, and Chris raced B. J. to the lobby door to hold it open for the ladies.

Hannah's eyes popped as she saw an impish-looking Gary Williams standing under a large white banner stretched from wall to wall on a cord. Big red letters announced:

COOPER'S GENERAL STORE
GRAND OPENING TODAY!

"Oh, Gary!" she exclaimed. "It's beautiful!"

"What's it say?" Patty Ruth said.

B. J. laughed. "Oh, Patty Ruth, can't you read anything?"

"Could you when you hadn't yet started school?"

B. J. blushed and Chris laughed. "She gotcha, B. J.!"

Gary's eyes sparkled. "We'll put up the banner Thursday morning before sunup, Hannah. It'll run all the way across the balcony. Nobody will be able to move down the street without seeing it."

"I don't know how to thank you, Gary."

"No need. It's my pleasure to help a little, seeing as how Glenda's had the joy of helping at the store, while I've had to stay here and slave over this hotel."

They heard heavy footsteps on the porch, and the door opened to reveal Colonel Ross Bateman and Captain John Fordham.

"Good evening, everybody," said Bateman. "Captain Fordham and I are here on official business with a Lieutenant Christopher Cooper. Would he be on the premises?"

Hannah smiled as her oldest son stepped up, clicked his heels, and saluted. "I am Lieutenant Cooper, sir."

Bateman looked up at the banner. "Did you make that great-looking banner for your mother, Lieutenant Cooper?"

"No, sir," Chris said. He pointed to Gary and added, "That lowly civilian made it, sir."

"Good one, Chris!" Captain Fordham said, laughing.

Williams scowled at the captain. "Oh, it was, eh? Who would protect you army dudes if it wasn't for us lowly civilians?"

Everybody had a good laugh, then Colonel Bateman said, "Chris, I'm going to have some spare time tomorrow afternoon.

I could give you the official tour of the fort then, if your busy schedule will allow it."

"I've already been in the fort, Chris," Patty Ruth said. "It's really neat."

"But you haven't had the soldier's tour—"

"I saw where they keep the guns!"

"That's enough, you two," said Hannah. "Colonel, Chris can come for the tour right after school tomorrow afternoon. Will that be all right?"

"It sure will, ma'am. Captain Fordham will pick him up at school and deliver him back wherever you say."

"How long will this tour take?" she asked.

"Probably about two hours, ma'am," Fordham said. "I'm going to show him a whole lot more after the colonel's tour."

"That will be about five-thirty," said Hannah. "We'll be at the Williamses' residence getting ready for supper. Do you know where they live?"

"Yes, ma'am. I'll have him there no later than five-thirty."

"You might just have to keep him in the fort, Captain," said Gary, with a twinkle in his eye. "I'm thinking that a lieutenant in the United States Army shouldn't eat in the humble home of a lowly civilian."

On Thursday morning, Hannah awakened and said, "Good morning, Lord. I love you. This is my big day. It's the grand opening of the store." Then she prayed her favorite verse. "Please cause me to hear thy lovingkindness in the morning; for in thee do I trust: cause me to know the way wherein I should walk; for I lift up my soul to thee."

When Hannah drew near the general store with Patty Ruth beside her, she saw the large banner in place and was pleasantly surprised to see the large crowd gathered in the street. Tears filled her eyes when they began to cheer and applaud.

Glenda was there, along with Julie Powell. Both women had volunteered to help Hannah behind the counter. And Betsy Fordham was there to take Patty Ruth home for the day.

Pastor Andy Kelly offered to pray for Hannah as she opened the store, and the crowd grew quiet. When he finished praying, Rebecca Kelly put her arms around Hannah. "God bless you, Hannah Cooper. We love you."

A rousing cheer went up, and Hannah brushed tears from her cheeks.

It was a bittersweet moment when she pulled the door key from her dress pocket and inserted it in the lock. She was thankful the Lord had provided for her and her children, but she missed the strength and the presence of her beloved Solomon. This was to have been their special moment—the realization of their big dream. As she turned the key, she whispered, "Help me, Lord."

The door swung open, and Hannah's two helpers followed her inside along with Betsy, Belinda, and Patty Ruth. The crowd surged forward behind them.

By midmorning, some of the shelves were showing bare spots, and Hannah sent Glenda and Julie to the storeroom to restock items.

Sundi Lindgren and her students arrived at ten-thirty, and Hannah passed out candy to them. Chris, Mary Beth, and B. J. watched their mother with pride as she graciously dealt with customer after customer.

Dr. Frank O'Brien and Edith purchased groceries and what supplies they could use in the clinic. Hannah tried to give them the items as payment for taking care of B. J., but they insisted on paying her.

Heidi Lindgren bought three bolts of cloth for making dresses, saying that she liked Hannah's stock better than much of what she received from her supplier in Denver.

The school children and their teacher had been there about twenty minutes when someone on the porch called, “Mrs. Cooper, look out here!”

Hannah was counting change to a customer and flicked a glance through the big window to the right of the door. She saw Two Moons and a large group of Crows dismounting from their horses.

“Glenda...Julie,” she called. “Would you take care of the customers for a few minutes while I talk with Two Moons. We met him on the trail and...oh, I’ll have to tell you the story later!”

Glenda laughed and said, “Go ahead, honey. Julie and I will be fine. We’ll just have to work a little faster!”

Hannah grinned at her friend and called to her three oldest children. “Come,” she said, beckoning with her hand. “Let’s go out and welcome Two Moons!”

The Crow Indian chief greeted Hannah and her children with a smile and congratulated them on the opening of the store. He introduced them to his squaw, Sweet Blossom, and his son of fourteen grasses, Broken Wing.

In turn, Hannah introduced her children to the chief’s family. “Where is small girl with bright red hair?” Two Moons asked.

“She’s staying with one of the officers’ wives at the fort—Betsy Fordham—who has a daughter her age.”

While Sweet Blossom and Hannah talked, Broken Wing asked his father if Chris could come to the village and visit him sometime.

“We will ask Hannah Cooper,” said his father.

Hannah gladly consented, saying they would work it out at another time when Two Moons was in town.

Many of the Indians came into the store and made purchases with white man’s money. When they had gone, Sundi

Lindgren took her students back to school.

Just past noon, Nellie Patterson entered the store.

"Hello," Hannah said warmly. "It's nice to see you, Nellie."

"You too, Hannah." Nellie walked on by and began to look around the store.

Glenda, Julie, and Hannah continued to work at a fast pace to take care of the steady stream of customers.

When Nellie was ready with her purchases, she made it a point to get in Hannah's line. As Hannah was totaling her bill, she said, "I can take a little break, Nellie. Could we talk for a few minutes? Alone, I mean?"

A trace of panic showed in the woman's eyes as she said, "I'd love to, Hannah, but I really have to get home as quickly as possible."

"Perhaps another time soon."

"Sure," Nellie said, and hurried out the door.

Little by little, nearly everyone in the town, the fort, and the surrounding ranches and farms came into the store for opening day. By closing time, Hannah and her helpers were tired.

"We'll get a good night's sleep, Hannah," said Julie, "and come back again tomorrow. There's no way we're going to leave you alone, in case you have another day like this one."

That night Hannah felt weary to the bone, but a thread of pleasure and excitement ran through her as she thought back through the day. The receipts had far exceeded expectations, and she was thrilled to share this with her children when the family gathered in Hannah's hotel room.

After kissing the children goodnight and making sure they were snug in their beds, Hannah found that in spite of her weariness, she was wound up. She walked to the Williamses' house, and Glenda made a pot of tea. They talked for nearly an hour before fatigue finally set in.

When Hannah finally climbed into bed, she whispered into the darkness, "Solomon, darling, it was a wonderful day. But I missed having you with me. You'd be proud of me, though. It really went well. Of course it would have been much better if you were here to run things. Oh, sweetheart, I miss you so."

Hannah wept for several minutes, then prayed, "Dear Lord Jesus, thank You so much for the way You have blessed me. Help me to be a strong witness for You. Give me wisdom, please, as I talk with people about their need to be saved. And Lord, I pray especially for the Pattersons. Please let me lead Nellie to You. Maybe I've been wrong. Maybe if Nellie got saved first, we could lead the children to You, then work to reach Alex. Help me to win them, Lord."

Moments later, Hannah Cooper, proprietor of Cooper's General Store, slipped into much needed sleep.

Chapter Nineteen

The next day at the store proved to be almost as busy as opening day, but Glenda assured Hannah that she and Julie could take care of the customers for a while.

Hannah walked to the fort and met Judge Carter at the telegraph office, where he showed her how to order goods and supplies by wire from Cheyenne City. Since Hannah was already low on many items, she sent a large order across the wire.

Judge Carter also showed her a catalog, and she ordered furniture from a company in Cheyenne City. It would take most of the savings she and Solomon had brought with them from Independence to purchase the furniture, but she didn't mind. The first day's operation of the store showed her it was going to go well.

According to return wires, the furniture would arrive in about two weeks. The store supplies and goods would come a week to ten days later.

Hannah returned to the store and found Clayton Farley waiting for her.

"Mrs. Cooper, the apartment will be ready for occupancy within another week."

"Thank you, Mr. Farley. We can't wait to get settled, but I just placed an order for furniture, and it won't be here for two more weeks."

Glenda spoke up. "You can stay right where you are, at no charge, for as long as you need to."

"I can't let you do that," Hannah said. "I'm perfectly able to pay you—"

"Nonsense! I insist, and that's all there is to it." Glenda's posture was almost comical as she stood with hands on hips, as if to say, "I have spoken!"

Clayton grinned at the two women and tipped his hat before heading back upstairs to his workmen.

During the next two weeks, the store did exceedingly well, and Hannah's bank account grew. Hannah was able to handle each day's commerce by herself now, and she was also keeping Patty Ruth with her at the store. The five-year-old stayed occupied by drawing pictures on paper at the table near the potbellied stove, having long conversations with Tony the Bear, and by doing little errands around the store for her mother.

Many times a day Hannah shot up little prayers of thanks to the Lord for the way He was blessing her business.

On Friday, October 7, Clayton Farley entered the store and told Hannah the apartment was finished. Chris, Mary Beth, and B. J. had just come into the store from school and wanted to go up and see it. Hannah made them wait until closing time so they could all go up together.

As soon as five o'clock came, Hannah locked the front door and took her brood upstairs.

Mary Beth took one look and said, "Oh, Mama! It's beautiful!"

"Can we stay here tonight, Mama?" asked Patty Ruth.

"Not until we have beds to sleep in, sweetheart. We'll just have to wait a little longer until our furniture arrives."

While the Coopers waited for their furniture, Glenda helped Hannah decorate the apartment and put things away. She stocked the kitchen cupboard with food from the store and put away pots and pans, dishes and eating utensils Hannah had brought from Independence. As the two women worked together, their friendship grew deeper and stronger every day.

The furniture arrived on October 13. That evening a group of men and women lent a hand, and by bedtime all the furniture was in place. When everyone had left but the Williamses, Gary said he would go home and get Biggie so he could be with his family on the first night in their new home.

The moment Gary walked through the door, the little dog jumped out of his arms and ran from room to room, sniffing about and checking everything out.

"All right, everyone," Glenda said, "let's take a tour and then Gary and I will leave and let you get to bed."

The "tour" began in the parlor, which had a green damask-covered sofa and chair, and a couple of glossy tables that held knickknacks and pictures. There was a daguerreotype of Hannah's parents on their wedding day, and one of Solomon's parents with their two sons, Solomon and Daniel, as boys.

Gary asked Hannah about Daniel and learned that he was married, had two children, and lived in Indiana. Hannah had not heard from him since about three months before she and Solomon left Independence.

There was a photograph of Hannah's parents with Hannah's four children, taken some three years previously. Gary commented on how much all four children had grown. He wondered to himself if there were any pictures of Solomon, but didn't want to upset Hannah by asking.

In the center of the parlor was a black wood stove for cold winter days. This room would get less use than the rest of the apartment, Hannah thought, but they would enjoy it when company came.

Gary looked around with admiration. "You're quite a hand at decorating, Hannah. You've made this place look so cozy and homey."

She looked at Glenda, who winked at her, and said, "I had some help."

"I just did what you told me," Glenda said with a chuckle.

Next, Gary was escorted to the large kitchen. The walls and cupboards were a glistening white. A large, round oak table with six chairs sat in the middle of the room, and a brand-new cookstove stood near the cupboard. There were paintings on the walls—some still life, and others of mountains or prairies.

"We'll probably spend most of our time in this room," Hannah said.

B. J. grabbed Gary's hand and pulled him along the hallway, eager to show him the room he shared with Chris. The walls were white, and there were blue-and-white quilts on the beds and matching blue-and-white curtains on the windows.

Mary Beth and Patty Ruth's room was painted a soft pink, and the curtains and bed coverings were white with tiny pink flowers and green leaves. A beautiful pink-and-white rag rug covered the hardwood floor. The girls had decorated their dressers with treasures they'd brought from Independence.

When the group stepped into Hannah's room, Gary immediately saw the gold-framed photograph of a ruggedly handsome man in a Union army uniform. There were captain's bars on his shoulders. He studied the picture and said, "Hannah...this is him?"

Hannah smiled faintly. "Yes. That's my Solomon."

"Handsome man. I think I see a little of each child in him, especially Mary Beth."

His words made all the children smile, especially Mary Beth, who said, "Over there on the bureau is their wedding picture, Mr. Williams."

Hannah led Gary to another gold-framed picture, this one of Solomon and Hannah standing just outside the door of the church where they were married. The long train of Hannah's white wedding dress was carefully placed around the step at their feet. Hannah held on to Solomon's arm as they smiled happily into the camera.

Glenda saw Hannah's chin begin to quiver. She slipped up beside her and put an arm around her waist. "They were a beautiful couple, weren't they, Gary?" she said.

He nodded. "I'm looking forward to meeting Solomon in heaven."

Mary Beth took her mother's hand, and the other children crowded close.

"We'll *all* meet together in heaven," Chris said. "Won't that be a wonderful day?"

"It sure will, son," said Hannah, patting his cheek. "It sure will."

Her room was painted light yellow. The bed had a yellow, white, and green spread that her mother had made for her a couple of years before. There were crisp white ruffled curtains at the windows, and an old rocking chair sat beside a small table in front of one of the windows. The chair had belonged to her paternal grandmother and was one of the few pieces of furniture she had put in the covered wagon.

After Hannah bid her guests goodnight and watched them walk down the outside stairs, she returned to her bedroom and closed the door. She quickly changed into her nightgown and robe and sat down in front of the mirror. She pulled the pins from her hair and let it cascade onto her shoulders.

After brushing her long tresses for two or three minutes, she laid the brush on the dresser and her gaze fell on the photograph of Solomon. She picked it up and stared into his face through a veil of tears. "Oh, darling, I miss you so."

She wiped her cheeks with the back of her hand and continued to gaze into Solomon's face. "At least I now have a place to call home. Of course, it will never be home like it would've been if you were alive. But at least I feel a measure of security here. My roots are planted once again. Goodnight, my darling. I love you."

She kissed the picture and placed it in the center of the

dresser, then laid her robe over the back of the chair and extinguished the lantern. As she walked toward the bed in the darkness, she gently patted her slightly swollen tummy and said, "I love you too, wee one."

On Saturday morning, Hannah was busy with a customer when she saw Justin and Julie Powell enter the store. After a few minutes she noticed that they were still strolling idly about the store but weren't gathering any items from the shelves.

Moments later, the Lindgren sisters entered the store and greeted Hannah warmly. Soon Heidi approached the counter with a few items to purchase, while Sundi chatted with the Powells.

When Hannah had bagged Heidi's groceries, Heidi turned to her sister and said she would see her later.

"Okay," Sundi said, and nodded. She then excused herself to the Powells and approached the counter. "I came by, Hannah, because I needed to see if I could talk to you sometime before Monday."

"You mean in private?"

"Yes."

More customers were coming through the door, including Marshal Lance Mangum.

Hannah glanced at Julie and said, "Honey, are you and Justin in a hurry to leave?"

The couple exchanged a glance, then Julie said, "No. Is there something we can do for you?"

"I wondered if you would take care of these customers while Sundi and I spend a few minutes together."

"I'd be happy to."

Hannah looked at Julie quizzically and said, "You and Justin have been here for a while. Is there something..."

Justin stepped closer to the counter and said, "We needed to talk to you too, ma'am, but we can wait till after you talk with Miss Sundi."

"I can come back later," Sundi said quickly.

"No need," said Justin. "You two go ahead; we'll wait."

Julie came around the counter, edging past Hannah to take her place. "Don't worry, Hannah," she said. "Take your time with Sundi. Justin doesn't have to be to work at the hardware store until noon, and it's not even nine yet."

As Hannah joined her, Sundi looked around. "Your children aren't here?"

"They're upstairs in the apartment. Dr. and Mrs. O'Brien are with them. Doc is taking B. J.'s last bandage off his arm, but there's more than that going on."

"Oh?"

"All four of my offspring are getting 'grandmothered' and 'grandfathered' real good, I'll guarantee you."

"Oh, yes," Sundi said with a giggle. "I've watched those precious people with your kids at church. They've definitely adopted each other, that's for sure."

"The O'Briens have really been a blessing, Sundi. Come on. Let's take a little walk."

The night had been quite chilly, but the brilliant Wyoming sun warmed up the air, so Hannah didn't bother to put on a coat.

As they strolled along the boardwalk, Hannah said, "What did you want to talk to me about?"

Sundi cleared her throat. "It's about Mary Beth."

"Mary Beth?"

"I'm concerned about her, Hannah. She's not getting good grades. It will show up when mid-semester report cards come out, but I wanted to talk to you about it first. Mary Beth's a very bright girl, and capable of getting top grades, but she seems preoccupied most of the time. I can't get her to concentrate on her schoolwork."

"It's her father's death that's preoccupying her. And you're right, Sundi, she is very bright. I can tell you that she's always brought home good report cards in the past."

"I thought so," Sundi said. "And I believe I can help her if you'll give me permission."

"Of course. What do you have in mind?"

"I've noticed that Mary Beth gets along well with the younger children. And they love her. Twelve grades is a lot for me to handle, and I desperately need someone to help me with the younger ones. That is, I need someone to keep an eye on them so I can give the necessary time to the older students. If it's all right with you, I'd like to tell Mary Beth she can monitor the younger students as soon as she brings her grades up to a satisfactory level."

"Oh, Sundi, she would love it!" Hannah said. "Mary Beth adores little children! Of course it's all right with me. I really appreciate your taking such interest in her."

"She's a wonderful girl, Hannah, and I want to help her all I can. I also want to help her because of her desire to be a teacher. I'll even let her do some teaching while she's monitoring the little ones."

In her excitement, Hannah reached out and squeezed Sundi's arm. "This is an answer to prayer. I've been asking the Lord to give me wisdom to help Mary Beth adjust to her father's death. What you've just proposed will help her immensely, I just know it. Those grades will come up fast, I guarantee you!"

"That's what I'm expecting," Sundi said, her eyes flashing. "I'll talk to Mary Beth at school on Monday. Or if you want, you can tell her about it ahead of time."

"Oh, no. This is your idea, and I think you should surprise her with it." She cocked her head and looked at the young teacher with loving eyes. "Thank you, Sundi. This will make her so happy!"

"That's what I want, Hannah. I want to see her happy.

Well, I need to get home. See you at church tomorrow."

Hannah turned and headed back toward the store, her heart thrilled at the way the Lord was answering prayer on Mary Beth's behalf. "Thank You, Lord," she said as she walked. "This will be such an encouragement to Mary Beth. And it will occupy her mind."

As she hastened along the boardwalk, the Lord spoke to her heart: *Hannah, there's something else that will help Mary Beth...*

Hannah pondered the words that had come to her mind and then said, "Yes, of course, Lord! I'll take care of it tonight! Thank You for speaking to me about it!"

Hannah entered the store and found Julie waiting on one customer. She could tell Justin had swept the entire store and it looked as though he'd straightened up the goods on all the shelves. Now he was using a feather duster. He paused and smiled at Hannah, then continued working.

When the customer left, Hannah said, "I can't leave this place for a few minutes but some little pixie sneaks in, sweeps the floor, straightens up the shelves, and dusts them."

"I don't like to be idle, Hannah," Justin said. "So if I can save you a little work, why not?"

"Well, I appreciate it very much." She headed for the counter where Julie stood. "Thank you, Julie, for filling in for me."

When Hannah glanced back at Justin, she could see that something was troubling him. "You two wanted to talk to me," she said. "What can I do for you?"

Justin cleared his throat nervously as Julie came around the end of the counter to join him. "Well, Hannah," he said a bit weakly, "we...ah...Julie and I had some unexpected expenses the past couple of weeks, and...well...our cupboard is pretty bare, and we don't have enough money to buy groceries. I'll get paid for last week when I get to work today, but that money is already spent. What Julie and I wanted to ask you was"—he cleared his throat again—"if you could extend us credit for a couple of months until we can get on our feet."

"Justin has tried to find night work, Hannah," Julie said, "but there just isn't anything in Fort Bridger."

Hannah shook her head and looked at Julie tenderly. "And just like Glenda, you wouldn't let me pay you for helping me in the store. Of course I'll extend you credit. And what's more, I'm going to pay you for the work you've done here."

"We don't want you to pay her anything, Hannah," Justin said. "Just let us buy groceries on credit till we can get on our feet. Business is getting better at the hardware store, and the Swensens told me I'll be getting a raise come the first of the year. We'll start paying you back what we owe you from each paycheck until you're paid in full."

Tears misted Hannah's eyes. "I don't want you to pay me back. I'm going to *give* you the groceries you need until the first of the year."

"But you can't do that!" Justin said.

"Just watch me! I'm extending you credit as you've asked, but come the first of January I will consider the bill paid. Now, don't argue with me. I'm a stubborn woman, and you'll just be wasting your breath!"

Julie burst into tears and wrapped her arms around Hannah. "Oh, Hannah, you're such a sweet Christian! And you're so generous!"

"Julie's right, Hannah," Justin said. "Thank you for being so good to us."

Hannah met his gaze with a look of serenity he had seldom seen before. "The Lord has been so good to me, Justin. The store has been showing a good profit already. Do you two remember what God's Word says in 1 John 3:17 and 18?"

Neither one could bring the verses to mind.

Hannah smiled. "Well, let me tell you. It says 'whoso hath

this world's good, and seeth his brother have need, and shutteth up his bowels of compassion from him, how dwelleth the love of God in him? My little children, let us not love in word, neither in tongue; but in deed and in truth.'"

Still smiling, she said, "Justin...Julie...I love you in truth, and I show that by loving you in deed."

Now even Justin was fighting tears as Julie hugged Hannah again and said, "We love you too, Hannah Cooper."

"That's for sure," Justin said. "Maybe someday the Lord will allow us to show *you* the kind of love you're showing us."

At nine-thirty that night, Hannah finished reading the Bible to her children, who sat around the big kitchen table, and said, "All right, my darlings, it's bedtime."

As chairs were shoved back, Patty Ruth announced, "It's my turn to have Biggie sleep with me tonight!"

"No, it's not!" argued B. J. "It's *my* turn!"

"Huh-uh! It's *my* turn. You had him sleep with you since he's slept with me!"

"No I didn't! I—"

"B. J.!" cut in Hannah. "I've kept track. It's Patty Ruth's turn."

B. J. looked as if he was going to disagree, but Hannah said, "Brett Jonathan!"

B. J.'s face straightened out quickly. "Okay. I guess you're right, Mama."

"You *know* I'm right."

"Yes, ma'am."

While Patty Ruth was carrying Biggie to the girls' room and Mary Beth was turning down both beds, Hannah prayed with the boys and kissed them goodnight. When she entered the girls' room, she said, "Mary Beth, I need to talk to you before you go to bed. We can talk in the parlor."

"Am I in trouble, Mama?"

"No, honey. You're not in trouble. There's just something I want to talk to you about before you go to sleep."

Hannah prayed with Patty Ruth—who was fitted tightly in her bed between Biggie and Tony the Bear—tucked her in, and kissed her goodnight. At Patty Ruth's request, Hannah kissed both Tony and Biggie on top of their heads.

Hannah could hear Patty Ruth giggling as she led Mary Beth to the parlor and they sat down on the sofa.

"Honey," she said, "I have something to tell you that's to be just between us for right now. Okay?"

The girl nodded slowly.

"My telling only you at this time, Mary Beth, is because the Lord has put it on my heart to do so."

Worry etched its lines across her young brow. "Mama, what is it? Is something wrong?"

"No, sweetheart. There's nothing wrong. There's something very right."

The lines on Mary Beth's forehead disappeared and a smile tugged at the corners of her mouth. "What is it, Mama?"

"Let me first say, honey, that I'm aware that Papa's death has been very hard on you. I've never looked in your diary, but the look on your face when you've written in it since Papa's death has told me your little heart is crushed. And, of course, we've talked about this."

"Yes, Mama."

"Because Papa's death has seemed to affect you in a different way than your sister or your brothers, I have something very wonderful I want to share with just you, for the time being."

Mary Beth's big blue eyes were riveted on Hannah's face.

Hannah kept her voice low and said, "This family has a special blessing coming. I'm going to have a baby in the spring."

"Oh, Mama!" Mary Beth gasped. "Really? You're going to have a baby?"

"Yes. Really!"

"How long have you known?"

"I was sure of it just before we camped at Devil's Gate. I told your papa at bedtime the same night he was bitten by the rattler. He was so thrilled about it."

Mary Beth began to cry. Tears welled up in her eyes and spilled down her cheeks as she opened her arms and wrapped them around her mother.

Hannah held her close. "Honey, are you upset?"

"Oh no, Mama! These are happy tears!"

Mary Beth eased back from Hannah and looked at her mother's face. "I don't understand why the Lord took my papa," she said, "but I can now praise Him because the same God who took Papa has given a new life to our family! The baby won't take Papa's place—no one could ever do that—but that little boy or girl will fill the empty spot we've had since Papa died."

"I don't want your sister and brothers to know just yet. I'll have to tell them soon, because I'm beginning to show a little. But for now, it's our little secret."

Mary Beth sniffed and nodded slowly. "Thank you for telling me, Mama. I'm so happy. You know what?"

"Hmm?"

"In my devotions a few days ago, I found a verse in the psalms that stuck in my mind. Or should I say in my heart? It has kept coming back to me. It's the first part of Psalm 18:30. 'As for God, his way is perfect.' God's way really *is* perfect, isn't it, Mama? He took Papa to be with Him, but He gave us this new baby to brighten our lives down here."

Hannah thought her heart would burst with joy at Mary Beth's words. "Yes, Mary Beth. We don't always see it that way, but the Bible always speaks the truth. Our God's way is perfect. It's up to us to believe it, even when we can't see it."

"Mama..."

"Yes?"

"I want to apologize."

"For what?"

"For not taking Papa's death better, and for not being more of a help to you in it all."

"Sweetheart, you don't have to apologize. You're only human."

"Well, this human promises to be more of a help to you from now on. As much as is humanly possible."

Mother and daughter had a sweet time of prayer together, thanking the Lord for the new little Cooper and the joy the baby had already brought to them.

On Sunday morning, just before she dismissed her Sunday school class, Sundi Lindgren told Mary Beth she wanted to talk to her for a moment. When the other students had gone, Sundi said, "I have something very important to talk to you about tomorrow. Can you stay after school for a little while?"

"Sure. I'll tell Mama I'll be a little late getting home."

On Monday afternoon, Mary Beth took a seat in front of Miss Lindgren's desk and watched her teacher with wide eyes as she moved behind the desk and sat down in her chair.

Sundi leaned forward on her elbows and said, "Mary Beth, I need to talk to you about your grades."

The girl's countenance fell, and she dropped her eyes to the floor.

Sundi quickly raised up and reached across the desk to touch Mary Beth's arm. "No, no, honey. I'm not going to scold you."

"You're not?"

"No. I understand why you haven't done well with your

schoolwork. It's because you lost your father, and you miss him so terribly you can't concentrate on your studies. Am I right?"

Mary Beth's lower lip quivered. "Yes."

Sundi circled the desk and sat down in a chair next to Mary Beth. She looked her in the eye and said, "I know exactly what you're going through. You see, my father was killed, too."

The girl's eyes widened. "Really?"

"Yes. I was older than you when I lost Papa, but it hurt just as much. I understand how losing your father affected you as it did."

Mary Beth listened intently as Miss Lindgren told her story.

"Heidi and I were born and raised on a farm in Minnesota—part of a Swedish settlement. My father raised us, because our mother died when Heidi was three and I was two. Neither of us remember Mama. Although Papa was a loving and tender man, he never married again.

"Both of our parents were fine Christians, and we came to know the Lord at an early age and committed ourselves to walk close to Him from then on.

"Papa raised cattle on the farm, and one day one of his bulls became enraged and attacked him. Papa was gored to death."

Sundi said she and Heidi were devastated when their father was killed. When Sundi described for Mary Beth her feelings and fears when she lost her father, of the loneliness she suffered, Mary Beth felt as if Sundi was describing the very things she had suffered with the loss of her own papa.

"I had just finished my college training and received my teaching certificate when Papa was killed. It seemed like a good time to think about a dream I'd carried in my heart for some time. I'd always yearned to move to the West and help settle this unknown frontier, so I talked Heidi into making plans to move west. I'd read about Fort Bridger in various newspapers and magazines, and saw an article that told of the town's growth and that they needed a schoolmarm. I wrote and applied for the job, and was accepted.

"We sold the farm and came to Fort Bridger in a wagon train in early August, not far ahead of you and your family. And the rest, you know."

Mary Beth looked at her teacher shyly and said, "It really helps to know you've been through what I'm going through. Thank you for telling me. I...I'm going to do better with my grades, I promise."

"Good!" Sundi said with a smile. "Because I have something else to tell you."

"Oh?"

"How would you like to be my assistant and help me with the children in first, second, and third grades?"

Mary Beth's eyes looked as if they would pop from their sockets. "Me?"

"You're the only person in the room with me, aren't you?"

"Yes. I—"

"The monitoring job is yours, Mary Beth, if I see an immediate improvement in your grades."

"Oh, you *will,* Miss Lindgren!" she said, leaping up to hug her teacher. "I promise you will! Oh, thank you, thank you, thank you! This is the best thing that could ever happen to me!"

Chapter Twenty

Hannah Cooper stood behind the counter, waiting on a lieutenant and his wife from the fort when she heard Patty Ruth, who was sitting at the table by the pot-bellied stove, say, "Mama, it's the kids! They're home from school."

Little sister ran to greet her brothers and looked behind them. "Where's Mary Beth?"

"She stayed after school to talk to Miss Lindgren," said B. J. "Don't you remember? We talked about it at breakfast this morning."

"Oh, yeah. I forgot."

Hannah looked past her customers. "Do you boys have homework?"

"Yes'm," Chris said.

"Go upstairs and get right on it. I want it done before suppertime."

"We'll do it, Mama," B. J. said.

The boys were about to head out the back door when Patty Ruth said, "Look, Chris! It's Broken Wing and his papa!"

Just then Two Moons entered the store, wearing his full headdress of brilliantly colored feathers. He was in buckskin shirt and pants, for the October air was cool. Broken Wing was in buckskins, too.

The lieutenant and his wife looked on with interest, being acquainted with three Crow army scouts at the fort who were from Two Moons's village.

Two Moons greeted them, then approached Hannah and asked if she and her children could come to the village tomorrow for the evening meal. Hannah accepted the invitation with delight, and Two Moons told her that he and Sweet Blossom, along with their son, would come in a wagon to transport the Coopers the twelve miles north to the Crow village. They would come at six on the white man's clock.

After the Indians left, Chris and B. J. raced each other up the stairs to the apartment. Hannah was still grinning to herself over their excitement about going to the Crow village when she looked up to see Nellie Patterson.

"Hello, Nellie," she said warmly. "Patty Ruth, can you say hello to Mrs. Patterson?"

"Uh-huh," Patty Ruth said, clutching Tony the Bear to her chest. "Hello, Mrs. Patterson. How are you? I am fine."

Nellie's sad eyes brightened a bit as she smiled and said, "Aren't you quite the young lady?" Then to Hannah: "Does Patty Ruth stay here with you all day?"

"She's been doing that, but just this morning, Betsy Fordham volunteered to keep her Tuesdays and Thursdays at her house. She and little Belinda have become close friends."

"I see. That's wonderful. Well, I guess I'd better get my groceries and head back home."

Three more customers came in while Nellie was gathering supplies. Though it took only a few minutes, she purposely waited until the others were gone before approaching the counter. While Hannah was adding up the bill, Nellie said, "I guess it won't be long now till you folks have your new church building finished."

"I think we're about a month away yet," Hannah said.

"That'll be nice, won't it? Having your own building."

"It would be even nicer if I could see you and your family sitting in one of the pews."

Nellie was silent.

"Nellie..."

"Yes?"

"I want to see you come to know my Jesus. He loves you and wants to forgive your sins and save your soul."

"I really need to be going," Nellie said quickly.

Hannah slid the groceries toward Nellie and said, "Honey, down in your heart, you have a thirst to know the God who created you, don't you?"

"Yes, Hannah."

"When a person gets saved, that thirst is quenched with the water of life. God made every human being with a thirst for Him. When they try to satisfy that thirst with other things, it only gets worse. The Bible says, 'Let him that is athirst come. And whosoever will, let him take the water of life freely.'"

Nellie nodded silently.

"Did you catch the word *whosoever,* Nellie?"

"Yes."

"That would include you, wouldn't it?"

Nellie's hands shook as she picked up the sacks. "I really have to be going, Hannah. Thank you for caring about me."

As Nellie started toward the door, Hannah said, "You know the most famous verse in the Bible, don't you, Nellie?"

The sad-faced woman stopped. "Do you mean John 3:16?"

"Right. Can you quote it?"

"It's about God loving the world, but I can't quote it."

"'For God so loved the world, that he gave his only begotten Son, that whosoever believeth in him should not perish, but have everlasting life.' Did you catch the *whosoever,* Nellie?"

"Hannah, I believe in Jesus."

"But this belief is more than just believing that He exists. It means putting your faith in Him to save your soul and wash away all your sins in His blood. You see, no one else could have died for you on the cross. No one else could raise himself up from the grave and be alive forevermore to save you. Only Jesus could do that, and *did* do that. To perish is to go to hell, Nellie. To have everlasting life is to go to heaven. Jesus will save you if you come to Him in repentance and ask Him to come into your heart and be your personal Saviour."

Nellie was trembling all over. "Hannah, I really must be going."

"Think about it, will you?"

"Yes. Thank you."

Hannah breathed a prayer as Nellie rushed out the door.

On Tuesday, Two Moons arrived at the store with Sweet Blossom and Broken Wing and took the Coopers to their village. They enjoyed a delicious meal together, and Hannah discovered a love growing in her heart for these people. She and Sweet Blossom had found many things to talk about.

The Crow children made Mary Beth, B. J., and Patty Ruth feel very welcome. Chris and Broken Wing, especially, found a true friendship growing between them.

Hannah noted the medicine men and the religious artifacts in the village and wondered if these kind people had ever heard the gospel of Jesus Christ. While she was getting to know them better, she would talk to Pastor Kelly about it.

By Wednesday, October 19, Mary Beth's grades had risen to near perfection, and she was given the monitoring job. Miss Lindgren's kind act had made her superbly happy, and her life took on new meaning.

While Mary Beth was assuming her new responsibility at school, Patty Ruth was helping her mother carry items from the storeroom to be put on the shelves. A soldier entered the store with a sheet of paper in his hand. Hannah recognized him as Corporal Eddie Slayton.

"Good morning, Corporal," she said with a smile.

"Corp'ral..." said Patty Ruth.

"Yes, little lady?"

"You don' shoot In'ians, do you?"

Slayton looked at Hannah, who shrugged.

"Well, honey, sometimes I have to shoot Indians."

"But they're good people. You shouldn' shoot 'em. I visited Two Moons's village. He's real nice. And so's his wife. And so's his boy. And so's all them In'ian people at his village."

"Well, little lady—"

"My name's Patty Ruth."

"Okay, Patty Ruth. You see, all Indians aren't friendly toward white people like the Crows are. Most of them want to kill us. So when they attack us, we have to shoot them so they won't kill nice little girls like you."

"Oh," said Patty Ruth, and walked away toward the storeroom, talking in a low tone to her bear.

Slayton handed Hannah the paper. "This came over the wire, ma'am. It's from the people who are shipping your supplies."

He excused himself, and Hannah read the message. The goods were on their way and would arrive in Fort Bridger on Monday, October 24, or Tuesday, October 25.

"Whew! It's a good thing they'll be here in less than a week," she murmured.

Several customers came and went during the morning. It was almost noon before Hannah had time to straighten up some shelves.

Nellie Patterson came in and purchased some small items,

but Hannah sensed she had come in for something else. She asked Nellie if she would like some coffee. The potbellied stove already had a fire in it to ward off the chill air, and it wouldn't take her long to heat up some coffee.

Nellie shied away, saying she had to get back home. Hannah felt certain the fear she saw in Nellie's eyes was put there by Alex.

The next day, Nellie came back. Even as she was placing Nellie's few purchases in a paper sack, Hannah prayed, *Dear Lord, I know the Holy Spirit has been working on her. Please let me lead her to You. I need some time with her, Lord. I need You to keep anyone from coming in so we'll have some privacy, and—*

Hannah's heart sank when she heard the front door open. She looked up and saw Glenda entering the store.

"Thank you, Hannah," Nellie said, and turned to leave.

"Ah...Nellie," Hannah said. "Wait a minute." Then to Glenda: "Honey, could you possibly watch the store for me while I talk to Nellie?"

"Why, of course. Is Patty Ruth here?"

"No. This is Thursday. Remember? She stays with Betsy Fordham on Tuesdays and Thursdays now."

"Oh, yes. You and Nellie go ahead. I'll take care of things here."

Hannah turned back to Nellie. "You do want to talk to me, don't you?"

Nellie's eyes filled with tears. "Yes," she whispered.

"Let's go up to the apartment then."

When they reached the apartment, Hannah sat her down at the kitchen table and dashed to her bedroom to get her Bible. When she returned, Nellie was weeping.

Hannah sat next to her and said, "You came to the store, hoping we could talk some more about Jesus, didn't you, Nellie?"

"Yes, Hannah. I can't put it off any longer. I want to be saved."

Hannah squeezed her hand. "Then you will. I just want to make sure you fully understand, so let's look at some Scripture." She opened her Bible and flipped some pages, saying, "I want to spend a little more time in the book of John, but let me first show you a verse I quoted to you the other day—Luke 13:3. Look at the words of Jesus right here that I've underlined: 'Except ye repent, ye shall all likewise perish.'

"In other words, Jesus says if we don't repent, we will go to hell. To repent means to change your mind, Nellie. Repentance is a change of mind that results in a change of direction. You must change your mind about your sin. Change your mind about Jesus, and do a 180 degree turn from the direction you're going and come to Jesus."

Hannah turned some pages and stopped at John 3. "Look again at John 3:16. 'For God so loved the world, that he gave his only begotten Son, that whosoever believeth in him should not perish, but have everlasting life.' Your faith must be in *Jesus* for your salvation, Nellie. Do you see that? Not a church or a religion or a denomination or some religious leader or baptistry water or communion elements or your own good deeds, but in *Him.*"

"It's getting clearer, Hannah."

"Look at the next verse. 'For God sent not his Son into the world to condemn the world; but that the world through him might be saved.' Through *Him,* Nellie. Not through anyone else. Not through our good works or the fact that we never murdered anyone or something like that. All men are sinners. Some are moral sinners, some are immoral sinners, but all go to the same hell if they refuse to put their faith in Jesus Christ and Him *alone* for salvation. Look at the next verse.

"'He that believeth on him is not condemned: but he that believeth not is condemned already...' See? God didn't send His Son into the world to condemn the world. The world was *already condemned.* Tell me, Nellie. Why are people condemned already? Because they haven't been baptized or because they haven't taken communion or joined a church? Or are they condemned already because they committed adultery or murder?"

"No," Nellie said softly. "It says here, because they have *not believed* in the name of the only begotten Son of God."

"Right! So it's unbelief that puts people in hell, isn't it? Their refusal to repent of their sin and put their faith in Jesus and Him alone to save them."

"I see that, Hannah," Nellie said, wiping the tears from her cheeks. "I know I'm a sinner. I know there's only one Person who can save me. I don't want to go to hell. I want to be saved right now. What do I do?"

"Nellie, do you believe that everything I've shown you in Scripture is true?"

"Oh yes. I believe it with all my heart."

"Then all that's left is found right here in Romans 10:13. Read that verse to me."

Nellie sniffed and read in a shaky voice, "'For whosoever shall call upon the name of the Lord shall be saved.'"

"Whosoever is *you,* isn't it?"

"Yes."

"Then let's bow our heads, and you call on Jesus, admitting that you're a lost sinner. Tell Him you're turning to Him in repentance, that you believe He died on the cross the pay the penalty for your sins, and ask Him to come into your heart and save you."

Hannah wept tears of joy as Nellie called on the crucified One to save her. When it was done, the two women clung to each other while Hannah prayed for Nellie, asking the Lord to help her be a testimony to her family. She asked the Lord that every one of the Pattersons would be saved, including Alex.

Hannah told Nellie that she'd been praying that whatever it took, the Lord would bring Alex to Himself. Hannah then explained to Nellie that she should be baptized, and Pastor

Kelly would talk with her about that. Then they went downstairs to tell Glenda that Nellie had just become a Christian.

As they entered the store, they were surprised to see the pastor and his wife at the counter with several bags of groceries. There was no one else in the store at the moment.

When the others saw the radiance on Nellie's face, they knew what had happened, but waited to hear it from her own lips.

"Tell these people what you just did, Nellie," Hannah said.

When Nellie said that she'd just received Jesus into her heart, there was a whole lot of rejoicing and hugging.

"Thank you, Pastor," Nellie said, "for the times you came to the house to give us the gospel." She then hugged Hannah and thanked her that she had cared enough to be persistent about her need for the Lord.

Nellie turned back to the pastor and said, "I want to come to church and bring the children so they can hear the gospel and be saved, too, but Alex will be furious when I tell him I've become a Christian."

"What do you think he'll do, Nellie?" Pastor Kelly asked.

She bit her lip and fear showed in her eyes. "He'll go berserk. I could hide it from him, but I don't believe the Lord would have me do that. I'm going to be honest and tell Alex what happened to me today."

"I'll go home with you," he said. "I'll be there when you tell Alex."

"Thank you, but I feel I must handle it by myself. I must do it this way."

Hannah put her hand on Nellie's shoulder. "You know best about it, honey, but you won't be alone. You have the Lord with you now."

Nellie's smile was brilliant as she said, "Yes. Yes, I do!"

"Let's pray right now and ask the Lord to go before you and protect you and the kids," Pastor Kelly said.

❦ ❦ ❦

That afternoon, when the Patterson children arrived home from school, it was obvious that something good had happened to their mother.

"Mama!" Luke said. "I can't remember the last time I saw you look this happy. What happened?"

"Oh, children! Hannah Cooper showed me from the Bible how to be saved!" She smiled from ear to ear, telling them it was the most wonderful thing that had ever happened to her.

Right away, Luke, Willa, and Joshua said they wanted to be saved, too. Miss Lindgren had mentioned salvation many times at school, and they wanted to know more about it.

"Then hurry, Willa," Nellie said. "Go get Pastor Kelly and ask him to come."

Pastor Kelly arrived with Willa, bringing a Bible as a gift to Nellie. He opened it and began showing the children the gospel story. They'd heard about Jesus dying on the cross for sinners and coming out of the grave, but had never clearly understood it. When the pastor made it plain, all three called on Jesus to save them.

Kelly hugged the children and told them how glad he was that they'd opened their hearts to Jesus. Just then, the back door opened, and Alex walked in.

When he entered the parlor, he saw Kelly. "What are *you* doin' here? I told you never to come into this house again!"

Nellie's scalp prickled and the flesh on the nape of her neck crawled. Despite her fear, she stepped between her husband and the pastor and said in a steady voice, "Alex, Pastor Kelly is here because I asked him to come."

Patterson's lip curled in a sneer. "And just why would you do that?"

"Nellie, would you like me to tell him?" Kelly asked.

"Tell me *what?*"

"I will, Pastor," Nellie said, her mouth going dry. She could feel her husband's burning eyes as she licked her lips and said, "I became a Christian today, Alex. I didn't plan to go against your wishes, but I had to obey God and repent of my sin and receive His Son into my heart. My fear of hell was greater than my fear of what you might do when I told you I was a Christian."

Andrew Kelly watched Alex's eyes grow wilder as he said, "Who forced this fanaticism on you?"

"It's not fanaticism," Nellie said. "It's salvation. And it wasn't forced on me. Hannah Cooper has been talking to me about it almost since she first came to town."

"I told you not to get friendly with her!" he yelled.

"I couldn't help it, Alex," Nellie said. "She cared about me. I went to the store today to ask her to show me from the Bible how to be saved."

Alex swore, spraying saliva, and said, "This wouldn't have happened if that woman hadn't come to this town! We were a happy family till she showed up!"

"Alex," Kelly said. "Cool down."

Alex drew a deep breath and was about to speak when Nellie beat him to it.

"Alex, when the children came home from school, they saw how happy I was. When I told them what happened to me today, they wanted to be saved, too. That's when I had Willa go fetch Pastor Kelly. He just led all three of our children to the Lord.

"It's not my intent to infuriate you, but the children and I must obey God. I promise you, I'll be a better wife than ever. Jesus will help me do that. I love you, Alex. The children love you. Please understand that. And Jesus loves you too, Alex. He'll save you if you let Him."

Alex stared hard at Nellie, then turned his hot eyes on the preacher. "I want you to get off this property! Get out now! Get out! Get out!"

Willa began to cry, and Luke put an arm around her, balancing on his crutches.

Alex pointed at his daughter. "Stop that bawlin'!" He turned back to Kelly and yelled, "Are you still here? I told you to get out! This is my property, and I told you to leave! Do I have to get the marshal? I have legal rights, you know!"

Kelly kept his voice calm. "Alex, I'm not leaving until you promise me you'll do no harm to any member of your family. In fact, I can have the marshal jail you if I have reason to believe you're going to unleash your wrath on them when I leave. Don't make me do it." Kelly looked steadily at Alex. "Do I have your promise?"

Patterson clenched his teeth and forced himself to calm down. Slowly, his rapid breathing subsided. "All right, Kelly. I promise I won't lay a hand on my wife or children."

"Do I have your word on that?"

"You have my word."

"Then I'll leave," said Kelly, heading for the front door.

"Thank you for coming, Pastor!" Nellie called after him.

When the door closed, Willa clung to her big brother, and Joshua stood close by, wide-eyed and frightened, as Alex wheeled about and fixed Nellie with stony eyes.

Before he could say anything, Nellie said, "Alex, the children and I want to go to church from now on. We want to learn more about the Word of God. We want to start this very Sunday, and we'd like you to go with us."

Alex swore and headed for the door. Over his shoulder, he said, "You fanatics can do whatever you want. I'm not goin' with you. If I told you not to go, you'd just do it anyhow."

"Where are you going?"

"For a walk. I need some fresh air."

"Don't be gone long. I'll have supper ready in a little while."

On Friday and Saturday, word spread to the Christians throughout the town and the fort that Hannah Cooper had led Nellie Patterson to Christ, and that her children had been saved, too.

Alex Patterson was now working on the new saddlery building in town, but had little to say when asked about what had happened to his wife and children. He was glum on the job and at home. When Nellie and the children tried to talk to him, he ignored them. As far as he was concerned, his whole life was ruined because of Hannah Cooper.

She needed to be taught a lesson.

CHAPTER TWENTY-ONE

Sunday morning came with a brisk wind blowing across the valley and the sky heavy with clouds.

When the Patterson family sat down to the breakfast table and Alex saw that Nellie was going to pray over the food, he left the room and didn't come back until his family had started eating.

During breakfast, Nellie looked across the table at her husband and said, "Alex, the children and I sure would love to have you go with us on our first day at church."

Alex lanced her with a poisonous look, but didn't reply.

Willa said, "Mama, are we going to get Bibles like you did? I know even the kids carry them to church."

"If you get 'em, it won't be with our money," Alex said. "That sneakin' pastor will have to give 'em to you."

"I'm sure Pastor Kelly will see that each of you has a Bible," Nellie said.

Alex was quiet a moment, then looked through the window at the heavy sky. "You'll all probably get caught in a snowstorm if you go to church. That wind sounds pretty cold, too."

"We'll bundle up good," Nellie told him.

The wind had died down and the clouds were breaking up by the time Nellie and her children arrived at the town hall for

Sunday school. The people welcomed them with open arms.

There was much rejoicing during the morning service when Nellie and her children walked forward to make their public profession of faith in Christ and to present themselves for baptism. When the service was over, the people crowded around the Pattersons to share their joy.

Hannah saw Justin and Julie Powell with their children, and she said to the young couple, "Seeing you two with these little ones makes me think of Solomon and me when we were your age."

"I wish we could have known your husband, Hannah," said Julie.

"Me, too," Justin said. "From what I've been able to pick up, he must have been quite a man."

"Oh, he was," said Hannah. "Handsome and rugged. Every inch a man. Strong as an ox...yet he was so gentle."

"Do you have any pictures of him?" asked Julie.

"Yes. I guess you haven't been up to the apartment since I unpacked our boxes. I have our wedding picture, and I have a picture of Solomon in his uniform."

"I'd sure like to see them," said Justin.

"Tell you what," Hannah said with a smile. "You can drop by this afternoon and see them."

"Oh, we won't be able to do it today," said Julie. "We're going to eat at the Swensens and spend the afternoon with them."

"Well...some other time," said Justin.

"Tell you what," Hannah said. "I'll bring them to the service tonight. I'm very proud of Solomon. I'd like to show his pictures off."

"Great!" said Julie. "We'll look forward to seeing them."

While his family was at church that morning, Alex sulked around the place, fuming and growing angrier by the minute at Hannah Cooper for what she had done to Nellie and the children. Their lives would never be the same, and neither would his. Alex Patterson's lot would be to live with a house full of religious idiots.

When Nellie and the children arrived home after church, the sky was almost clear, but there was a stiff breeze, punctuated periodically by strong wind gusts. The air was cold. Winter was on its way.

Alex waited till Sunday dinner had been prayed over before arriving at the table to eat.

"Pa, you should have been in church with us this morning," said Luke. "The pastor told the story of how David killed that big ol' giant, Goliath. It was really good when he got to that part about—"

"I don't want to hear it, Luke," Alex said. "We had better things to talk about before that Cooper woman came to town and stuck her nose into our business."

Luke looked at his mother, who shook her head, telling him with her eyes to leave it alone. The rest of the meal was eaten in near silence. When Alex finished, he got up and went outside without a word.

"Mom," said Willa, "Pa's really miserable, isn't he?"

"He's letting his anger toward Hannah eat him up. All we can do is pray for him."

That evening, Alex stood at the barn and watched his family leave the house and head for town. He noticed with disgust that every one of them was carrying a Bible.

When Nellie and the children were out of sight, Alex headed for the house, cursing the name of Hannah Cooper. He stepped into the kitchen and hung his coat and hat on wall pegs by the door, then went to the cupboard. Taking out a half-full whiskey bottle, he popped the cork, cursed Hannah again, and took a long pull.

Shep lay on the floor in a corner, eyeing the man skeptically.

At the Cooper apartment, Hannah and her children were putting on their coats, getting ready to leave for church. Patty Ruth had her small New Testament in one hand, and Tony in the other.

Hannah carried a small canvas satchel, bearing the two gold-framed photographs she treasured with all her heart.

When Biggie saw them heading for the door, he ran ahead of them wagging his tail as if he was going, too.

"Mama, Biggie wants to go to church with us," B. J. said.

"He can't, honey."

"Why not?"

"You know dogs aren't allowed in church."

A sly look captured B. J.'s eyes as he gave a sidelong glance at his little sister and said, "Well, how come *bears* can go to church if dogs can't?"

"B. J.," said Patty Ruth, "bears like Tony can go to church 'cause they don't make noise or messes like Biggie would."

"Come on, children," said Hannah. "We don't want to be late to church."

Biggie started to follow the children out the door in front of Hannah, but she commanded him to stop. The little dog whined, then ran and jumped on a chair next to a small table by the parlor window. From the chair, he hopped up on the table and pressed his nose to the glass.

Outside, as Hannah pulled the door shut, Chris said, "Look, Mama. Biggie's smudging up the window with his nose."

Biggie wagged his tail and yipped at them as they started down the stairs. "Guess we'll have to keep that chair away from the table so Biggie can't get up there," said Hannah.

Alex Patterson sat at the kitchen table, gripping the whiskey bottle. He had almost drained it, and a flush was on his face. There was savagery in his eyes as he said to himself, "Yep. I'm gonna do it. That Cooper woman needs to be punished, and that's that."

Rising to his feet, he put the bottle to his mouth and emptied it, then banged the bottle on the table and went to the cupboard. He pulled open a drawer and took out several wooden matches.

Alex Patterson made his way through the darkening streets of Fort Bridger, moving from one alley to another, making sure nobody saw him. He was glad that many of the townspeople were at the church service.

He reached the alley that led to the rear of Cooper's General Store, then headed toward the Cooper barn, which stood some forty feet across the alley behind the store. He looked around the corral in the gloom for some sight of Buster. When he didn't see him, he opened the gate, entered the corral, and rounded the corner of the barn to the big double doors. Buster nickered at him in the deep shadows as he opened the doors.

"Come on out, Buster," Patterson said, swinging the doors wide. "I don't wanna harm you for what that woman did."

Buster nickered and rushed past him into the corral.

Alex moved deeper into the darkened barn to the three

large windows in the west wall. He flung each one open.

He noted a pitchfork leaning against the wall and used it to throw several large clumps of hay over the belt-high wall of the mow, scattering them across the floor. Buster stood outside in the corral and neighed at the intruder.

"Shut up!" Alex hissed. He pulled a match from his pocket, knelt down, and struck it, cupping its flame against the breeze that came through the barn door. He made sure the flames took hold in the dry hay, then lit more matches, starting small crackling fires all over the barn floor. He then used the pitchfork to pick up a large flaming clump and toss it into the mow.

Alex dashed into the corral and saw that the horse had retreated to the farthest corner. Reaching the corral gate, he looked around, making sure no one was there to see him. Then he opened the gate, stepped out, and closed it. Smoke was already billowing out of the windows and the double-wide doors.

Alex ran behind a barn further down the alley, then looked back. To his amazement, the gusty wind was tossing clumps of burning hay through the open windows toward the general store. Buster was neighing shrilly.

Alex stood wide-eyed as he saw burning hay blow against the back porch of the store. Soon smoke tinged with orange flame began to race across the porch, driven by the wind. "No! No! I didn't mean for the store to burn!"

Alex watched the flames take hold on the clapboard wall, licking their way upward. It took only minutes for the back door of the store to burst into flame, and soon the entire rear of the building was ablaze.

Mesmerized by the rising, spreading flames, Alex made his way closer to the fire without realizing it. His mind was fixed on the crackling, popping flames and the black billows of smoke rising toward the night sky. He thought about hell. He recalled the preacher telling him he was going there, and he cringed at the prospect of such a horrible thing.

Alex stopped when he realized he was almost between the two burning buildings. The barn was now almost fully ablaze.

Suddenly his attention was drawn to the apartment on the second floor. Biggie was barking in terror and scratching at the window next to the apartment door.

From the direction of the fort, Alex heard men shouting, and seconds later the fire bell at the town's center began to clang loudly.

At the town hall, Pastor Andrew Kelly was just winding down his sermon when the fire bell began to clang. People on the street were shouting about a fire.

"Folks," said the preacher, "the service is dismissed. We've got volunteer firemen in this building, and they need to go."

By the time the congregation had spilled from the hall into the street, the sky above Fort Bridger was alight with a saffron glow.

The O'Briens and the Coopers were together as they left the building and looked down the street toward the orange sky.

"Hannah," said Edith, "the fire has got to be close to your store!"

"Yes! It looks like it's in our block!"

Hannah and her children outran the O'Briens and passed many people as they ran toward the fire. When they were within a block of the store, Chris cried, "Mama! It *is* our store!"

"Oh, no!" Mary Beth said.

Hannah ran ahead of them toward her blazing store. As she drew near, she saw the volunteer firemen working the pump of the town's fire wagon and spraying the store with water. Dozens of men had set up bucket brigades and were dipping from the watering troughs along Main Street, handing the buckets along the lines. Amongst the firefighters in one of the brigades was Alex Patterson.

Men on both sides of the burning store were dousing the walls and roofs of the adjacent buildings in an attempt to keep them from bursting into flame.

Hannah's heart was in her mouth as her children stood beside her, weeping. She felt an arm go around her waist and looked to see Glenda Williams, who said, "I'm sorry, Hannah. I'm so sorry!"

Hannah bit down hard on her lower lip, her face devoid of color.

Justin Powell came running up and said, "Hannah, your barn's on fire, but Buster's all right. He's in the corral, and he's frightened, but he's all right. The entire back of the store is on fire, though…all the way to the roof."

Chris cried Buster's name and took off running as fast as he could toward the alley.

"Chris, don't go back there!" Hannah shouted. But the roar of the fire and the loud voices in the crowd drowned out her words. In seconds, he disappeared, racing around the edge of the crowd while shouting Buster's name.

Justin took off after him.

The O'Briens were there now and tried to comfort Hannah, but her mind was filled with confusion and frustration. Her knees were like water, and her whole body was trembling. The entire building—the store, the apartment—was engulfed in flames. The flames were devouring all she had worked for, making ash of all her efforts.

Suddenly Mary Beth blinked against her tears and cried, "Mama! Biggie's in there!"

B. J. and Patty Ruth set wide eyes on her. In all the excitement, they had forgotten about their little dog.

Almost like a sleepwalker, Hannah looked at her children and said, "It's too late to save Biggie."

Hannah and the children stood huddled together with Glenda, weeping as the wind-swept blaze devoured their home and store. All three were sobbing Biggie's name as if their hearts would wrench themselves from their chests.

Every able-bodied man in town except Dr. Frank O'Brien—who felt he was needed more at Hannah's side—was fighting the fire, or struggling in the eerie, dancing light of the flames to keep the adjacent buildings from turning into like infernos.

Fiery sparks were everywhere, raining down on the crowd, who batted them away. The men with the water pump gave up on the store and began dousing the nearby trees.

Soon Patty Ruth was in her mother's arms, drained of strength from repeatedly crying Biggie's name.

Many women came by to comfort Hannah. Most of the words didn't register. At times, Hannah stared straight ahead, feeling the heat on her cheeks, smelling the smoke, holding her little daughter close to her heart.

Soon one of the porch uprights made a grating sound, sagged, and collapsed. Several people cried out as the porch roof made its own groaning sound, then fell in a heap. Smoke rushed upward and sparks swirled about in the wind, racing for the orange sky.

Chris returned, telling his mother that Buster was all right, but he had just realized that Biggie must have died in the fire.

"I know," Hannah said, her face wet with tears.

Another quarter hour brought the final thrust at Hannah's heart when the building made a strange sound, almost as if it were in pain, then collapsed within itself in a loud roar. There was a massive shower of sparks, followed by an upsurge of flame...then the ruins were enveloped in thick, back billows of smoke.

Glenda held on to Hannah, who now was trying to fold all four of her children in her arms as they wept together.

Rebecca Kelly moved in, speaking soft words of comfort to Hannah. Julie Powell was close by, with her two children, wanting to be of help. Frank and Edie stayed within arm's reach.

As the Coopers wept over the loss of their home, the store, the barn, and their little dog, the rest of the people made a circle around them. The crowd cleared a path for Pastor Kelly as he made his way to the little knot of people gathered close to the Coopers.

The wind had died down some, but was still gusting. The weeping began to subside as Kelly stepped up and said, "Hannah, I don't know exactly what the church can do for you at this point, but I know the people will rally to help you. I'll call a special meeting as soon as possible."

Clinging to her children, Hannah could only stare at the burning, smoking rubble, and nod.

Gary Williams had crowded in close to Glenda, and said, "Hannah, you can have your hotel rooms back, along with your meals. It will all be free."

Hannah continued to stare at the black heap that was once her store, and nodded slowly. Gary wasn't sure she had heard what he said.

Suddenly a familiar sound was heard. It was a little dog's bark, coming from somewhere out in the darkness.

"Mama!" gasped Mary Beth. "That sounds like Biggie!"

No sooner were the words out of Mary Beth's mouth than a small white dog with black spots came running from the back side of the smoking rubble, weaving among legs. Biggie yapped excitedly when he saw his family, and he hurried to them.

The crowd laughed and applauded as Chris picked Biggie up, hugged him, and the Cooper children made over him, shedding tears of relief and joy. For the moment, the loss of the building was forgotten. Hannah petted Biggie's head as Chris held him, but her eyes had a vacant look.

"Mama," said B. J., "how did Biggie get out of the apartment? You closed the door tight when we left for church."

Hannah shook her head, blinked several times, and said, "Honey, I don't know how he got out."

"I do, Mama," said Patty Ruth. "*God* let him out."

"Looks like He might've," Doc O'Brien said.

Then, one by one, the crowd began filing by the Coopers, speaking words of comfort and encouragement to Hannah and her children. Hannah was once again staring blankly at the rubble, and barely heard them.

When Judge and Mrs. Carter drew up, the judge said, "Hannah, you can be thankful for one thing...your new shipment hadn't arrived yet. If it had, you'd have lost all of it."

Hannah nodded, but did not reply.

"You can use the sutler building until a new store can be built," Carter said.

"The town will still have a store, Hannah," said Mrs. Carter.

The judge saw the look in Hannah's eyes and said to his wife, "Come on, dear, we'll talk to her later."

Glenda smiled at them. "That would be best."

Clayton Farley was next, along with Marshal Lance Mangum, who was covered with soot. Farley said, "If you can come up with some way to purchase the materials, I'll supply the labor at half what I usually charge, Mrs. Cooper."

Hannah Cooper felt as if she were living a nightmare, wishing she could wake up.

"Ma'am," said Mangum, "do you have any idea what could have started the fire?"

Hannah turned to look at him. "Hmm?"

"I asked, Mrs. Cooper, if you have any idea how the fire got started."

"None whatsoever," Hannah said in a monotone.

"Were there any lanterns left burning when you went to church?"

"Hmm?"

"There was just one lantern burning in the apartment, Marshal," Mary Beth said. "I doubt it could have caused the fire. It was hanging on a closed hook over the kitchen table. There was no way it could have fallen off."

"I see," nodded the marshal. "I'll talk about it with your mother later."

Hannah, with her children, the Williamses, the Kellys, and the O'Briens, moved slowly toward the hotel. When they arrived there, Hannah's mind was beginning to clear. When Dr. O'Brien offered to give her a sedative, she kindly refused, saying she would be all right.

Pastor Kelly led the group in prayer, asking the Lord to help Hannah and her children through this trial, and to supply their needs.

The O'Briens and the Kellys offered to stay with Hannah and the children through the night, but Hannah told them it would not be necessary. Again Doc offered to give her a sedative so she could sleep. Hannah thanked him, saying she would rather not take the sedative. Glenda told them that she would stay in Hannah's room with her for the night. If Doc or the preacher were needed, she would send for them.

When the O'Briens and the Kellys were gone, Gary excused himself, saying he would take Biggie to the house.

Still somewhat in shock, Hannah put her children to bed, telling them not to worry. Everything would be all right. Though she did not believe it herself. Patty Ruth was thankful she had taken Tony with her to church.

Glenda was waiting in Hannah's room when she entered, moving like a sleepwalker. Glenda took her by the hand and said, "Come on, honey, let's get you into that bed."

Suddenly Hannah clung to Glenda and sobbed as though

her heart had been shattered into a million pieces. Glenda guided her to the bed and sat her down, then held her while she wept.

After several minutes, Hannah looked at her friend and said, "There's nothing left for us here, Glenda! The only thing I can do is take the children and go back to Missouri to live with my parents. We have nothing left...not even the money it will take to go back. Oh, Glenda, I don't know what I'm going to do! I have nothing...nothing...nothing!"

"You have the Lord," Glenda said softly.

Still sobbing with a heavy heaving of her chest, Hannah threw her hands to her face. "God doesn't care about me, Glenda! If He cared, why would He let my store and barn burn to the ground? Have I done some terrible thing? Is that it? Is God punishing me for something? He took my husband, now He's taken everything I own in the world, except my children!"

"Hannah, listen. The Lord hasn't forsaken you...and he's not punishing you. I don't have all the answers, but Jesus still loves you and cares for you. Everything will work out. Mr. Farley's offer certainly will be a help."

Hannah met her gaze. "Offer? What offer?"

"Didn't you hear him? He offered to charge you only half on the labor when you build the new store."

"I do remember something like that now," said Hannah, running splayed fingers through her disheveled hair. "But... where would I ever get the money to pay half on the labor and buy all the materials? We're talking about better than ten thousand dollars, even with Mr. Farley's offer. I might have four hundred dollars in the bank."

"Well, at least you have the judge's offer, too."

"What's that?"

"He said you could use the sutler's building till you could build a new store. And he said that your shipment is on the way...that if it had already been delivered, you'd have lost it, too. So you have goods coming. You can use the sutler's and go back into business."

"It won't work, Glenda. Not for a long period of time. That's why the judge wanted to get out of the business. That tiny building can't carry the goods this growing town needs. Besides, my children need a home. It's wonderful of you and Gary to let us live here in the hotel, but we need a home. There's no way I could afford a house."

"The Lord can supply it all for you, honey," Glenda said, gripping her hands and squeezing them.

"He doesn't care, Glenda," Hannah said, breaking into sobs again.

Glenda held her in her arms, patting her back while she wept, and prayed silently for God's help. She let Hannah cry till the heavy sobbing began to subside, then pulled back from her and said, "Hannah, where's your Bible?"

"It's...oh, I left it at the town hall. It was in that small canvas satchel I had with— Oh! With Solomon's pictures! Oh, I still have those pictures! If I hadn't taken them to church with me, they'd have been gone, too! I still have them, Glenda!"

"I'm so glad, Hannah. I know they are treasures to you. Listen. You sit tight. I'm going to run downstairs to the office. I have a Bible down there. I have something I want to show you."

Hannah was still sitting on the bed when Glenda returned. Sitting down beside her, Glenda opened her Bible and said, "Now, Hannah, you've been through what I can't even imagine, losing your husband and now the store and your home. No wonder you're at a point of despair and wondering why God has let all of this happen to you. I don't pretend to understand what you're going through right now...but I know and *you* know that the Lord has *not* forsaken you. He has some great purpose for it all. I just want to share a truth from Scripture with you that has long been a strength to me. All right?"

Hannah's hands were trembling. "Yes, all right."

Glenda read Matthew 6:25–32 to her friend, then went back and said, "Hannah, listen once again to Jesus' words:

> 'Consider the lilies of the field, how they grow; they toil not, neither do they spin...for your heavenly Father knoweth that ye have need of all these things.'

"Hannah, dear...the lilies trust their Creator so explicitly to provide for them, that they do not toil nor spin. They don't fret and worry, Hannah. Is that right?"

"Yes," nodded the young widow. "The lilies trust Him completely, with the assurance that He will take care of all their needs."

Glenda smiled. "You're seeing it, aren't you? Hannah's heavenly Father knows that she needs a new store and apartment. He knows that she and her children need new clothing and household goods. He does care, doesn't He?"

New tears bubbled from Hannah's eyes. With trembling lips, she said, "Yes. He does care. It was so wrong of me to say He doesn't. Oh, please forgive me, Lord." She took a deep breath. "Yes, Glenda, my heavenly Father will take care of my children and me."

Glenda embraced her, and while Hannah clung to her, she kept repeating, "Consider the lilies...consider the lilies...consider the lilies..."

The Holy Spirit was using the words *consider the lilies* to bring a flood of peace to Hannah Cooper's shattered heart. In spite of all that she faced, she knew it was going to be all right.

When Hannah awakened the next morning, with Glenda asleep in the overstuffed chair beside her, she smiled and said, "Thank You for my sweet Glenda, Lord. And Lord Jesus, thank You for those precious words, *consider the lilies.* I know You will care for us even as You do for the lilies. Help me not to toil or spin, but to trust You to take care of us."

Later, when they were eating breakfast at the Williamses' house, Hannah read Matthew 6:25–32 to her children, telling them how the Holy Spirit used the words *consider the lilies* to bring her peace about their situation. She went on to carefully explain what Jesus was saying when He made His statement about the lilies.

The children listened intently.

Patty Ruth's little eyes sparkled as she said, "Jesus wouldn' lie, Mama. He takes care of the lilies, so He will take care of us!"

Fresh tears flowed down Hannah's cheeks as she reached across the table, caressed the little redhead's cheek, and said, "You are so right, honey. I don't know how He is going to do it...but Jesus is going to take care of us."

CHAPTER TWENTY-TWO

The Coopers and the Williamses were just finishing breakfast when there was a knock at the door. Gary left the kitchen, and moments later, returned with Pastor Andy and Rebecca, who had come to talk to Hannah and the children and to pray with them. They also brought the canvas satchel containing Hannah's Bible and the two photographs in the gold frames. As the preacher handed it to her, Hannah rose to her feet and thanked him.

Rebecca put her arms around her. "Hannah, how are you doing?" she asked.

Hannah looked over Rebecca's shoulder at her pastor and said, "I'm fine. With Glenda's help, the Lord gave me sweet peace last night about our loss."

"Well, tell us about it," said the preacher, smiling broadly.

Hannah took her Bible from the satchel. "Let's go into the parlor, and I'll tell you."

Hannah chose an overstuffed chair, and her four offspring sat on the floor at her feet. While opening her Bible, Hannah's eyes misted. "Pastor...Rebecca...I'm going to read you something in Matthew chapter six that I have read no doubt hundreds of times. But last night, in my darkest hour, Glenda read it to me. There were a few words in the passage that gripped me to the core of my soul. They were exactly what I needed, and the Lord knew it. It's Matthew 6:25–32." The Kellys listened intently as Hannah read the passage:

> Therefore I say unto you, Take no thought for your life, what ye shall eat, or what ye shall drink; nor yet for your body, what ye shall put on. Is not the life more than meat, and the body than raiment? Behold the fowls of the air: for they sow not, neither do they reap, nor gather into barns; yet your heavenly Father feedeth them. Are ye not much better than they?
>
> Which of you by taking thought can add one cubit unto his stature? And why take ye thought for raiment? Consider the lilies of the field, how they grow; they toil not, neither do they spin: And yet I say unto you, That even Solomon in all his glory was not arrayed like one of these. Wherefore, if God so clothe the grass of the field, which to day is, and to morrow is cast into the oven, shall he not much more clothe you, O ye of little faith?
>
> Therefore take no thought, saying, What shall we eat? or, What shall we drink? or, Wherewithal shall we be clothed? (For after all these things do the Gentiles seek:) for your heavenly Father knoweth that ye have need of all these things.

Brushing tears from her eyes, Hannah said, "The whole passage is filled with encouragement for our very predicament. But the part that gripped my heart above all was where Jesus said, 'Consider the lilies of the field, how they grow; they toil not, neither do they spin.' I was toiling last night, and I was spinning...doubting my Lord and worrying about what was going to happen to these precious children and me. But no more. Pastor...Rebecca...I don't know how the Lord is going to bring about a new store building, apartment, and barn for us, but I know He's going to do it. And just like Jesus said in this passage, our heavenly Father clothes the grass of the field and feeds the birds He created...and we are better in His sight than they. So I know He will take care of us."

Rebecca left her seat, leaned over Patty Ruth and Mary Beth, and hugged Hannah. "Oh, thank You, Jesus!" she said. "Thank You for giving Hannah such peace!"

Andy Kelly spoke up. "Let's pray and thank the Lord for the peace He has given Hannah, and thank Him in advance for the way He's going to provide what she and her family need."

When the preacher had finished praying, there were hugs all around.

"Well, Hannah," said the pastor, "today I'm going to put out the word that we're having a special meeting of the church tonight. We'll see what God does through the church to help you."

Hannah thanked him, and the Williamses told him they would be at the meeting. Then the Kellys left.

Hannah said to the group, "I'm going to go see what the rubble looks like in daylight."

"Not by yourself, you're not," Glenda said. "I'm going with you."

"Not by yourselves, you're not," Gary said. "I'm going with you."

"Could we go too, Mama?" asked Chris.

"You've got to get ready for school, son."

"Couldn't we be a little late, since it was our store and home, too?" asked Mary Beth.

"Well..."

"Oh, good!" B. J. said. "Whenever she says, 'Well...' like that, it means we can!"

"You're pretty smart, B. J.!" Patty Ruth said.

"Sure I am," said the eight-year-old. "I picked *you* for a sister, didn't I?"

Everyone laughed but Patty Ruth. Squinting and cocking her head, she said, "Mama...did B. J. choose me for his sister?"

"Not exactly, honey. But I'm sure if he'd had the opportunity to choose between you and all the little redheaded girls in the world, he'd have chosen you."

The O'Briens had joined the Cooper family when they stood on Main Street with the Williamses and looked at the black rubble. Doc had one arm around B. J. and the other around Chris. Edie held the girls in the same way.

There were still chunks of wood that gave off little tendrils of smoke.

Many townspeople and folks from the fort passed by slowly, but they did not interrupt the solemn moment for the Coopers.

"I'm so glad I'm saved," said Hannah. "What would a lost person feel, standing here as I am right now? They can't claim God's promises like His children can."

"I wouldn't trade what I have in Jesus for anything this old world could offer," said Doc.

"Mama, look," said Mary Beth, her gaze set up the street.

All eyes turned to see a band of Indians riding their pintos toward them, with a wagon out front. Two Moons guided the horse-drawn wagon to the side of the street where Cooper's General Store had stood, and raised his hand in a gesture of warmth and respect as he drew rein.

While the mounted Indians—male and female—were drawing up, Broken Wing alighted from the wagon and hurried toward Chris. Two Moons hopped down and helped Sweet Blossom from the wagon seat. The two of them stepped to Hannah and her little group and the chief said, "Mrs. Cooper, we only learned of fire at sunrise this morning. We have brought blankets made by our women, and there is also food in wagon for you and your children. We are in hope that these will be of help to you."

"Thank you so much," Hannah said. "The blankets and the food are very much appreciated, Chief Two Moons."

Sweet Blossom stepped to Hannah, embraced her quickly, then stepped back beside her husband. "We are your friends, Mrs. Cooper," she said softly.

"You certainly have shown that, Sweet Blossom," Hannah said. "There is no way I can thank you enough. And please, tell your people how very much these gifts are appreciated."

Two Moons smiled, looked toward the mounted Crows, and told them in their own language what Hannah had just said. Smiles broke out on their dark faces.

"Would you like me to take the food and blankets to our house, Hannah?" asked Gary.

"Yes, that would be nice."

"We will take the wagon there," Two Moons said.

"All right," Gary said. "I'll lead you."

"Before this," the chief said, looking toward his son, who stood beside Chris, "Broken Wing has something for Mrs. Cooper."

The fourteen-year-old boy moved up to Hannah, smiling. In his hand was a Crow-made headband with beads forming bird wings all around it. Bowing, the boy looked up into Hannah's eyes and said, "This is token of love from Crow to white lady friend." As he spoke, he extended the headband with both hands.

Hannah blinked at the tears that welled up in her eyes as she accepted the gift and placed it on her head.

"Mama!" Mary Beth said. "It looks beautiful on you!"

"Your mother is very beautiful lady," the chief said in his deep baritone. "She is beautiful on outside *and* on inside."

"That she is, Chief," Dr. O'Brien said.

Two Moons smiled. "We will go now."

"Thank you so much," Hannah said with feeling. "Your kindness and generosity will never be forgotten."

Two Moons nodded and helped his squaw back onto the wagon seat. When he was in place, and Broken Wing was seated beside his mother, Gary led the wagon and mounted Crows down the street.

Hannah turned to see Marshal Lance Mangum standing nearby. He approached and said, "I've looked the whole situation over, Hannah, and I have to say the fire started in the barn. In fact, I'm positive it did not start in the store building at all."

"Why do you say that?" she asked.

"The wind was blowing from the east last night. So if the fire had started in the store building, it would've blown the flames *away* from the barn. I believe the fire started in the barn and the flames blew across the alley. Did you have a lantern burning in the barn?"

"No. We didn't even have a lantern in the barn."

"Then I think that leaves only one option as to how the fire was started."

"And that is?"

"Arson."

Hannah blinked. "You mean—?"

"Somebody set the barn afire on purpose."

"But who— Why...why would anyone do a thing like that? I—"

"Either it was a random thing, set by some demented person, or it was someone who had some reason for wanting to burn you out."

The morning breeze ruffled Hannah's dark brown hair, blowing wisps across her forehead. "Is there such a demented person in this area?"

"Not that I know of, but drifters do come through."

"Well, I'd rather believe it was a drifter than someone who

purposely set the fire to burn me out."

"Of course, he might have only meant to burn the barn. The stiff wind came up about the time the fire had to have started."

"But, still, Marshal…who would want to do such a thing?"

"I can't say, ma'am."

"It gives me the creeps to think there might be a person around here like that, Marshal."

"Well, since he didn't leave any clues, I don't have a thing to go on, ma'am."

"I understand. All we can do is pray that whoever it is doesn't do this to me again."

"Yes, ma'am. Something strange here, too."

"What's that?"

"Was your horse closed up in the barn when you left for church?"

"Yes."

"He sure was, Marshal," Chris said. "I put him in there myself, and he whinnied at me through the window when we were leaving for church. He was inside, all right. And the door was latched. You're thinking how did he get out of the barn, right?"

"There's only one way. Somebody let him out."

"There's another mystery here too, Marshal," said Hannah. "Do you know about our dog?"

"Only that he showed up on the street last night during the fire."

"That's the mystery. When we left for church, Biggie was in the apartment. I closed the door myself, and I made sure it was tight. Biggie couldn't have opened that door by himself. Somebody let him out."

Mangum scratched his head. "That's a mystery all right. Well, I'm gonna nose around a bit and see if I can find some answers."

At that point, Hannah told her three oldest children to head for school. They were to tell Miss Lindgren why they were late, and if she had any questions, she could send home a note.

When Chris, Mary Beth, and B. J. were gone, the O'Briens excused themselves saying they had to get to the office. As they walked away, Glenda said, "Well, Hannah, the Lord knows who the arsonist is. We'll have to trust Him to take the man in hand."

"That's all we can do." Hannah sighed and ran her gaze over the black rubble. "What a mess here, huh? Almost eleven thousand dollars in that heap, Glenda. And that doesn't include the goods on the shelves. I don't know where I will ever get the money to build it again."

Glenda put an arm around her. "Remember. Jesus said, 'Consider the lilies.'"

Hannah's face brightened. "Here I go again. O me of little faith." She wrapped her arms around her friend and said, "I love you, Glenda."

The Coopers and the Williamses had just finished supper when Marshal Mangum knocked on the door. Gary answered the knock and ushered the marshal into the kitchen.

"Hannah, I've talked to every man who was on the scene at the fire last night. Including Gary, here. Not one of them had let the horse out of the barn, nor the dog out of the apartment."

"I know who did," Patty Ruth said. "*God* did."

Mangum smiled. "You may be right, Patty Ruth."

"Just in case it wasn't God," said Hannah, "do you suppose it was the arsonist?"

"Had to have been," Mangum said.

"Well," said Gary, "at least he's kind to animals."

As serious as things were, this brought a laugh from everyone.

Hannah and her children were at the hotel during the special church meeting, talking together in Hannah's room. At eight-thirty, the Williamses and the Kellys came to the door, and were ushered in by B. J. There were smiles on the faces of all four.

"Hannah," Pastor Kelly said, "you know the church is in a building program, and we're paying for the construction as we go."

"Yes."

"Well, in spite of the financial load that is on the people right now, we took up a special love gift for you and your children of four hundred forty dollars."

"Really?" gasped Hannah.

Kelly reached in his pocket and handed her a fat envelope. "Here it is...minus my commission, of course!"

Hannah laughed. It felt good to laugh. "Whatever that commission is, Reverend Kelly, sir, you are entitled to it! Seriously, Pastor, how will I ever be able to thank you and all those wonderful people for their sacrifice?"

"None of us are concerned about being thanked, Hannah. We just love you and these youngins of yours, and it's our joy to help in this way."

"May I have a moment in the service Sunday morning to thank them?"

"The pulpit will be yours. But only for that moment. No preaching now!"

"Mama used to preach to Papa sometimes," Patty Ruth said.

"Yeah, and she did a pretty good job," Chris said. "Papa always got his heart right when Mama preached to him!"

Hannah gave Patty Ruth and Chris a mock scowl. "No more private family secrets, you two!"

On Tuesday morning, six wagonloads of goods and supplies arrived in Fort Bridger from Cheyenne City. Judge William Carter and Hannah Cooper supervised the unloading at the sutler's building and four other buildings in the fort where the goods would be stored.

Hannah went to work, stocking the shelves, and several of the women in the fort helped her. She would open again for business by Thursday.

While the shipment was being unloaded inside the fort, Justin Powell was busy at the hardware store and gun shop, helping his boss add new shelves. Business was steadily increasing, and Hans Swensen was reminding Justin that he would be getting a raise in pay come the first of the year when they looked up to see Cade Samuels and Lloyd Dawson enter.

"Good morning, gentlemen," Samuels said, smiling. "We know, Justin, that you're a member of the church, so you probably gave your gift for the Coopers at the special meeting last night."

"Julie and I did what little we could, sir," Justin said.

Then to Swensen, "We feel the rest of the town should help Hannah too, Hans. Would you like to contribute?"

"I sure will," Swensen said.

The two men were about to leave after receiving Swensen's generous gift when Abe Carver came in. They greeted the blacksmith, and Samuels said, "We're soliciting gifts for the Coopers, Abe, but you no doubt gave last night."

"Yessir, that Mandy and I did. We plan to give Miz Cooper some more in the nex' few days. But let me say that I 'preciate what you gentlemen is doin'. Miz Cooper and her family deserve the best we all can do."

Samuels and Dawson left, and Abe was making a purchase at the counter when Corporal Eddie Slayton came in with a sheet of paper in his hand. "Good morning, Abe...Hans."

Both men greeted Slayton warmly.

"I'm looking for Justin," said the corporal. "I've got a wire for him from back east."

"He's building new shelves back there," Swensen said, throwing a thumb over his shoulder.

Slayton headed toward the back of the store. "Justin..."

"Yeah!" Justin said from behind a row of shelves. "You say I have a wire from back east?"

"Yes."

"Good news or bad?"

"Guess."

At the sutler's, Hannah was unloading a box of candy at the counter when she looked up to see Nellie Patterson come in. Hannah rushed to her and embraced her. "It's good to see you, Nellie."

"You, too, Hannah. I was at the special meeting last night, and I was so happy to see how much money was raised for you." Leaning close, Nellie whispered, "I had to sneak some from my secret piggy bank to do my part, but it was a joy to do it."

"Oh, thank you. Thank you so much."

"My pleasure."

Hannah thought how wonderful it was to see the change in Nellie. The sad look had been replaced with a happy one by the Lord.

"I haven't been able to see you since the fire," Nellie said, taking hold of Hannah's hand, "but I just wanted to see you for a minute and tell you I'm praying the Lord will drop every dollar you need out of the sky so you can rebuild."

Hannah laughed. "Well, I'll take it whether He drops it out of the sky, or whatever way He chooses."

Clayton Farley and three of his men were working on the new saddlery building at the south edge of town. While Alex Patterson sawed boards and pounded nails, his conscience was eating at him. He recalled Nellie's repeated warnings that one day his temper was going to cause him to do something he'd truly be sorry for.

Alex wrestled with his conscience until midafternoon. Finally, he went to his boss and said, "Mr. Farley, I have somethin' real important I have to do. Could I have a little time?"

"You mean right now?" Farley asked.

"Yes, sir."

"How much time do you need?"

"Well, I'm not sure, sir. Whatever time I take off, I'll make it up in the next day or two by workin' late."

Farley hunched his shoulders. "All right. Go ahead."

Hannah had left the fort to eat a late lunch at Glenda's Place, and was at her hotel room with Glenda before leaving for the sutler's again. Glenda was going to go with her and help stock shelves.

They were about to leave the room when there was a knock at the door. Hannah was at the dresser dabbing at her hair.

"I'll get it," Glenda said, and opened the door.

Hannah heard Alex Patterson's voice say, "Oh, hello, Mrs. Williams. I was wantin' to see Mrs. Cooper. Is she here?"

"I'm here, Alex," said Hannah, appearing with a comb in her hand. "What can I do for you?"

"Well…I…I need to talk to you, ma'am."

Glenda glanced at Hannah. "I can wait down in the office."

"No need, Mrs. Williams," Patterson said. "What I have to say to this lady will be no secret pretty soon, anyhow."

"Well, come in," Hannah said.

The two women sat on the bed while a shaky Alex Patterson sat in the overstuffed chair. He had hardly eased into the chair when he began to weep. "Mrs. Cooper, I'm the one who set your barn on fire," he blurted.

Hannah and Glenda exchanged glances.

Before either could speak, Alex's words were tumbling off his tongue. "You know how I talked to you that day in your apartment… Well, my feelings toward you got a lot worse when you made a Christian out of Nellie."

"I didn't make her a Christian, Alex. Jesus did."

"You know what I mean. It was your influence. And then my kids were next. I hated you for it. I mean, *really* hated you. I wanted to punish you bad." His voice broke, and he choked up, tears streaming down his face.

Hannah left the bed and laid a hand on his shaking shoulder. "Mr. Patterson, if it's forgiveness you want, I forgive you."

He looked up at her, stunned. "You do?"

"Yes."

He wept the more, shaking his head. Hannah sat back down beside Glenda. Alex brought himself under control and said with a quivering voice, "I didn't mean to burn the store. I only meant to burn the barn. The wind carried the burnin' hay to the store. I…I didn't want your horse harmed, so I let him out of the barn before I set the hay on fire."

"And you let my dog out of the apartment when you saw the store catch fire."

"Yes. I saw him up there at the window, barkin' and

scratchin' on the glass. So I let him out before the flames caught the stairs on fire."

Wiping tears with his palms, Alex said, "I know you'll have to turn me over to Marshal Mangum for this, Mrs. Cooper, but I don't care. Whatever the law does to me, I deserve. More than anything, I just wanted to hear you say you forgive me. But I didn't think if it came at all, it would come this easy."

"I can forgive you, Alex—may I call you Alex?"

"Yes, ma'm."

"I can forgive you, Alex, because the Lord Jesus Christ forgave me for the sins I committed against Him. He taught me how to forgive. Because you've come to me like this, I'm not going to press charges. I'm going to ask Marshal Mangum to be lenient with you."

Alex sniffled and said, "You'd do that for me?"

"Jesus did more than that for me. And you know what? He'll forgive you of all your sins too, Alex."

"Yes, ma'am. That's another thing I came for. I want you to show me how to be saved."

It was all Hannah could do to keep from shouting. Holding her voice steady, she said, "I'll show you in just a moment, Alex, but I want to ask you something."

"Yes'm?"

"If only the barn had burned, would you have felt as bad as you do?"

"No. I don't know. I mean...I meant to burn the barn."

"Then it was God's wind that carried the fire to the store, wasn't it?"

"I guess you'd have to say that, yes."

Hannah's eyes filled with tears. She turned to Glenda and said, "So many times I prayed for Alex's salvation. I always asked God to save him, whatever it took."

"Yes," said Glenda. "I've heard you say that to the Lord."

"Well, I guess when we say 'whatever it takes' to God, we'd better mean it. It cost me my store, my home, and my barn."

"I'm sorry, Mrs. Cooper," Alex said.

"I'm not, Alex. You're about to be saved from going to a burning, eternal hell. The loss is worth that to me."

Nellie Patterson and her three children stood in a tight cluster, weeping as Hannah Cooper remained beside Alex in their small parlor while he told them he had just become a Christian.

Alex opened his arms as they rushed to him. Nellie felt as if she were dreaming.

While holding his joyous family close to him, Alex said, "I told Mrs. Cooper that I knew she'd have to turn me in for what I'd done. So I went with her to the marshal's office. She pled with Marshal Mangum not to jail me, saying that I'd learned my lesson."

"And what did he say?" asked Nellie.

"He said he wouldn't jail me, but since I did break the law, I have to stand trial. But because this dear lady isn't pressin' charges, and is askin' for leniency for me, Marshal Mangum said he'd recommend that the judge give me a light sentence. Whatever the judge does, I deserve."

"The Lord will take care of it all, Nellie," Hannah said.

"Hannah, if God can save my husband, He certainly can take care of us until whatever sentence the judge gives him has been served. We'll make out fine because now this is a Christian home!"

The entire town was buzzing that evening as the news of Alex Patterson's confession and conversion spread. Pastor Andy

Kelly visited the Pattersons and welcomed Alex into the family of God. Alex was quite obviously a new man. Alex asked the preacher to forgive him for his past behavior, which Andy was more than willing to do.

Hannah was telling her children the whole story in her hotel room just before bedtime when there was a knock at the door. Justin Powell was there, smiling, as Chris opened the door.

"Come in, Justin," Hannah said warmly.

As Justin stepped in, he said, "Julie and I heard about Alex getting saved, Hannah. Praise the Lord!"

"Yes, praise the Lord," Hannah said.

"I won't stay but a minute," Justin said. "I came to invite you to our house for supper tomorrow evening. Julie and I really want you to come."

"Well, we'd be glad to," Hannah said.

"Great! You know where we live, don't you?"

"Sure do."

"Six o'clock all right?"

"That'd be fine."

"See you then," he said, heading for the door.

As he was about to close the door behind him, Hannah said, "Can we bring something?"

"Only yourselves," Justin said, chuckling, "and five empty stomachs!"

Chapter Twenty-three

It was five minutes till six on Wednesday evening when Hannah Cooper and her four children turned the corner on the block where the Powells lived and headed down the dusty street.

"Which house is it, Mama?" asked B. J.

"It's right in the middle of the block. It sits back a ways from the street. You'll be able to see it in a minute."

Hannah had worked hard all day, with the help of several women from the fort and town, including Nellie Patterson. Alex had encouraged her to spend the day helping Hannah get the store ready.

The circuit judge would be in Fort Bridger in three weeks. Clayton Farley was so amazed at the change in Alex that he kept him on even though he would be facing the judge. Hannah was praying that the sentence would be light.

The small store in the fort was ready for business, and Hannah would be there at eight tomorrow morning to open the door. She had thanked the Lord a number of times that the goods from Cheyenne City had not come before Alex had set the fire.

As they drew near the middle of the block, Hannah said, "There, B. J. That's the Powell house, back there near the alley."

"It sure is little," Patty Ruth said.

"Well, the Powells don't have much money. That's why we're helping them with their groceries for a while."

"I'm glad we can do that," Mary Beth said. "It's always such a good feeling to help people."

Hannah smiled. "It's like the Lord said, honey, it is more blessed to give than to receive."

"That's really true," Chris said. "It always gives you such a warm feeling to give something to somebody."

The Coopers turned into the yard of the small house and saw Justin open the front door, a wide smile on his face. "They're here, Julie!" he called over his shoulder. "Come on in, ladies and gentlemen! Supper's just about ready!"

A pleasing aroma met their nostrils as the Coopers stepped past Justin into the small parlor. Julie met them there and asked, "Is everybody hungry?"

"*I* sure am!" said B. J.

"Well, come on into the kitchen," Julie said, leading the way.

As they moved into the kitchen, Hannah looked around and asked, "Where's Casey and Carrie?"

"We decided to have supper in peace tonight," said Justin, coming in behind them. "So we let Mandy Carver take them home with her. Mandy takes care of them whenever we need to go somewhere or do something that would be easier without two small children."

"Well, we'll miss them tonight," Hannah said.

Julie pointed out where she wanted each of the Coopers to sit, and while they were taking their places, she set the last of the hot dishes on the table. When all were seated, Hannah looked at both Justin and Julie, and it seemed their eyes shined as she had never seen them shine before.

Justin said, "Chris, would you lead us in prayer, and thank the Lord for the food?"

"Sure," Chris said with a smile.

Chris not only thanked the Lord for the food, but he also thanked Him for saving Alex Patterson. He closed by thanking God that since He took such good care of the lilies, He was going to do the same for the Coopers in the face of all they had lost.

As they began to eat, Julie said, "Chris, what was that about the lilies? Were you referring to that Scripture where Jesus told us to consider the lilies whenever we have the tendency to worry over how our needs are going to be met?"

"Yes, ma'am. I sure was. Why don't you tell her, Mama?"

Hannah was glad to tell the Powells about how in her darkest hour after the fire, Glenda had taken her to the passage in Matthew 6. She explained with tears in her eyes how Jesus' words about the lilies had driven away her fears, picked up her spirits, and given her peace.

They all discussed the passage for some time while they ate. When it appeared the last word on the subject had been spoken, Julie said, "Hannah, I'm so glad for what the church did for you."

"It meant more than words could ever express," Hannah said.

Justin took a sip of coffee, set the cup in the saucer, and said, "Hannah, when the Lord makes it possible to replace everything you lost...what kind of a figure are you looking at? Not trying to be nosy, you understand. It's just that we care about you, and we'd like to know."

Hannah smiled. "I don't consider your question being nosy, Justin. Looking at what it cost us to build the store and barn before, and what it'll cost to replace all other losses, I'd say we're looking at somewhere in the neighborhood of twelve thousand dollars. That's allowing for the cut in labor cost Mr. Farley promised. And...we now have over four hundred dollars, thanks to the church, to put against that figure."

"I see," Justin said. "And you have no doubt that the Lord is going to take care of every need you have, just like He does the lilies who don't toil nor spin?"

"That's right," she said with confidence. "Hannah Cooper, here, toiled and spun for a while after the fire...but the sweet Holy Spirit has given me absolute peace in my heart that the Lord is going to do it. I have no idea how, but that's His business."

Justin glanced across the table at his wife. They smiled at each other. "Honey, do you want to tell them?" Justin said.

Suddenly Julie's face tinted and tears gushed to her eyes. "I can't," she said, choking on the words.

There was puzzlement on the faces of all five Coopers.

Justin was having some trouble of his own. He blinked at the moisture that rose in his eyes, cleared his throat, and said, "Hannah...Chris...Mary Beth...B. J....Patty Ruth...Julie and I know how the Lord is going to do what you're trusting Him to do."

"You do?" Hannah said.

"Yes. I received a telegram today from an attorney in Maryland. My Uncle Jason Powell died last week. He was a bachelor, so he had no children, nor did he have any other close family. The attorney said the entire estate was willed to me. It is just over a hundred thousand dollars."

Mary Beth's eyes popped. "Wow!"

"Mama," asked Patty Ruth, "is that a lot?"

"Yes, it is," Hannah said.

"The wire said the money is being transferred to our account at the Fort Bridger Bank early next week, Hannah," Justin said. "Julie and I discussed it, and we are in agreement that because of your generosity to us in our desperate need...we're going to give you the money it will take to rebuild the store and barn and to replace every bit of your loss. We'll start by writing you a check for fifteen thousand dollars. If that doesn't cover it, you'll get another check when we know what's lacking."

Hannah was speechless.

"Now, don't you even think of refusing the money, dear lady," Justin said. "You would be insulting the Lord. This is His way of taking care of five precious lilies, if you please. Besides that, we'll have more joy in this than you will, because it's more blessed to give than to receive!"

Hannah's children looked at her. She swallowed hard, thumbed tears from her cheeks, looked skyward, and said, "Thank You, Lord! Oh, thank You!" Then to the Powells, "And thank *you,* Justin...Julie!"

"Don't thank us," Justin said with a laugh. "Just think of the blessing we're getting out of this!"

Gary and Glenda Williams were sitting in their favorite chairs in the parlor of their home, reading, when they heard footsteps on the front porch, followed by a knock on the door.

"I'll see who it is," Gary said, laying the book on the small table next to his chair.

Glenda was already up. "Just stay there, sweetheart," she said, heading for the door. "I'll get it."

When she opened the door, she saw five happy smiles and ten gleaming eyes as Hannah said, "Glenda! Wait'll you hear what the Lord has done for us! Talk about *consider the lilies!*"